THE RESORT

SARAH GOODWIN

avon.

Published by AVON
A division of HarperCollins*Publishers* Ltd
1 London Bridge Street
London SE1 9GF

www.harpercollins.co.uk

HarperCollins*Publishers*
Macken House,
39/40 Mayor Street Upper,
Dublin 1
D01 C9W8
Ireland

A Paperback Original 2023

First published in Great Britain by HarperCollins*Publishers* 2023

A catalogue copy of this book is
available from the British Library.

ISBN: 978-0-00-859154-0

Typeset in Sabon MT Std by
Palimpsest Book Production Ltd, Falkirk, Stirlingshire

Printed and Bound in the UK using
100% Renewable Electricity at CPI Group (UK) Ltd

MIX
Paper | Supporting
responsible forestry
FSC™ C007454

This book is produced from independently certified FSC™ paper
to ensure responsible forest management.

For more information visit: www.harpercollins.co.uk/green

This novel is dedicated to my brave and beautiful Mum.

Prologue

I love a mystery. That's what this whole trip was meant to be about. Chasing a puzzle, a myth, all those ghost stories and unexplained events. This place has so many secrets. A history of either violence or misfortune, perhaps both, has made its mark on every bit of it.

If ghosts are real I wonder what these ones have seen. What stories they might tell if only I could hear them. Perhaps they could answer some of my questions or spark new ones. Or else whisper their last words to me.

Perhaps they might have warned me.

The ground underfoot is only lightly dusted with snow, not yet frozen. My boots slither in the mud beneath as I try to run. It's pitch black under the trees and out of the moonlight I can hardly see two feet in front of me. I'm already exhausted from the long walk and my muscles are screaming at me to stop. I have to keep going but fear can only give me strength for so long. It's so hard to make any progress. I'm stumbling, sliding, my legs straining.

Am I still being chased? I can't hear anything over my own blood roaring in my ears. The panicked gulps of air I'm sucking in. I twist and look, catch sight of a shadow between the trees and whip back around with a whimper. Oh Christ. The figure isn't even hurrying after me. As if my escape attempt is completely futile and I just don't know it yet.

The cabins loom out of the early morning mist. The same cabins that only a few hours ago I was happily poking around in. Looking for clues. Now, as I throw myself up the porch steps and slam the door behind me, I wonder what clues I will leave behind for the next person unlucky or stupid enough to come here.

Pressed to the door I flick the latch and brace myself to hold it shut. Perhaps I had enough distance that I wasn't seen coming in here? A moment after that thought I realise that I must have left a trail in the mud. Footprints leading right to my hiding spot. A place so obvious a child could find me, let alone . . .

Straining my ears I listen for footsteps or voices. With my lip clenched between my teeth I count inwardly. I reach ten, then twenty, and after sixty seconds my heartrate slows ever so slightly. Maybe I got away? Surely I wasn't that far ahead. Only a few seconds at most when I looked back before. But then again, perhaps I'm not the only one fleeing the scene? Maybe that figure wasn't striding after me, but slipping away?

I wish I had my bag, the phone in there. The GPS. Anything to help me get out of here, find help. But I put it down to rest my back and that was when I saw the blood. Fresh blood steaming on the ground, peppering the light snow. I feel sick remembering it. The blood and the sounds that man was making. The terror and pain on his face.

Then I hear it. Footsteps on the porch, slow and deliberate. A convulsive shiver runs over me and despite my instinct to hold the door shut, I back away. There's a creak and a click. For a moment I think I see a black eye glinting between the warped boards. Then, everything is agony.

Chapter 1

Getting to the airport was the usual struggle. I'd been awake half the night worrying I'd sleep through my alarm. The other half of the night was taken up with nightmares that I'd already overslept and that I had gone to the wrong airport by accident. Not exactly a restful start. Ethan, of course, slept like the dead, because it wasn't his sister's wedding we were going to. He had nothing to prove, unlike me.

In the end I woke up half an hour before the alarm went off and decided I couldn't take it anymore. So whilst Ethan slept on I tiptoed around getting into my airport uniform of leggings and a hoodie. In the cheap fluorescents of our bathroom I already looked like death. I'd had my hair cut and dyed for the wedding into a dirty-blonde shag that was meant to look mussed yet cool. Fresh from bed it just looked limp and sad.

I made a tea and drank it looking out at the empty street. Well, empty except for two rats going through a capsized recycling bin across the way. Until a seagull bullied them away and started ripping into a black bag. The Bristolian equivalent of watching the deer emerge and sip morning dew. I picked my cuticles and wondered if I ought to have booked a manicure.

Just before the alarm I crept back to the bedroom with a tea for my husband. He opened wary eyes and then glanced at the time, groaned and accepted the mug. As he lifted one hand to rasp his stubble, he exposed the tattoo on his ribs. A faded flash-art skeleton from his teen years. Both of us had patches of embarrassing ink, but thankfully most of it was easy to hide. I ruffled his mop of dark hair and he said something that sounded like 'fucking destination weddings'.

Our pre-booked taxi was ten minutes late and we hit traffic on the way to Bristol airport because of some kind of vintage car fair happening nearby. Normally I'd have enjoyed seeing so many old-fashioned cars and motorbikes, but not today. Even the sight of an honest to God omnibus didn't make me squeal in delight. Today was not the day for it. Not when we had a strict timetable to follow.

'We should get a stall at that next year,' Ethan said, watching as several ancient VW campers chugged past our stationary taxi. 'Bet they'd love some proper vintage vinyl.'

I nodded, inwardly screaming at the traffic to just please move.

I was practically hyperventilating by the time we got checked in at the airport and headed for security. Ethan had forgotten to take his phone out of his carry-on and we got pulled aside to dig it out and re-scan. At least he'd not worn his Docs. All that lacing and unlacing would have driven me mad. The whole time we were waiting I was watching the multiple giant clocks in the airport and getting tenser every minute. If I was late to the start of Jess's wedding week, I would never forgive myself. I wasn't sure she would either, though she'd never say anything.

Finally, we passed security and reached the far less stressful part of the airport. Though my level of anxiety barely dipped.

'Do you want a coffee?' Ethan asked doubtfully, eyeing my bouncing leg.

'Tea, please.'

It was only after he'd gone that I remembered my water bottle. It was empty, as per airport rules, but I'd intended to get a drink for the flight. One of my fussy little 'quirks', as Ethan called them, was not liking to drink from bottles I'd bought. I'd worked at a super-market one Christmas and seen rats running all over the flat packs of drinks. Damn it, maybe I could still get a drink before we had to move on. I opened my bag, then realised the bottle wasn't in there. I must have moved it to Ethan's bag when I had to fit the wedding present into mine. At least I hadn't forgotten that. Even the thought of doing so made me feel a bit ill.

Oh well, they'd have water on the plane. They didn't charge for that, right?

I was pleasantly surprised though, when Ethan returned with two cardboard cups and my water bottle.

'You remembered?' I said, gratefully taking the full plastic flask.

'A husband's duty,' he said, tipping an imaginary hat. 'I got you iced tea because there was a queue for the water fountain. But it's in the bottle because I know you're a fusspot.'

'Even better.' I kissed him on the cheek and for a few minutes we escaped the stressful rush of the airport, sipping our hot drinks in an oasis of calm. Then they announced our gate and we were off again like tired horses on their third race of the day, dragging our bags with us.

The flight to Bavaria was just under two hours. Not that it mattered much because we'd have gone for economy even if it was twenty hours. We couldn't afford anything else. Not yet anyway. My inheritance was still pending and I didn't want to think about what it would mean when the money finally came in. For me and for my relationship with Jess. That money had started to symbolise everything that remained unresolved between us. The rift in our relationship packed full of pound coins.

Desperate not to think about it I plugged my head-phones in and put on a children's audiobook from when I was about five. Something to calm me, that familiar story in a voice whose tone and rhythm I knew off by heart. Both Ethan and I liked old things, found them comforting in a weird way. After all, if a piece of uranium glass or a shellac record could survive for decades without a scratch, we could survive anything. He put that in his vows.

'Bugger, I forgot my—' Ethan was saying as I pulled a spare set of earbuds from my bag. 'Cheers.'

'At least you always forget the same things,' I said.

I sipped my iced tea and leant back against the headrest. My sleepless night caught up with me in a rush and before I knew it, Ethan was gently shaking my arm. I struggled upright and he tugged my head-phone from my ear.

'We're here,' he said, amused by my confusion. 'You didn't even snore. I've never seen you sleep that deep.'

I nudged his knee with a playful frown. Still soaked in sleep I helped gather our bags and we joined the tail end of the queue to get off the plane. Outside the air was cold and I hugged myself, wishing I'd thought to put my coat on before hefting the bags. I couldn't be bothered to drop everything now and struggle with it. It had been enough of a bother at security, but I was putting up with it instead of bemoaning our lack of checked luggage.

Our flight was one of those little planes they never bother pulling in to the airport. Instead you have to gather on the tarmac and wait for a bus in the morning chill. I just wanted to get into our rented car and go back to sleep.

Eventually we got through the airport and out to the blocky little office in a car park with rows of shiny cars outside, their insides lined in paper. I waited whilst

Ethan went in to sign some final paperwork and then came out to look over our car. It wasn't a great model; no heated seats or fancy sound system. Just a basic level run-around. We'd even brought our old satnav from home instead of paying out to borrow one. I only hoped our maps were still good. I felt a bolt of panic at the thought of not being able to find the resort. Had Ethan remembered to check the map updates? Was that what was going to undo all our planning?

I checked the time on my phone. We were on schedule. I'd been hoping to be a little bit ahead of ourselves by now. It was very important that we weren't late. Just this once I could not be late. I'd let Jess down enough over the years. This was not going to be one of those times. Everything was going to be perfect for her wedding week.

'We need to stop for fuel,' Ethan groused as we pulled out of the car park. 'They only put a bit in. You better believe they're getting it back with less than a quarter of a tank. That's if I don't push it back into the car park on fumes. Fucking rip-off.'

He chuntered away like any English person on holiday whilst the satnav guided us to a petrol station. I was already struggling to keep my eyes open. Even with all the slightly abnormal normality of another country to watch as it flew by the window. The different logos and sign colours, how the plants at the side of the road weren't quite the same as back home and the way the radio had German announcers and adverts in between American pop songs.

At the station Ethan dug a paper wallet out of his bag and handed me some euros.

'Do you want to get some snacks for the journey? Can you grab me a coffee, oh, and some cigarettes?' he asked.

I nodded.

'Don't forget a lighter!' Ethan called after me.

I went in and picked up sandwiches, chocolate bars and crisps. There were coffee machines at the back, but I couldn't work them out. Either they were the most complicated ones I'd ever seen or my foggy brain just couldn't grasp them. My coins kept being returned and none of the options I pressed ended with a cup being dispensed. So I opted to get Ethan an energy drink instead. Unlike me he was happy to swig from the can, but I'd go over it with an anti-bac wipe just in case.

The cigarettes were the worst part, because I had to point and mime to get them and a cheap lighter. The woman behind the counter was obviously trying to be nice about it but I felt so stupid. I should have at least bought a phrase book. I left the shop with my cheeks on fire.

'I have these by the way,' Ethan said, digging two pre-packaged waffles out of the front pocket of his hemp hoodie when I returned to the car. 'They brought them around while you were—' He tipped his head and snored with a whistle.

'You said I didn't snore!'

'I was sparing your feelings. The woman in front of

us tried to smother you twenty minutes in, took me and two flight attendants to pull her off you.'

'My hero.'

Ethan grinned and tucked a cigarette behind his ear for later.

I set the satnav with the address Jess sent me. Her wedding was being held at a ski lodge and she was paying for our stay there – room, food, everything. Even my dress and Ethan's suit, which were probably already waiting for us there. All we had to do was get there on time. I would not fuck this up. According to the satnav's estimation we'd arrive with some time to spare. Just not as much as I'd originally planned in. We'd been delayed on landing and then the queues in the airport held us up even longer. We'd lost about an hour. Hopefully we'd make it up on the drive. Otherwise we'd have just enough time to freshen up before the welcome dinner Jess told me about when I rang last week.

I sipped from my bottle and hoped my outfit for the dinner wasn't getting too creased in the bag. Not that I wasn't going to look like a heap of shit next to Jess anyway. I think she travelled with an iron and maybe even a mini-dry-cleaning set. Jess was always called a 'natural beauty'; soft dark hair, big dark eyes and perfect skin without even trying. The kind of woman made for pearl earrings and shift dresses. The kind who looked expensive and professional. I'm the one who changes hair colour like I change my underwear, with healed piercings all over and bad tattoos on my lower back and legs. I'd never seen Jess look anything but perfect and polished. I could barely keep polish on for a day without picking it off. But that wasn't a big deal anyway. Maybe I was just freaking out because this would be our first time meeting face to face since the funeral. This was meant to be her week, her day. Honestly, the fact that I couldn't compete with her on a good day could only help me here.

We were moving over the city's roads so smoothly it almost felt like we weren't going anywhere at all. Before too long I felt my eyelids droop. My forehead met the cold glass of the window and I missed whole stretches of the songs on the radio.

Ethan reached out and turned the volume down, then gently patted my knee. The satnav piped up and told him to take the next left. I closed my eyes, relieved that we were going to make it. This time, I wouldn't let my sister down.

Chapter 2

The car jolted suddenly, knocking my head against the passenger window. The inside of my mouth was dry and my eyes felt sticky. How long had I been asleep for? I remembered the ramp to the motorway or whatever it was called here. Then I must have completely passed out. I had that headachy, dehydrated feeling you get from midday naps in stifling rooms.

'We there?' I managed.

'Not . . . just yet,' Ethan said, after a long pause. A pause that said something wasn't quite right.

Peeling my eyelids open I squinted out into a blindingly white world. Snow covered everything and the weak sun was bouncing off it straight into my eyes. I groaned, closed my eyes again.

'Mila?' Ethan said over the drone of the windshield wipers.

I groaned again in response and prised my eyes open to look out at the road ahead. Like everything else it was covered in snow, hemmed in on both sides by tall trees. Thick dark pines which were quite soothing to look at in all that whiteness. Though their branches were weighed down with snow which dropped heavily onto the car as we passed underneath. Big dollops of snow, interspersed with the whirling flakes coming from the sky.

'Where are we?' I asked, sitting up and reaching for my water bottle. My lips felt like paper.

'Right . . . So, the thing is, I'm not really sure?' Ethan said.

That woke me up. Fast.

'What do you mean? What about the satnav?' I looked at my husband and found him biting his lip, eyes crinkled at the edges as he squinted out at the road. A sure sign that he was anxious and getting overwhelmed. I realised what was missing from the atmosphere in the car; the robotic prompting of the satnav. My eyes flew to it but the screen was completely blank, not showing a map and comforting directions. It was dead.

'It stopped working about half an hour ago. I've been following this road ever since. We must be nearly at the resort, right?'

'Did it say to do that before it turned off?'

'No . . . it just said to go straight for however many kilometres but I don't really know how to judge those. And it didn't say what to do after that. I did pass some turnings but no signs for this place we're meant to get to. I thought it was best to just keep following the road.'

A twisty feeling made its home in my stomach. A feeling I was very familiar with. It was the sensation that came when I knew I was going to be late for something important. As Ethan was always pointing out, that was pretty much everything. I was not a punctual person. But today had to be different. This was Jess's wedding after all, and I'd already done enough to spoil it, what with that misunderstanding over Pete's phone.

'What time is it?' I glanced at the digital display in our rented car and swore. 'We were meant to be there an hour ago! Jesus! I need to ring her.'

'No chance – I already tried using the map app on my phone and there's no signal at all up here. No calls, no internet.'

I grabbed my mobile from the cup holder between us and checked. No bars at all.

'Oh well, that's just great!' I detached the satnav from the windscreen and shook it, like that would help.

'Calm down, the wedding isn't for a few days. It's just the welcome dinner tonight. She'll understand.'

'That only makes things worse! Jess always understands and says it's no big deal. That's who she is. But this is her special week – I owe this to her after . . . everything.'

'What happened with Pete wasn't your fault,' Ethan said gently. 'She understood why you had to say something.'

I sighed. Pete was my sister's fiancé. Still. Even though a few months before I'd picked up his phone instead of mine and found some nudes on it. Nudes sent to him by several different women. Pretty surprising really, given that Pete looks like a geography teacher, all tucked-in check shirts and neatly parted pale brown hair. Ethan and I have long speculated that he irons his jeans.

Obviously I'd gone straight to Jess. She'd been absolutely devastated, almost cancelled their whole wedding and broken up with him, even though they'd been together for years. Longer even than Ethan and I. That was until Pete convinced her he'd never even opened the messages in case they were malware. That he thought it was just spam. He still hadn't told her about them, but Jess forgave him so I had to as well. I liked Pete before that whole incident but since then things had been a bit strained. Even before Mum and Dad died. Before Mum's funeral.

'I wish I'd never said anything,' I said, watching the wipers scoop snow off the windscreen. 'She probably thinks I was trying to ruin everything on purpose.'

'Jess doesn't think like that,' Ethan soothed. 'All that is in the past now. You two are all the family you've got – she knows that. Just like she knows you're not to blame for your parents.'

I knew that; a few months ago I'd even believed it. But since the funeral I wasn't taking anything for granted. Ethan didn't know what went on with Jess and me that day and I couldn't bring myself to tell him.

Even before all that it was hard not to feel like I had a lot to make up for when it came to Jess. When I came along as the baby of the family, she was five. I was premature and had a host of health problems, and she had to be the responsible one, the helpful one. For our entire lives nothing she did was ever as important or interesting as what I was doing, at least as far as our parents were concerned. They babied me and relied on her, expecting her to do well. She did, but it was just what she was meant to do, so they never gave her much credit. I'd always looked up to her, this girl who was half a decade ahead of me and absolutely crushing life. Growing up had meant beginning to realise how unfair our parents had been to her.

Now she was marrying Pete at long last. I think the reason she delayed it so long was to stop Mum and Dad comparing her wedding with mine. That or she was worried I'd pop out a grandkid right before and steal her thunder. Not on purpose but, it wouldn't be the first time I'd accidentally fucked things up for her. There wasn't any worry about Mum and Dad not giving her wedding enough importance now. Though I knew it killed her that our parents wouldn't be there. They'd both passed in the last eight months, first Dad, then Mum.

Their deaths only made the situation between Jess and me more tense. They'd left me about ninety per cent of their estate because 'I was starting my family and needed it more'. It hadn't come through yet but it was only a matter of paperwork. I'd planned to split it with Jess but now I wasn't sure she'd accept anything from me.

'I think this sign's for a town,' Ethan said, interrupting my thoughts. I followed his gaze and saw a sign, though not of the modern roadside kind. We were pretty far into the Alps by now after all. The sign was carved from a great slab of wood and nailed to a tree stump. The wood, as the headlights hit it, had a grey weathered look, like it had been there for decades. Maybe more. Between the weathering and the flurries of snow I could just about make out the name on it as Ethan slowed the car: Witwerberg.

'They might have a map or someone can give us directions,' Ethan said.

'Not sure how helpful that'll be. Neither of us speak German.'

'I have faith in the German education system. The lady at the car rental place spoke better English than me,' Ethan pointed out. 'Besides, if they have wifi I can use my phone and get a map myself.'

Ethan took the turning and I zoned out again, my anxiety slightly curbed by the thought that we might make it. Not on time, but at least we'd get there in time for most of dinner and not miss it completely. I'd cling to that.

I watched the road ahead as it narrowed and the trees closed in around us. On my side the snow-covered ground began to dip down and soon we were driving along the top of a steep ridge. At the bottom, in a deep gulley, I saw snowdrifts and a few dark shapes that might have been rabbits. It was hard to tell in the gathering night. The wheels skidded slightly on the road and I gritted my teeth, but we carried on slowly and after a few minutes I managed to relax.

I let out a breath and tried to untangle the stress in my belly. I was so determined not to be late for once. To show up on time and make sure Jess had a perfect wedding. I owed her that after so many years of my life taking precedence. She deserved a perfect wedding with her as the centre of attention for once. It was up to me to make sure it was the best day of her life and here I was, more than an hour late on the first day of the week of events she had planned.

The hypnotic wipers began to slow. I blinked, not sure if I was mistaken. Then the whole car began to shudder and slow down, finally coasting to a stop.

'Fuck,' Ethan breathed. 'Fuck, fuck, fuck!' He punched the steering wheel then tried the ignition. A sputter. One more. Then nothing. The car was completely silent, dead. The cold outside immediately began to leach away the heat around us. Snow silently gathered on the windscreen, blocking out the light, flake by flake.

He'd been quite composed about the satnav failing but now Ethan looked ready to rip the steering wheel off the dashboard. He kept trying the ignition but nothing was happening.

'What is it?' I asked stupidly, looking at the fuel gauge which said we still had over half a tank.

'I have no idea. Hang on,' Ethan snapped as he struggled out of his seatbelt and opened the door. A cold blast of air threw snow into the car and I winced.

The hoodie and coat that had kept me cosy in the confines of the airport were not cut out for Alpine snowstorms. Ethan, still only wearing his hoodie, slammed his door shut and a moment later the bonnet of the car obscured my view. I heard him unsnapping things and muttering to himself. I had no idea what he was doing. Neither of us were good with cars. I could just about add the oil and water to ours, back when we still had a car. Ethan was worse than me; he once fuelled up with diesel instead of petrol and brought us to a stop on the M5. It wasn't really a surprise when he slammed the bonnet down after a few minutes and got back into the car, shivering.

'I've got no idea what's wrong with the fucking thing. Maybe something froze up or got disconnected when I went over that hump that woke you up.' He tried the ignition again and nothing happened. 'Could be the battery?'

'OK,' I said, trying to stay calm. 'Let's walk to this town and get someone to come back with us to jump it. That's what you do with dead batteries, right?'

Ethan shrugged. 'I suppose. We don't know how far it is to town though.'

'We'd better wrap up warm then.'

Our bags were in the back and it took a few minutes to hunt through them for the scarves and hats we'd brought but not bothered to wear in the warm car. Ethan shouldered his coat on and I donned my gloves, wishing I'd thought to wear fleece-lined leggings or actual trousers. I was a bit warmer with the hat and stuff on but getting more and more anxious by the minute. We were getting later and later for the welcome dinner and I couldn't even call Jess to explain. What would she be thinking? That I didn't care enough to get there on time? That maybe I wasn't coming at all?

'Hey,' Ethan said, and I looked up at him. I knew my eyes were welling up. I was always quick to tear up in frustration. 'We'll get there. I promise.'

'OK,' I said, forcing myself to breathe slowly and calm down, taking the hand he offered me. He gave my fingers a reassuring squeeze.

We didn't have any kind of rucksack, so I put my water bottle and the packed food we'd brought for the journey into my handbag, along with the a cheap torch from the car. The kind you buy by the till in pound shops. Not the kind you ever want to actually rely on. Above the snow-topped trees the sky was a deep, dark blue, steadily deepening to black. Night was coming fast and we still had no idea how far away Witwerberg even was or if we'd be able to walk there.

Side by side, Ethan and I began to hike up the narrow road, leaving the lifeless car behind.

Chapter 3

I learned that day that night falls very quickly when there are no streetlights or welcoming buildings to hold it off. Before too long we were stumbling through the snow, following the narrow beam of the torch. Darkness was all around and I kept jumping at every little noise: snow falling from branches, trees creaking in the wind, a twig cracking underfoot. I'd not looked at much info about where we were going for the wedding, but on the resort website I had seen a warning about wolves. I had no idea how common wolf sightings were but in the pitch blackness I wasn't thinking about odds. Only teeth.

Ethan insisted on going ahead of me so I could follow his footprints on the uneven ground. He always joked that I could fall over from a standing start but it didn't seem funny at all just then. Especially not when I hit a rut, broke through the icy crust on it and twisted my ankle. I went down with a shriek that echoed through the trees.

'Mila!' Ethan lifted me back onto my feet but the damage was done. I winced as I set my foot back down. 'Is it broken or sprained?'

'Sprained, I think. Shit!'

'Do you have painkillers?' Ethan asked.

'Somewhere. Can we just get to town and I'll find them when there's more light.'

I leant on him and together we limped along, our progress now even slower than before. How far away were we from civilisation? There'd been no distance mentioned on the Witwerberg sign. Were we too close to need telling or had the fateful words 'twenty miles' been erased by time? Like in a horror film where the hapless teens miss the part of the sign covered by a loose plank – 'danger – do not enter'.

Neither of us said much. I think we were too focused on reaching the town, straining our ears for any hint of civilisation: an engine, a TV blaring, even a voice. But there was nothing. I was cold, in pain and absolutely going to pieces over being so late for Jess's dinner and the possibility that we were about to encounter a wolf.

We'd been walking for ages, but the silence said we were still really far away from town. My leggings were doing nothing against the cold and were now soaking up snow and sticking to me, making me even colder. Likewise my trainers, so comfy on the concourse, were wet through now. I was preparing myself for a long, painful walk, when we came over a low hill and found ourselves staring at a town. More accurately, a village.

The road, more like a track at this point, snaked past it at a short distance, like it was avoiding the sad little ring of buildings. Ethan shone his torch around. At the centre of the ring was a stone well with a thick beam of wood over it, worn but still carved with the name 'Witwerberg'. If that hadn't been there, I never would have believed that this was the place we'd been heading for. The place we'd pinned all our hopes on.

There were six buildings, all log cabins with wide roofs and shuttered windows. The kind cuckoo clocks and Christmas villages made famous. Each one had a low porch outside, some of which were carved and decorated. But I wasn't thinking about the cuteness of it all at that moment. All I saw were six buildings in utter darkness. Not a light on in any of them. More than that, the crookedly hung shutters, fallen-in roofs and rotting porch steps all told one unpleasant story; this place was abandoned. Probably had been for over a hundred years.

'Shit,' Ethan said. 'You've got to be . . . This place is a ghost town.'

Another rush of frigid air gusted over us and I shivered, feeling the cold sink deeper into my body. I needed to get warm soon; we both did.

'I can't go any further. We need to get under cover,' I said.

Ethan took one look at me and nodded. I could tell he was reluctant to give up on finding civilisation. He was so determined he'd probably have hiked all night if my ankle wasn't hurt. That sheer force of will was the reason we had a livelihood. He'd thrown everything into starting our record shop and repair business. We'd started out on a market stall right after uni, but now had a proper shopfront. I only wished either of us could fix a car like we could a turntable.

'Over here,' Ethan said, guiding me towards the first cabin in the row. Unlike the one next to it, it looked intact and stable. At least the roof was still on. He left me leaning on the porch rail whilst he prised the door open, hanging his full weight on the handle. It was thick wood, swollen with damp. When it gave in and flew open a smell of decay wafted out. From inside came a skittering sound which I hoped was just dry leaves caught in the sudden draught. I could not handle rats right now on top of everything else.

Ethan shone the torch around. I'd expected the little cabin to be mostly empty but it looked as though it had been completely stripped. Not even a broken chair or discarded book remained. Whoever had last occupied the place had taken everything with them. The floor was covered in dried pine needles, leaves and dust. One window was an empty hole, the shutters either fallen off entirely or hanging on broken hinges. The window on the other side was tightly shuttered. Opposite the door was a fireplace with a tiny, very rusted grate.

'Cosy,' I muttered, trying to make a joke, but it came out flat. Ethan just glared around the cabin as if it, over everything else, was the worst part of this whole ordeal.

I took a step inside and realised that under the debris on the floor there was some kind of matting that caught the tread of my shoe, too thin to be called a rug. More like rotten fibres pasted down with dirt. It slightly muffled the sounds of my movements as I hopped in and leant against the wall.

'We need some wood to get a fire going,' Ethan said. 'My lighter's in your bag, right?'

'Yup, first time I'm glad you smoke,' I said, trying, with slightly more success this time, to lighten the tense atmosphere.

Ethan snorted, then pulled an apologetic face. 'I'm going to have to take the torch with me. You OK being in the dark?'

'Yes,' I lied. 'I'll try and get something going with what's blown in.'

'All right, I'm just going to the other cabins to look for planks or something we can use. I'll try and get that window covered too. Keep the heat in. Just sit tight and take some painkillers for your ankle.' Then he ducked out, taking the only light with him.

Gingerly, I used my injured foot to push some of the debris aside then lowered myself until I could drop into the clear patch. Manoeuvring into a sitting position hurt a bit but being off my feet was worth it. Inwardly praying that I wouldn't suddenly touch anything alive, I scooped leaves and pine needles into the grate and felt around in my bag for the lighter. I was never going to give Ethan shit about being a smoker again, that was for sure.

It took a bit of shuffling around and I burned my fingers twice, but eventually I got a tiny, if very smoky, fire going. Lighting illicit bonfires in the woods to drink around had finally paid off. It was mostly leaves, plus some sticks off the floor, but it gave a bit of light. I slowly fed needles and some receipts from my bag into it whilst I waited for Ethan to come back. He'd been gone quite a while and I couldn't hear him anymore. I told myself that if he'd been attacked by something I'd have heard him shout. Or scream.

Trying to stay calm I opened my water bottle and took two ibuprofen for the swelling in my ankle and some paracetamol for the pain. Aside from my water bottle of iced tea there was Ethan's can of energy drink and the snacks we'd bought for the journey. Sandwiches, crisps, chocolate bars and the waffles from the plane. I'd over-purchased, which was fortunate. At least we'd have fuel to keep our bodies warm for the night.

Still no Ethan. I checked my mobile again. He had his with him. Still no 4G and no signal either. My battery was also at less than half because I'd fallen asleep and not charged it in the car. Great. I wasn't about to waste it by using the torch.

A sudden noise behind me had me jerking around.

'It's me,' Ethan called from outside, banging around trying to get the shutters closed. 'Hold on.'

After a moment he came in with an armful of wood. Some bits of plank and a few bits of log with moss and lichen on them.

'There was more but I didn't want to take even longer.

Should be enough to keep us warm tonight. Oh good, you got a fire going already.' He fed a few bits of damp wood into the fire and it spat, smoking a lot more. Together we watched, hoping for it to catch. When the flames grew higher they swayed with our collective sigh of relief.

Ethan peeled off his wet gloves and warmed his hands. 'Any chance of a sarnie?'

'Beef and horseradish or ham and cheese?'

'Half each?'

We divided them up and ate quickly. The sandwiches were practically frozen from being in my bag and didn't do much to lift the chill in my belly. Still, at least we wouldn't go hungry. I could tell Ethan was still just as worried as I was, because he didn't make his usual crack about me being happy to eat from packages, yet not drink from bottles. He only munched in silence, glaring into the fire, deep in thought.

I thought of Jess and the welcome dinner which would be nearly over by now. What was she thinking just now? Perhaps she was trying to phone me. Maybe she'd even realised something was off and had some people out looking? I wanted to believe it but the fact was that she probably just thought I was late, as usual. Late to the flight, maybe even missed it. When her calls didn't go through she might put it down to us still being in the air. God, I was going to owe her such an apology when we finally got to the resort. OK, so none of this was strictly my fault, but it felt like it was. I'd just wanted to do this one thing right. Now it was all ruined.

'Hey,' Ethan said, breaking my anxious train of thought. 'Jess won't care about this once she knows what happened. It'll make for a great story to tell at the reception.'

'I don't want a great story – I want her to have a perfect wedding. This is just going to put me in the spotlight – "Everyone, look at Jess's mess of a sister, arriving late with this crazy story." This is her day, it shouldn't be about me. Like everything else has always been about me.'

'All right, so tomorrow we find some help, get a lift to the resort and just play it cool. We got delayed, we're here now and everything will go as planned.'

'Promise?'

'I promise,' Ethan said, putting his arm around me. 'Tomorrow everything will look different and tonight will seem like a bad dream.'

I sighed but I knew he was right. Kind of. Usually Ethan knew exactly what to say but this time he had no way of knowing the way Jess and I had left things when we saw one another last. Still, that was behind us now. Almost. I just had to make sure nothing else happened to ruin her wedding.

With the fire crackling beside us, we bedded down on the hard floor to try and get some sleep. Despite the long nap I'd taken in the car I felt exhausted. My ankle was throbbing and I could barely keep my eyes open. Normally I couldn't sleep without turning over about five times and could always feel the slightest lump in a hotel bed. But hiking through the night with frayed nerves was singularly draining. I fell asleep so fast that damp cabin floor might as well have been a memory foam mattress.

The last thing I felt was Ethan putting his arm around my waist and resting his head against my shoulder. I remember thanking God he was there with me, keeping me calm on the worst night of my life. I couldn't imagine going through the past twelve hours without him.

Chapter 4

'*Mummy!*'

I heard Jess screaming and Mum's answering shout. It had all happened so fast. A second ago I was high up in the old apple tree, shaking the branches to make the best apples fall. I could feel one under my back, round and hard. They made a great sound when they hit the grass. I didn't make that sound.

Mum appeared next to me, looking down. My head hurt and one of my legs was burning. I must have scraped it on the hard grey bark. My fingers still ached from gripping it tightly.

'What happened?' Mum asked, poking me all over. 'I told you to watch her, Jessica. You know you're not meant to climb the tree – it's dangerous.'

'I did watch her!' Jess insisted. 'She said she was going in to get some squash while I got the swing ball out of the shed.'

'It doesn't look like anything's broken,' Mum said.

'But go and get your dad so he can take her to the hospital. She might have a concussion.'

I heard Jess's jelly sandals squeaking as she ran up to the house.

'Millie, you know that old tree is dangerous. A whole branch fell off last year. Didn't Jess tell you not to climb on it?' Mum asked me, smoothing my hair off my face.

'She . . .' I stopped, thinking of my new bike in the garage. I'd only had it for two days. Would they take it away if they found out I'd changed my mind about the squash and wanted an apple instead? That I'd seen Jess in the shed and realised that if I got up the tree quick enough she wouldn't catch me?

'Yes?' Mum prompted.

'She told me to,' I said. 'Jess told me I could climb the tree.'

Mum huffed, shaking her head. I felt my tummy flip over. Now she was mad with Jess. But I'd only wanted her to not be mad at me.

Dad and Jess came back, Dad with the first-aid book and a torch, which he shone in my eyes. Whilst he did that I saw Mum grab Jess's arm and pull her aside, wagging a finger in her face.

Jess's eyes met mine, teary and confused. I looked into the torch beam.

They took me to hospital to get looked at, then got me a Happy Meal on the way home. I asked if we could get an extra toy for Jess, because it was Beanie Baby week. Mum said I was a thoughtful sister and the lady at the counter gave me an extra toy.

At home, Jess was in our room when I brought the beanie lobster to her. I crawled it across the pillow and tapped her nose with its claws. Her eyes were red and all her beanies were in a heap on the floor where she'd thrown them.

'Here, his name's Pinchy,' I said. 'He's a twin.'

Jess sniffed, but took the lobster and made it crawl over my arm and up my neck, which tickled. Then she got the old fish tank out to make Pinchy and Snapper a house. Outside I could hear Dad sawing the bottom branches off the apple tree. I felt bad, because now Jess and I couldn't play house under them. But at least everything else was back to normal.

Chapter 5

The cold woke me up.

I peeled my eyes open and the first thing I saw was the empty grate and the ashes of our fire. It must have burned out in the night. I let out a groan as I realised one of us should have stayed awake to keep it going. Now the cabin was freezing again. We'd also used up all the wood Ethan gathered the night before. Not that there'd been much of it. So one of us would have to go looking for more if we wanted to warm up before deciding what to do now. A quick wiggle of my toes told me that my trainers were still sodden. My socks squelching in snowmelt. Ugh.

After shutting my eyes against the seemingly impossible day ahead of us, I tried to imagine what our options were. Head back to the car and try to get it started, wait in this abandoned cabin and hope help came eventually, or try to walk somewhere else. I flexed my foot experimentally and felt an immediate spike of pain. Walking somewhere else was out then. Great.

I realised then that I didn't have Ethan's warmth at my back. I struggled to sit up and felt my ankle throb again. The pain chased away the lingering fuzziness of sleep. Ethan was gone? Where?

'Ethan?' I croaked.

No answer. I couldn't hear him outside either. Maybe like yesterday he'd gone to the other cabins to look for wood and was out of earshot? I fought to calm my racing pulse and reached for the painkillers. My water bottle was empty so I had to dry swallow them. All the while I told myself not to panic, that Ethan would be back in a moment with more firewood and a plan for how we were going to get out of this mess.

But he didn't come back, with or without firewood. I waited in the cold, longer than I wanted to, until I couldn't take the waiting anymore. Then I hauled myself onto my feet and limped out of the cabin. Standing on the porch I leant on the railing and looked around slowly, alert to any sign of him, until I was facing towards the opposite cabin, the last in the line. No sign of him anywhere.

'Ethan!' I called out. The sound of my voice rebounded from the trees. There was no way anyone around the village couldn't hear that. But still, I got no reply.

I stood there a moment, my uneven breathing and racing heart blotting out any other sound. What if he'd gone for more wood and somehow become trapped? His foot might have gone through the floor of one of the cabins, severing an artery. Or else a beam had fallen and knocked him out. The only way he wasn't answering back was if he wasn't able to. I couldn't waste any more time. I had to look for him.

I could walk, though it was painful. I went to the next nearest cabin, the one with a fallen-in roof. No sign of him inside between the jutting timbers. The next one, missing a door. No Ethan. On and on, I went to each cabin in turn and looked inside, finding debris, fallen logs, rotten floors, but no Ethan. On my way round I snagged a fallen branch and used it to steady myself and take the weight off my ankle, but it did nothing to alleviate my sense of helplessness.

Where was Ethan? Had he wandered into the woods to pee? Was he being chased by wolves or had he seen someone in the distance and run off to get help? My mind conjured and dismissed a dozen scenarios. But none of them felt right. None of them put my fears to rest. I still felt like something was very wrong here.

Finally, I stood on the porch of the last cabin in the semi-circle and took the weight off my injured ankle. I could feel the top of my trainer clamped around the swollen foot, but that wasn't even on my list of concerns. A list that began and ended with 'what has happened to my husband?'

I was satisfied that he wasn't nearby but unable to answer me. But what if he'd gone further than the cabins and something had happened? How was I meant to find him? I limped back to the cabin we'd spent the night in and checked for any kind of note. I even went as far as checking my phone for messages, even in the notes app. Nothing. If Ethan had left the clearing, he hadn't left me any way of finding him.

Images of my husband lying at the bottom of the gulley or being savaged by wolves in the forest filled my brain. Oh God, what was he thinking? It was too dangerous for us to split up, even if he just needed the loo. Why would he just go off on his own? Unless maybe he'd tried to wake me up but couldn't? I had been sleeping really heavily. If he was just going to pop into the trees and come back he might not have thought to leave a note. But that had to have been ages ago. What if he'd lost his way in the snow?

I went back out and circled behind the cabins. My ankle was swollen to twice its normal size and radiating pain, but I couldn't just do nothing. Ethan might have fallen and hit his head on a rock, or blundered into a branch. In this cold he wouldn't last long.

The ground under the trees was uneven and humped with fallen branches covered in snow. I couldn't see any sign that Ethan had gone this way. Still, I limped out further and called his name, over and over, desperate to catch sight of his military greatcoat or red hat in all that white. But there was nothing.

I stumbled back into the clearing, now thoroughly panicked and in a huge amount of pain. If he wasn't in the woods or the cabins, where could he have gone? Maybe he'd had to go further than the treeline and having no paper, hadn't thought to leave a note on my phone?

There was only one place I could think of that he'd

need to go and that was back to the car. Maybe he thought he could find the problem in daylight, or was just hoping it would start again spontaneously. He used that tactic a lot at home and called it 'giving things time'. When he couldn't find a fault in a player he'd shrug and say 'needs time' and leave it for an hour or so. Sometimes it even worked. Mostly it didn't. But he was probably desperate enough to try.

The more I thought about it the more certain I became that he'd gone back to the car. Perhaps he decided to go whilst I slept so I wouldn't panic about being alone? Which was obviously working really well. If that was what he'd done I'd give him such an earful when he came back.

I stood there, frozen by indecision. If I was right and he had gone back to the car, he'd be back soon with either good news or bad. I just had to wait for him. Unless he was hurt, of course. And what if he got the car working and then had to come and get me? The car would never make it down the narrow track we'd taken. He'd have to walk and by then the engine might have crapped out again. No, if he got it going we had to leave right away and try to reach the resort or some kind of help. Besides which, he might be hurt or stuck somewhere and I had no way of knowing how long he'd been gone. I had a sudden vision of the car suddenly jolting forward and crushing his foot. Anything could have happened. I had to go to him.

With my improvised walking stick in hand I limped to our cabin, slung my bag on and scraped 'gone to car' in the snow on the porch. If Ethan came back he'd know where I'd gone. As I did so I wondered why it hadn't occurred to him to do the same. We had no paper but the white expanse outside was available.

I started to walk back the way we'd come in the dark. All the while my blood fizzed with anxiety. What if I was wrong and Ethan was somewhere else? What if the car was truly fucked and I'd have to make the whole painful walk back again? What if I met a wolf or even a fucking bear on the way? If they even had bears here. That last thought made me stumble to a stop but the image of Ethan lying in the snow, slowly turning blue, was enough to get me moving again.

I couldn't even stay annoyed with Ethan for leaving me asleep on my own. I was just so worried about what might have happened. Once I knew he was OK I could probably muster some outrage, unless he'd got the car going, in which case I'd marry him all over again.

When I finally reached the wider road where we'd broken down I nearly cried. Here was the ridge we'd driven along. It couldn't be much further. It had started to snow again and a strong wind was blasting me in the face, the flakes like sand. My ankle was on fire and my back had started to hurt from the awkward way I was walking. My legs trembled with pain. I desperately wanted to sit down and rest, but there was nowhere to do so and no way was I stopping until I got to Ethan.

Then I reached the spot where we'd broken down. We'd left deep wheel ruts in the snow and a chaotic whirl of footprints as we got stuff from the boot and paced around. Though all the tracks were blurred by snow they were still there. They were the only things that told me I was in the right place, because the car was gone.

I stared stupidly at the wheel ruts in the snow where the car had clearly been. This was where it had broken down, there was proof, but the car was gone. For a moment I was too shocked to process anything other than the complete absence of our rental car. Then it hit me that this was the last place I'd imagined Ethan might be. If he wasn't here, then where could he possibly have gone? Not to mention, how could a car that didn't even start just vanish like this?

I was dumbstruck for a moment, my thoughts refusing to settle or connect. Then my mind started grasping on to details, like the direction of the wheel ruts. There was the trail we'd made as we coasted to a stop and yet there were newer tracks slanting left. Not in a turn to get the car facing back up the road, but going straight off the road.

I limped to the side of the road and looked down into the deep gulley. It cut away from the road steeply, down so far I doubted I'd be able to climb up the side even if my ankle wasn't hurt. At the bottom, wedged between two pines, was our car. It had cut a weaving trail through the snow on its way down.

My insides turned to ice. Had Ethan managed to get the car going and been trying to manoeuvre it round, only to lose it on the slippery road and crash? It didn't look like he'd got out if so. No footprints accompanied the car's winding ruts. No sign that a driver had struggled out and walked away. Was he still in there, unconscious . . . or worse?

'Ethan!' I called down, trying to glimpse any movement from the inside of the car. Nothing. If he was in there he wasn't moving at all. I didn't want to think about what that meant.

I had to reach him – but how, with my ankle as bad as it was? If I tried to get down there I'd probably just get stuck at the bottom with the car. But it was better than standing around up on the road whilst Ethan succumbed to a concussion.

It was only as I looked around for a way down that I remembered, with a cold twisting in my stomach, where the car keys were. I dug through my bag, for a second hoping that Ethan had just taken them, but then I felt the unfamiliar keyring with the rental office details on it. I still had the only set of keys. I'd put them in my bag when Ethan thrust them at me so he could put his gloves on.

Ethan wouldn't have been able to drive the car even if it suddenly started to work. He hadn't had an accident. The car had rolled off the ridge, somehow. Surely if Ethan had seen what had happened he'd have come right back to tell me about the car. Without it we were both trapped. Which meant . . . he hadn't come this way at all.

'Ethan!' I shouted, desperate for an answer, but none came.

The back of my neck prickled and I turned, suddenly

scared that I'd find someone watching me. A stranger. But there was nothing. Just the snow swirling as the wind gusted and moaned. I had to get into cover; this didn't seem like a normal snow shower. A storm was blowing up. There was nowhere to go but back to the village. Without Ethan. Without knowing where on earth he'd vanished to.

On the journey back I was in a lot of pain, but fear was my real concern. I kept hearing twigs snap or branches sway. I turned or looked to the treeline and every time I was certain that I would see someone. Not Ethan, someone else. I felt like I was being watched. Not only watched, but followed by someone just out of sight. It made my skin crawl no matter how many times I told myself that I was just scared for Ethan and afraid to be alone.

It was almost a relief when the village came into view through the curtains of snowfall. At least it was familiar and I could get inside and out of the growing storm. Perhaps Ethan had returned from wherever he'd gone to and I'd find him in the cabin, worried for me. Maybe he'd just been looking for wood after all, with his hat pulled down against the cold, muffling the sound of my voice.

I happened to glance down as I picked my way, finding my footing. Then I froze. All thoughts of a woodland stalker quickly replaced by a new and horrifying realisation.

There on the ground were my footprints from the night before, with Ethan's. The new snowfall had blurred them a bit, but I could still see them. Beside them were my footprints from only an hour or so before as I checked the cabins and the woods, then finally left in the direction of the car.

There were no other prints.

As far as I could see, mine were the only fresh footprints in the snow. There was no evidence on the white ground that suggested Ethan had left the cabin or hiked off in the direction of our car. Let alone returned to our shelter.

Slowly, I walked into the village and looked at the ground. There had to be something. I must just be looking at things from the wrong angle. But after a circuit of the village, dragging my swollen foot, I was certain that I wasn't missing anything. The proof was in the footprints. Or rather, the lack of footprints.

There, in the snow, were my tracks. A crazy daisy chain from one cabin to another. And there were Ethan's slightly blurred prints from yesterday alongside them as he went from house to house looking for firewood. Some snow had fallen, making them fuzzy around the edges, partially filling them, just like the tracks we'd made when we entered the clearing.

No one else had walked through the village between us arriving and me looking for my husband. There was no sign of him going to look for wood that morning, of him doing anything at all since we went to bed the night before.

Slowly I made my way back to the cabin we'd spent the night in. I was hoping that on closer inspection,

I'd be able to see what I expected to see. Evidence of Ethan leaving the cabin. But there was nothing. It was impossible but . . . Ethan wasn't in the cabin and, as far as I could see, he hadn't set foot outside it either.

He was just . . . gone.

Chapter 6

With the storm howling through the woods my only choice was to shut myself back in the cabin. It was the last thing I wanted to do. Less than twenty-four hours ago that little house had looked like salvation, shelter, safety. Now it made me shudder just to look at it. This was the place where my husband had vanished.

There was no other word for it. I could no longer come up with any explanation other than that. Ethan wasn't looking for wood, fixing the car or even having a pee in the woods. He was just . . . gone.

I suppose I could have chosen any of the other cabins. But just then I couldn't deal with another unknown. With missing doors or shutters, or the possibility that the roof might leak. Besides which, every single one of them was part of what had happened. The whole village felt wrong, like I'd stumbled into a horror film.

I limped into the cabin and shut the door. Momentarily relieved to be out of the rising storm. I don't know why it almost surprised me to find the place as empty as when I'd left it. Almost like I'd imagined Ethan would reappear if I gave him some time. As if he was part of a magic trick that would end with everything being the same as it was before.

Helplessly I looked around at the four bare walls and featureless floor, then up into the rafters. What had happened to Ethan and where had he gone? How had I not heard him go and how had he been whisked away without leaving a single footprint outside in the snow?

The impossibility of it all made me even more uneasy than in my earlier panic over Ethan's whereabouts. It wasn't just that he was gone, it was that he'd gone without a trace. Taken, or spirited away, leaving no evidence. There was nothing I could hold on to, no fact or explanation to keep me grounded in reality. Without that anchor my mind was going wild, unable to settle on any of the terrible theories it had conjured up. There was something eerie about the lack of evidence, the unexplained disappearance. Something that tapped into the childish part of me that still believed in monsters and ghosts, but only when it was dark. Only when I was all alone.

I looked around me, desperate for a clue. A hint as to how to find my husband. The cabin had two windows, one in each short end, and both were shuttered. Ethan had closed one set himself from the outside. I went to it and shook the heavy wooden shutters. They refused to open and I guessed he'd somehow wedged them shut from the other side. The other shutters were latched on the inside as they'd been intended to be. Had Ethan opened them and climbed out? Why though? And to where? I'd heard of people going a bit weird when hypothermia set in, like stripping off their clothes in the snow. But not climbing out of windows for no reason.

Chilled, I tried to remember if I'd looked at that side of the cabin when I was out. What if Ethan, for some reason, decided to open the shutters and look out, only to be seized by something and dragged outside? What if as well as wolves there were bears in these woods and one had scooped him up with a clawed hand and left him, savaged, by the cabin wall? I'd slept so deeply, perhaps I hadn't heard him scream. Or else his throat was slashed open too quickly for him to make a sound.

Afraid of what I'd see on the other side, I opened the shutters. The wind took them at once and clattered them back against the house, throwing snow in my face. Squinting against the icy shards I looked down. There was nothing there. No blood, no body and no prints under the window. Ethan hadn't left that way, unless he'd climbed up onto the roof. Which seemed even less likely than a bear attack. Where would he go from up there, even if he had a reason to climb up that way? The other cabins were too far away to jump to.

With difficulty I dragged the shutters closed against the wind and forced the latch home. Suddenly feeling every bit of exertion I'd expended since that morning,

I let myself slide to the floor. My ankle was badly swollen and I ached from my night on the floor, never mind the long hike to and from the car. Or where the car should have been. I had no explanation for that either. How had it ended up down the gulley? The pain in my ankle was getting worse and I couldn't think straight.

Unsure of the time, I dry swallowed some more anti-inflammatories and hoped I wasn't double dosing. Outside the snowstorm was gathering strength and I heard trees groaning as they were pummelled by the wind. Inside the cabin was just as cold as outside, my breath a dense white fog. Was Ethan out in that? Had I missed something, walked right past his body on the ground? But if he was out there unconscious in the snow, I had no answer as to how he'd got there.

What the hell was going on? I buried my head in my hands and fought to calm myself. I could feel panic rising like water, ready to close over my head. Ethan was gone and I had no idea where or how. I was stuck in an abandoned village and my one potential method of escape was sitting at the bottom of a gulley.

Sitting there, I managed to hone in on the bad feeling that had been brewing since I returned to the village, feeling as if I was being watched. It all felt . . . personal. That's the only way I could explain it. The satnav, the breakdown, the car, the unexplained disappearance of Ethan – this no longer felt like bad luck. This felt like I was being toyed with. As if this was someone's intentional trap. Someone had shoved our car off the road and taken Ethan. Something that left no footprints. Something that watched from the woods.

'Get a grip, Mila,' I whispered to myself. 'Get a bloody grip.'

But I was whispering because I was scared of being heard even over the howling storm. I couldn't quite convince myself that I was alone in that place. Even as the storm raged around the cabin and I huddled into my coat, covering my ears against the screams of the wind, I felt the presence of something outside. Something that wasn't a storm or anything natural. Something evil.

The storm went on so long that I couldn't tell if night had fallen or if the shutters were just crusted in snow. I eventually uncurled myself and crawled to the grate to light another fire. There wasn't much to fuel it; some charred sticks from the night before and the end of a log that hadn't completely burned away, plus some leaves. It barely warmed one third of the cabin. I huddled in close to the light and heat, like it was some kind of holy fire that would keep my creeping dread away. As much as I told myself it was just the panic, the anxiety, I couldn't make it go away.

Whilst I waited out the storm, burning every leaf and twig in the cabin to stay warm, I thought of Ethan and Jess. The two people I loved most. Ethan was missing. Possibly taken against his will, trapped or held somewhere. Was he hurt or afraid? What was going to happen to him and could he get away? What if he needed my help? What was he going through right now and why? Why was this happening to us?

Helplessly I thought of Jess, waiting for me still on day two of her wedding week. Was she worried now? Had she called the police, the mountain rescue, or whatever Germany had to save hapless tourists? Was someone looking for us? Would they even find me out here in Witwerberg and how would they find Ethan if I didn't even know where he was?

Finally, my thoughts turned to the village itself. Why was it abandoned? What had happened there to make it feel like this? What was it that I could sense, that my mind kept trying to explain away – the sense of being watched. Of being haunted.

Eventually there was nothing left on the floor to burn. The fire was slowly dying and the temperature, which had already been far too cold for comfort, was plunging dangerously as the storm went on. I needed something else to burn or I would freeze to death within hours. Of course the building I was in was made of wood, but ripping into my shelter wouldn't do me much good. It was so old it might even start crumbling if I removed so much as a floorboard. Not that I had anything with which to pry at them.

I waited as long as I could but eventually I realised it was useless. It didn't matter that I was in pain, that the weather was like a living creature prowling the woods. I was going to have to go outside. There was no avoiding it.

By this time my ankle was slightly less swollen,

though still painful. Just in time for me to aggravate my injury all over again. I was already wearing every bit of clothing I had and was still cold to the bone. As I looked at the door though, that wasn't what was holding me back. I knew that outside I'd be even colder, buffeted by winds and blinded by snow. Yet the thing keeping me inside the icy cabin wasn't fear of the weather. It was fear of what might be out in that storm. Fear of what had happened to Ethan and of whatever had made him vanish so completely.

I got to my feet and rested my gloved hand on the door latch. My other hand cupped the phone in the pocket of my coat. I'd need to use the torch after all in the unnatural darkness.

'You need firewood,' I told myself sternly. 'This is all just in your head. You're freaking out, but you need to stay warm.'

I was trying to be like Ethan – practical, logical. He was the one who normally talked me down when I started spinning out. The one who assured me that I had locked the door, that the noise outside wasn't our car window being smashed and that we weren't going to get flooded out of our shop just because record rain was forecast. He called it my 'inner doom prophet' and he was my reality check. Now I'd have to do it for myself.

'Come on, Mila,' I muttered to myself. 'The sooner you go, the sooner you bring wood back and get warm in front of a nice bright fire.' Before I finished the sentence I yanked open the door and stepped out into the blinding snowstorm.

As bad as I'd been expecting it to be, it was nothing compared to the reality. Outside the snow might have been falling noiselessly, but it was flying so fast it took my breath away. The wind more than made up for the silent snowflakes. It screamed in my ears, freezing them painfully fast. The crashing and creaking of trees was loud and constant.

I couldn't see anything. The snow was flying like fistfuls of sand and I could hardly open my eyes to see the absolute darkness through each blinding flurry. The light from my phone couldn't reach anything, it only bounced off the snow. With my head down I held out one hand, feeling for anything solid.

Stumbling along I gritted my teeth and tried to breathe as little as possible. Each mouthful of frigid air hurt my chest and made my teeth ache. My nose was running uncontrollably after only a few seconds and I felt the snot freeze to my top lip.

My feet suddenly hit something solid and I fell onto my knees, dropping the phone. Scrambling around with both hands I felt my fingers hit it and send it spinning off somewhere. Fuck.

The surface under me was flat and uniform. After feeling around for a moment I realised I'd tripped on the steps to a porch on one of the cabins. Frowning I remembered that the cabin next to mine was mostly collapsed. The roof had fallen in and the porch was rotted through. I must have walked straight past that one in the storm and ended up further than I'd planned. How was I going to find my way back?

Panic started to take hold of me, making my heart race and my thoughts trip all over themselves. This was a terrible idea. I'd have been better off staying in the cold cabin instead of plunging out into the middle of a blizzard. Even when I was trying to be sensible I still made terrible choices. Typical.

I clawed my way across the porch, feeling like I'd just been dunked in a tub of icy water. I made it in through the open door of the cabin. This one was almost identical to mine, except that the floor was mostly covered in snow. I tried to feel for the door and shut it, then realised that this was the cabin with no door. The third one in the semi-circle. Well, at least now I knew where I was.

Out of the barrage of snow I checked the floor and found dark shapes between the mounds of snow; bits of stick and branch that had blown in over the years. I realised I'd brought nothing to carry this stuff in and groaned. Stupid. I'd need at least one hand free to feel my way back to the right cabin. After a moment's thought I took off my beanie hat and started shoving sticks into it as a makeshift bag. Now I'd be bareheaded in the storm. Wonderful.

After grubbing up enough wood to fill my beanie, plus a few chunks in my pockets, I decided I needed to get back to the cabin. I was freezing cold even under all my layers and desperately needed to get a fire going. I'd been hunched over for a while, my back to the snow coming through the door. Standing up I cracked my spine with a wince and looked out into the storm.

That's when I saw him.

Them.

It.

A human-shaped shadow in the snow. It was hard to see with the shifting, maddening waves of snowflakes, but just for a moment it was there. A person on the edge of the clearing. A person I could sense looking right at me.

I was too stunned to call out. Logically I should have thought it was Ethan but the crawling on my spine and the prickling of my neck told me this wasn't my husband. There was nothing familiar or reassuring about its presence. This was the stranger I'd sensed watching me. The evil hiding in the woods.

Whoever, whatever it was, it vanished between heartbeats. One moment I was sure I was looking right at the outline of another person. The next it was just the snow and the wailing of the wind.

I ran. It was stupid, infantile, but I couldn't think in that moment. I just wanted to put a door and four walls between myself and whatever it was that had looked at me and then vanished. I fell down the porch steps into the deeper snow and floundered my way back towards my cabin, following the tracks I'd left before. I practically had my nose to the ground and they were already blurred by snowfall. Within another half hour they'd have disappeared entirely.

At the cabin I almost threw myself inside, latched the door and leant against it. If I'd had a chair or any other piece of furniture I'd have barricaded myself inside. As it was I just stayed there. Holding the door shut with every bit of strength in my frozen body, praying that I wouldn't feel anything on the other side.

Chapter 7

The only thing that prised me away from that door in the end was cold. Without it I might have stayed there until help came and found my body still holding tightly to that latch.

I have no idea how long I sat there on the floor, hand going stiff on the icy metal, my shoulder against the wood. An hour? Two? Enough time for my mind to come back from that place of deep fear it had gone to. The kind of fear that holds you in a trance like a rabbit watching a car barrel towards it. Enough time for my brain to start working properly again. It told me that spectres in the woods weren't as deadly as hypothermia. That the door wasn't going to protect me from the creeping cold and the prickle of numbness in my wet shoes. That's what got me up and frantically relighting my fire. Though not before I shoved a bit of plank under the door to wedge it shut.

Stupidly I'd burned all my dry tinder whilst trying to put off going outside to look for wood. Now I only had the damp sticks I'd just gathered. The torch had also vanished along with Ethan, so I was groping around in the dark. I clicked the lighter for a little light then tried to set a fire, but the wood only spat and smoked. Finally I gave up and turned out every pocket of my bag, hoping for one last scrap of paper to get things going. Right at the bottom of an inner pocket was an extremely battered looking tampon. I'd never needed one more.

The tampon and cardboard applicator burned well, enough to get some of the sticks to catch. It took a bit of careful positioning but eventually I had a good blaze in the grate and had arranged the larger logs to dry in the warmth. I took off my wet gloves and trainers and held my hands towards the fire, propping my feet as close as I dared and letting the heat chase away the stiffness. There wasn't much I could do about my wet leggings except wear them until they dried in the heat from the fire. Even though I was glad of the warmth, it was the light I appreciated more than anything else. Light to keep the shadows away.

Had I really seen what I thought I'd seen – a person out there in the snow? The fact that I was no longer sure it was a man, just . . . someone, probably meant no. It had to have been an illusion created by all that snow and my own fear. Who would be out in this storm? Besides, if it had been a person, not just in the clearing but looking right at me, they would have said something, surely? Called out, come to me to find out why I was there. They wouldn't have just stood there and watched me crawl around on the floor of the cabin. Watched as I ran back here and slammed the door shut. They'd be worried, want to know what I was doing.

Unless they didn't care, I thought, that fear resurfacing. Unless they weren't just walking into the village by chance, but there watching me. Stalking me as they'd been doing all day. The tickle on the back of my neck, the crack of branches in the woods. The feeling that I was being watched. What if they'd been out there since our car broke down? What if they were to blame for Ethan's disappearance and I was next?

I shook myself. Ethan hadn't left any footprints, never mind anyone else. As far as I'd seen, no one had come near the cabin or left it until I woke up and went looking for Ethan. The only thing telling me that there was someone in the woods was my own frightened brain. If there really was someone out there and they'd taken my husband, why would they leave me to run around all day? Surely I was an easier mark, injured and panicked as I was.

Looking at it logically, like Ethan would have, it all had to be paranoia. Woods were full of animals making noises, and swirling snow could make thousands of random shapes. Shapes my mind was interpreting as a person. Maybe because a person could be fought or shut out of a cabin, whereas hypothermia, starvation and the fear of never being found could not. I was creating an enemy I could potentially reason with or fight, instead of coping with the more terrifying things I couldn't escape.

If I kept telling myself that, I was sure I would start to believe it. That eventually the more basic, instinctive thoughts of ghosts and spirits would fall in line and be controlled by my more logical mind. I just had to distract myself and keep my thoughts on an even keel.

By the light of the fire I tried to be organised and went through my supplies. There wasn't much. What had looked like a lot of food when it only had to last us the night wasn't much now I was stuck with no way out of the village. The sad little pile of rations held four bags of crisps, three chocolate bars, a can of energy drink and two individually wrapped waffles from the plane. In my panic after finding Ethan missing I hadn't eaten anything or even had a sip of drink all day. Now hunger and thirst were catching up with me, no longer pushed down by the urgency of my search for Ethan.

Whilst searching my bag for kindling I also found some sachets of instant coffee, sugar and milk which I'd taken from a hotel ages ago and forgotten to remove. I was lucky airport security hadn't picked up on them. There was also one ketchup packet from a long forgotten McDonald's meal. Not exactly rations for climbing Everest, or surviving in a deserted village.

I spent a few minutes moving these sad little packets around, trying to work out how long I could stretch them for. Two more days? Three? What if rescue hadn't come by then? I had a sudden thought of someone stumbling across my skeletal remains, curled into the foetal position by the long-dead fire. Starved to death. I swallowed, my throat dry, and told myself not to think about that. Help would come. I just had to last that long.

At least I wasn't going to die of thirst; there was plenty of snow outside for me to melt, though the thought of what bacteria and bugs might be hiding in that 'clean' snow made me shiver. How could I purify it? I wished I had a pot or something to boil the water in. Or some of the water purification tablets Dad had bought that one time, for our holiday in Greece. He was always over-prepared. I should have learned from him.

I wished I hadn't thought about that holiday. It was another sore spot in my memory, because once again, Jess was left out. She'd had her final year exams at uni when our parents booked it. But rebooking would have meant going two weeks later and I'd have missed my end of year prom at school. Which was unthinkable to teenage me, but shouldn't have been such a big deal to them. So Jess didn't get to come and I had the whole twin-bed room to myself.

God, I hoped she realised soon that I was missing. But honestly, I couldn't blame her for not immediately jumping to the conclusion that I was in trouble. She probably just thought that once again my wants had come first and I'd bailed on her wedding to enjoy myself elsewhere.

My belly howled then, bringing me back to the present. Having not eaten since the sandwiches last night, panic had been dampening my appetite. But the cold was waking it up and my stomach was beginning to cramp. I had one of the waffles, even licked the sugar off the inside of the packet. The energy drink had quite a lot of sugar listed in the ingredients too, so I wiped the top with my sleeve and cracked it open. My anti-bac wipes were in the car at the bottom of the gulley. As I drank the too-sweet fizz I felt a stab of loss at the thought of Ethan making fun of me for breaking my rule about cans. What if I never heard him make fun of me again? What if he was never coming back?

I forced back the lump in my throat and chugged the energy drink. It would keep me awake but that's what I wanted. There was no way I would willingly sleep in that cabin at that moment. Last time I'd let my guard down my husband had vanished. I hadn't imagined that. The figure in the snow might have been the result of fear and illusion but Ethan really was missing.

Slightly re-energised I started a more thorough search of the cabin. I'd been distracted before, acting on impulse and not being rational. Now I took it inch by inch. Even so it didn't take long. The walls were solid logs with windows cut into them. One with shutters I could open, one lot jammed shut from outside. Overhead there were only rafters and shadows, though I couldn't see much up there without my phone which was now lost in the snow outside. The floor had that weird burlap covering on it, more visible now without the leaves and debris on top. I tried lifting it at the edges but it was either glued to the floorboards or had become plastered down with dirt and foot traffic. In places it was worn to near invisibility or stained with dirt, just a couple of fibres clinging on.

Lastly I felt my way along the walls. I wasn't sure what I was feeling for; secret switches or a knothole that was really a doorknob? A door to where I had no idea. But there was nothing, until I got to the back wall.

My fingers hit a jagged spot and then fumbled into a rough hole, maybe an inch across but deepest in the middle. I was crouched down and the hole was maybe two feet off the floor. I would have written it off as random wear and tear but it was the only thing in the cabin that stood out as being out of place. Turning so the firelight could reach the wall I examined the hole. It was rough and irregular like something had scraped at it. On one side there was a straight cut though. Like it was made with a tool. I tried poking it, even put my eye up to it as if it was a peephole. But there didn't seem to be anything more to it than just a hole in the wall. Maybe something to do with how the logs were felled? An aborted attempt at a notch?

I sat back with and sigh and rubbed my hands over my face. None of this was helping. Where the hell had Ethan gone? And why? How? It didn't make any sense. There was nothing in the cabin that gave me even the slightest idea of how a fully grown man could get out without leaving footprints on the snow. Was I on the right track earlier? Had he actually climbed out the window onto the roof?

I looked up at the shadowed rafters. Was that it? I

was being facetious but . . . how else would he have done it? But still that didn't tell me why. Either he'd been taken by someone, or something, or, as much as I didn't want to believe it, he'd left of his own accord. But even that made no sense. Why would Ethan leave me alone in the village without telling me where he was going? He knew I was injured and he knew I didn't have any more firewood. If he wanted to go for help and leave me behind to hold tight, he'd have told me, gathered wood for me. Fetched our case from the car so I had more clothes and supplies. He'd have left footprints.

No, I refused to believe that Ethan left on his own. Something had made him go, made him disappear. The same thing that had been watching me and following me as I looked for him out by the car.

The car. That was another thing. What the hell happened there? I was so annoyed at myself for not thinking to look for any extra sets of footprints whilst I was up there. Now they'd been obliterated by the storm. I wouldn't be able to work out what had happened. But it had to have been someone doing it on purpose, right? I had the keys but they'd probably just pushed it into the gulley. Whoever 'they' were. I realised I was getting carried away again, giving in to paranoia. Yesterday it had all happened so quickly. What if Ethan hadn't put the handbrake on before we left the car?

I let a reluctant smile take hold as I remembered when we'd bought our first and only car as a couple.

It was right after we'd graduated and he hadn't driven since passing his test three years before. He'd been so excited to show it off to my parents and had been utterly speechless when he threw open the curtains and it wasn't on the driveway. He'd left the handbrake off and it had rolled into the road. No one was hurt, thank God, but I teased him about it mercilessly. Then a few weeks later he realised that the persistent 'whooshing' noise I'd been complaining about was because I'd left the passenger door slightly open and driven it like that for five days. We were even after that.

My smile faded. I wanted to know where he was so badly. Just to know that he was OK. Still, remembering that little mistake made me doubt my theory that our car had been pushed off the road by some mystery stalker. We'd probably just fucked up and left the brake off and it had rolled.

I'd been more focused on what had caused it to move than on what that meant: anyone driving by wouldn't find the car. There was now nothing on the road to attract rescuers who might be out looking for me after I'd not arrived at the resort. If in fact Jess had decided I was now late enough to qualify as missing. I cringed internally as I realised that maybe she wasn't worried yet. She knew I was usually late to stuff, but there had been times that I hadn't shown up at all. One time in particular.

Back then she was just turning twenty and I was only fifteen. That doesn't excuse it but it was what she always said when I tried to bring it up and apologise.

She was graduating with a first, naturally, and I now knew she was super excited to take pictures in her gown and go out for a celebration dinner. She probably even expected a little gift or something. Hell, when I scraped by with my third in Music Tech I got a sterling silver treble clef necklace.

I was meant to take the train up after school on Friday and meet my parents at their hotel. They hadn't wanted to leave me behind but I'd insisted I was fine and Mum wanted to do some sightseeing. Only I decided in my teenage wisdom, to go on a camping trip with a few friends instead. Without telling my parents and claiming afterwards that I missed the train and didn't want them to buy another ticket.

My friends and I took our DoE gear into some woods with several large bottles of cheap cider. We lit a fire, smoked some spliffs, blasted some music and inevitably attracted attention. The farmer whose land we were on called the police and I got arrested at two in the morning, six hours before Jess's graduation breakfast.

Mum and Dad instantly dropped everything to drive home and get me. I must have been a sight, muddy, still drunk and wearing a lost-property sweatshirt because I was topless at the time of arrest. Really classy. They took me home, put me to bed and then stayed with me. Jess went to her graduation breakfast and ceremony alone. She never got her celebration dinner and, to cap it all, my parents hadn't bought her a gift.

She was nice about it. I was underage; obviously they couldn't just leave me at the police station. But that was the first time I started to feel bad about Mum and Dad always picking me over her. Why hadn't one of them stayed for her graduation? Why hadn't they bought her something? It wasn't like we didn't have money. It was like they didn't think about her at all. If she didn't tell them straight up that she needed something, it just didn't occur to them.

Maybe Jess was sitting in that resort and thinking I'd just decided not to come? That I'd decided to go to a music festival or gone on holiday and just forgotten that her wedding was this week? I was, after all, the one who sent Christmas presents too late to arrive before New Year, and nine times out of ten failed to send thank-you notes and birthday cards. The fact was I had a lot of years of being a terrible sister under my belt. A lot of shit I needed to make up for.

What if it was days until she finally realised I wasn't coming? What if she assumed I'd fucked up again and just never called me? Hell, maybe she thought I was still angry about the funeral and decided to cut off all contact. If Ethan really had vanished, no one would ever find me in Witwerberg.

That thought worked better than any energy drink. After curling up in a ball on the hard floor I was awake for hours. Still hungry but too scared to use more of my rations. I just laid there and imagined the worst. That no one would ever find me and my body would freeze to the floorboards of that tiny cabin unmourned and unmissed.

Chapter 8

I knew as soon as I heard Jess shouting that she'd found her makeup set. For the past three days I'd been worried about when she'd next use it. Hoping that maybe she'd just forget about it. Fat chance. She'd saved up for two months to buy it from Woolworths.

The set was really nice. A big pink heart full of eyeshadows and two little gold hearts with lipstick and blusher in them. It came with three brushes with handles full of floating glitter, and three sponges in the shape of little hearts. Around the edges of the packaging were six bottles of nail polish with sparkly lids. I'd seen them all up close when she brought it home and unwrapped it, putting each thing onto her dressing table.

'Can I have one?' I begged Mum that night. 'Please, please, pretty please?'

Mum laughed. 'Millie, you're only ten, that's far too young for makeup. Jess is a teenager, what she does to her face is her business, but I won't have you ruining your skin at your age.'

Jess was in the room, but she didn't say anything, just lifted her Maths textbook a little higher. Dad, watching Countryfile, didn't seem to be listening.

'Jess, can I play with it?' I asked her that night, once we'd both had our baths.

'No, Mils, it's not a toy. You'll muck it up and I just got it.'

'But—'

'I said no,' Jess said quickly. 'Be told.'

I did listen to her. I didn't touch it for a whole week after that. But then she went out to the cinema with her friends and I wasn't allowed to go to that either. So I went into her room to look for something to do.

I didn't mean to ruin the kit. I only wanted to open up the hearts and look at the colours, maybe try some on. But the pink one was really stiff to open and I pulled a bit too hard. It slipped out of my hands, hit the table and went face down on the carpet. When I picked it up a couple of the eyeshadows were smashed and there was a crack in the case.

I didn't know what to do or how to fix it. So I just shut the kit and put it back where it was before, with the crack facing the wall. But clearly Jess had just picked it up and seen the damage. She wasn't stupid – who else could it have been but me?

'You cow!' She threw open my bedroom door, waving the pink heart. 'You did this on purpose, didn't you?'

'I didn't mean to!'

'That's crap – you've been on about it since I brought

it home and you couldn't stand me having something that you didn't.'

'No, I just wanted to look at it. It was an accident, I swear!'

'What's all this?' Mum asked, coming up the hallway. 'Jess, don't use that kind of language around your sister.'

'Mila broke my makeup,' Jess said, showing Mum the damage. Mum took the set, turned it over and sniffed.

'Oh dear, well, it was a flimsy thing. What do you expect when it's that cheap?'

'It was two months' pocket money,' Jess said, angry tears gathering in her eyes. 'She needs to get me another one.'

'You should have kept it in a drawer if you didn't want your sister to play with it,' Mum said. 'She's only a little girl, Jessica. She doesn't know any better.'

I wanted to say I wasn't little. I was ten, not six, and it was an accident. I wasn't 'playing' with it. But Jess interrupted me before my mouth was halfway open.

'It was in my room! She shouldn't have even been in there.'

'It might be your room, but it is in my house, young lady,' Mum said, her nostrils going thin the way they did when she was extra-cross. 'You do not make the rules.'

Jess stiffened and her cheeks went bright red.

'Now, I will take you to Woolworths tomorrow and give you some of your birthday money to buy a new set – even though that money is meant to be savings. But for now you will go to your room and calm down.'

Jess ran to her bedroom and slammed the door. Mum looked at the broken makeup in her hands.

'I'll put this in the bin.' She half turned away, then looked back. 'Do you really want a set like Jess's?'

I nodded, but I felt all twisted up inside. Jess was upset because of me and now Mum was annoyed with her. I shouldn't have touched her stuff. I promised myself I never would again.

'I'll talk to Daddy and see if he agrees, and I'll buy you one tomorrow,' Mum said. 'For your dollies, not your face – OK? I don't want you running around like a little madam. People will think you weren't raised right.'

Chapter 9

I must have eventually worried myself to sleep, because I was woken up by the burning need to pee. Barely aware of my surroundings I left the cabin and squatted behind it. The cold cut through my clothes like a knife. I was shivering before I'd gone half a dozen steps. It wasn't until I was done and hurrying back that I thought to be afraid of whatever else might be out there. Sleepiness had done what bravery could not – convinced me to go outside.

I looked around in sudden fear, almost expecting to see the same figure that had terrified me before. But the clearing was empty and quiet. A thick layer of fresh snow covered everything and mine were the only foot-prints on the ground. Leading from the cabin to where I now stood. Any traces I'd left the night before had been wiped away. Likewise any evidence of my mystery figure was gone too, if it had ever been there to begin with.

Without the howling wind and with all other sounds

deadened by the thicker coating of snow it was eerily quiet in the village. I couldn't hear much except the soft rustle of branches and my own breathing.

Standing there in the daylight I almost felt embarrassed at how scared I'd been yesterday. Ethan was missing and that was scary enough without me inventing monsters in the dark. I needed to keep a level head or I'd end up hurting myself – I'd already twisted my ankle and tripped over some porch steps. I was lucky I hadn't got lost in the snow whilst running in terror. I could easily have frozen to death in the woods or fallen and broken my leg. I needed to be sensible and keep myself going until help arrived.

I ignored the little voice inside that told me help might never come. Those thoughts had kept me awake but I was trying to silence them now. There was no point in imagining the worst. I had to deal with what was in front of me now. Anything else was just panic talking.

The first pressing problem I was going to address was the lack of any signal to potential rescuers. To attract anyone passing on the road I needed some kind of sign. An SOS. That meant hiking all the way back out to the main road on my bad foot, but it couldn't be helped. I also needed firewood to keep me warm, probably a few days' worth in case another storm hit. Some water would be good too. I eyed the well sceptically, but there was no sign of a bucket. It would have to be snowmelt. I just needed to find a way to boil it clean.

First though I needed to get my sign in place. I didn't want to be messing around with water and firewood whilst cars drove past and missed me completely. The thought that I might already have missed the only person to drive past in months was already firing my blood with anxiety.

Writing the sign wouldn't be a problem; I had a red lipstick in my bag that promised twenty-four-hour wear, which would hopefully stand up to the snow. I just needed something to write on. Obviously I could write on the sign for Witwerberg, but I wanted to catch the attention of anyone going in the opposite direction. I needed another piece of wood. I figured a plank would do nicely. I just needed to find one that could be easily prised up. The ones in my cabin were a no go thanks to the matting. That and I didn't want to have to keep skirting a hole.

I ate the second airplane waffle as my breakfast. As I made my way back out of the cabin I wondered what my chances would be if I took what little food I had and just tried to walk to the ski resort. I was still using my stick, now that I didn't have to feel my way in a storm, but my ankle felt slightly better for the overnight rest. Was that my best hope of survival?

This bright idea quickly died out. I had no idea where the resort was or even which direction to take on the road. I didn't want to wander off and get attacked by animals or lost in the woods. Even walking the road didn't guarantee me rescue. Who knew how well travelled it was? I knew I was better off staying where I had shelter and somewhere to light a fire. Staying near the car was probably also a good idea. I had no idea what kind of tracking methods were used on rental cars but if it was something that brought people to the car's location when it crashed I needed to still be around for them to find. Making a sign was my best hope.

The fallen roof of the next cabin over had pretty much blocked the doorway so getting inside to have a look around wasn't possible. Instead I eyed up the damaged porch. Whilst the sides were made of half-logs, the top was planked. It creaked underfoot and I hoped that meant something was just loose enough for me to pull up.

After scraping the snow off the porch with my foot I found that one plank was cracked all the way along. Maybe from the force of the roof coming down or just through age. Still, if I could get that broken plank out I'd be able to reach under the next one and hope-fully have enough leverage to pull against the rusted nails.

That was easier said than done. The plank, though cracked, was still wedged in there very securely. If I'd had a hammer or some kind of crowbar it would have been easy but after clawing at it with my fingernails for a while I realised I'd never get a good enough grip. Pulling the plank up wasn't happening. I'd have to break it.

I stood over the plank, gripped the porch rail and stamped with my good foot. The plank didn't budge. I tried again, using my heel to hammer down on the broadest part of the crack. It sort of bounced but didn't break. Again, I stamped. This time there was an encouraging cracking sound. A few more hefty whacks with my foot and the board split entirely. A large shard of it fell into the hole, leaving a gap just wide enough to reach into and pull the rest out.

I kneeled on the uneven boards and started to pull up the broken pieces of wood. Then I turned my attention to prising up a usable board. Even after what had to be decades of neglect, the nails didn't want to give in. I found myself wishing for Jess's toned muscles. I was skinny but not fit in the least and just breaking the board in had sapped my energy. I had to put my whole body weight into pulling against the plank. Finally, with a series of popping cracks, the nails gave way and I flew backwards into the porch rail.

I got to my feet and tried to brush snow off my leggings before it had a chance to melt. They were still damp from my fall the day before and I couldn't face sitting by the fire, half naked, to dry them properly. Maybe I could try and reach the car later and get my bag?

Turning over this idea, I glanced down at the hole I'd just made and froze.

Underneath the porch was a space just under a foot high. The floor was compacted dirt, weirdly dark to look at after staring so long at the snowy ground. Like putting shades on after looking at the sun-spangled sea. But shadows weren't the only thing down there. I could only see a sliver of it through the hole but lying on the dirt was a bundle, wrapped in cloth. Cloth that was weathered and frayed, clinging to the shape it was wrapped around. Shrunken in enough for the outline of a human skull to be visible through it, mouth open in a soundless scream.

I dropped the board I'd been holding and threw myself backwards like I'd just seen a poisonous snake. My foot twisted sideways on the uneven step and I cried out in pain and fear. For a moment I thought I might fall onto the porch, my face beside that gaping skull. Instead I slithered down the steps and stood, heart pounding.

From there I couldn't see into the hole. But the image of that skull in its shrunken shroud was painted across the inside of my eyes. The fabric sucked into the open mouth like the skeletal remains were still breathing.

I gripped the porch rail in my hand as my vision swam. Nausea rose up and I gulped against it, my skin prickling with a shiver unrelated to the cold. A body. There was a body under this cabin. I'd slept only a few feet from it for two nights. Feeling all the while as if something bad was lurking just out of sight. Was this it? Had I found the reason for my unease? A sort of sixth sense for death that millions of years of evolution hadn't quite erased?

As the shock faded and was replaced with fear, I inched forward. I felt a compulsion to investigate. To remove the element of uncertainty. I needed to know what those bones meant. Whether they could tell me anything about what was happening here. Where Ethan had gone or what might have happened to him. Just as with a poisonous snake I couldn't turn my back on the skull. As if once I did, I'd be opening myself up to danger.

So I crept back up the porch steps and looked into the hole I'd made. I stood there, trying to make the sight in front of me into something that made sense as a larger piece of the situation I found myself in. That close I could see the pattern on the dirty, rotting cloth: a sprinkling of flowers in threes, faded and hard to spot against the stains of dirt and . . . whatever else had seeped into the cloth over the years.

It was only after several minutes of gazing into that dark opening that I noticed the edge of another scrap of fabric, peeking out beside the first. A piece that wasn't so much cloth as knitting.

I didn't want to put my fingers back under the boards. As if the bones down there might spontaneously re-animate and reach for me. But I was caught in the sway of curiosity. The kind that leads people into dangerous places and stupid acts. So I reached down and levered up another board, straining against the nails, and another after that. I was panting, my sweat turning chill under my clothes, but morbid fascination overcame my exhaustion. Eventually, I uncovered more of the knitted thing beside the body.

The first body that is.

The knitted object looked like a blanket and it was coming apart, fraying to holes in spots. Through those holes I could see the off-white bones of whoever had been wrapped in it. Like pale peeled sticks in the darkness. A second skeleton.

I took in a breath, a great gasp. I'd been holding my breath as I looked at those bodies I realised. But with that intake of air came a smell; musty, part earth and part decay. Acid flooded my mouth and I barely made it to the porch rail in time to vomit onto the snow. Trembling, I wiped my mouth with the back of my hand and turned slowly to look down at the bodies once more.

There was no going back now. I was shaking but determined. As if by forcing myself to uncover everything hidden beneath that porch I could somehow escape future shocks to my system. If I saw all the horrors now, I wouldn't have to be surprised by them later. Maybe I was just tired of not being in control of my surroundings. Of being at the mercy of chance. I pulled up more boards and looked down at the third and final skeleton concealed beneath the porch. This one was the smallest and had been wrapped tightly in something thick and tough, like sacking. I couldn't see the outline of a single bone, yet there was no doubt in my mind that this was another body.

I sat back, my fingers aching from ripping at the planks, several nails torn and weeping blood. Below me the three skeletons lay innocently, as if they were meant to be here and I was the one out of place. An intruder.

What the hell were they doing there? Who had done this and when? Why? I whirled to look behind me, around at the other cabins and the treeline. That terrible feeling was back only stronger, the feeling of being watched. I suddenly felt incredibly vulnerable. I'd been out here for ages, making noise, working away with no awareness of my surroundings. All the fear from last night flooded back. The figure in the snow, Ethan's disappearance and now these skeletal remains. What was this place? What had happened here?

I grabbed an armful of boards and hurried back to my cabin. Like a child turning off a light and bolting into bed I felt somehow that the cabin was safe. Even though it was where Ethan had vanished. Even if it was only next door to the pile of bones I'd just discovered. So far it had kept me from harm.

Inside I shut and wedged the door, then sat opposite it, knees to my chest. The fire was mostly out but I didn't get up to feed it. I couldn't bring myself to do anything but stare at that door and think of those bones, almost glowing in the darkness under the porch. Three dead bodies only a few feet from where I'd slept for two nights. Was that why I had this awful sense of dread? Had I somehow felt the presence of death that was right on the doorstep? Something primal and animal left over from pre-human days. The sense that there was decay and death nearby and therefore, danger.

Part of me thought that was ridiculous, but what was the alternative? That I really was being watched? By whom, or what? Something that left no footprints, made no sound and could appear and vanish in the blink of an eye. Nothing could do that. Nothing human anyway.

A chill that had nothing to do with the dying fire ran up my spine. What was it that I was thinking? That I was being watched by something . . . otherworldly? A monster or a shadow, a ghost? After all I was in a ghost town. I didn't want to think about the possibility of being haunted, yet those bones swam before me. Evidence that something awful had happened here. Something that had to have left a mark, even if it wasn't a physical one. Especially if it wasn't a physical one.

I clenched my hands, pressing my nails hard into the flesh beneath. I had to stop letting these thoughts in. I wouldn't accomplish anything if I scared myself silly again. I'd just waste more time hiding away instead of taking steps to keep myself safe and to get myself out of Witwerberg.

I had to be logical, to focus on my survival. I needed to make a sign and gather more firewood. I needed to take hold of what I could control and keep myself alive until help came. The last thing I needed was to start believing in ghosts and goblins in the woods. All that would accomplish would be distracting me from the necessary work of staying alive. I couldn't afford to let my paranoid imaginings run away with me.

Still, there were things I could not explain, starting with Ethan's disappearance. Then the figure in the snow and now these shrouded skeletons. I'd almost managed to rationalise the car going down that gulley as just an error in judgement, leaving the handbrake off. But what if that wasn't it at all? What if there was something out there, whether human or . . . not?

Sitting there, watching the fire slowly die, I realised that it didn't matter if my stalker was human or inhuman. I had no way to combat either. The only thing I could do was try to keep myself alive and wait for their next move.

Chapter 10

I did the only thing I could; carried on. I had the board and could now make my sign. That was the one thing I could do to help myself. If I didn't want to stay stranded with those skeletal remains in that weird little village, I had to attract help.

The hike out to the road took longer this time than it had the day before. I had to carry the board and it meant leaving my walking stick behind. Though my ankle had felt better that morning I jarred it when I leapt away from the skull I'd uncovered. Under strain on the journey it quickly started to make walking difficult. It got to the point that I could feel my lip throbbing as I sank my teeth into it with every step. All the while the cold was pressing in on me, working its way through my clothes and under my skin. I could almost hear the calories in my system ticking down as I moved. Thinking of the tiny amount of food I had left drove me on. I needed to get out of Witwerberg.

The plank was hard to carry because of the rusty

nails sticking out of it and the fact that it dragged in the snow if I let my arms sag even a little. More than once the end of the plank caught in a mound of snow and jerked out of my arms. Fortunately my coat, though not too good at keeping the cold out, protected me from the rusty nails.

It wasn't just the pain from my ankle and the awkward plank that slowed me down however. I felt eyes on me from the second I left the cabin. Whether they were real or purely in my imagination, I had the intense feeling of being followed. If anything it was worse than it had been the day before. Every few paces I couldn't help but look into the treeline or glance behind me. Each time I expected to see someone there. Whether a real person or the shadow figure that had appeared in the snowstorm.

Far from reassuring me, every time I found myself looking at the empty path, my unease only grew. I could feel that something was there. I could sense it watching me, following me. Not being able to see it only made it more frightening. Like a monster in a horror film that always manages to stay out of shot and is somehow more terrifying than any CGI or special effects could make it. Not knowing what was watching me or why only made me try to go faster on my injured ankle. I was so on edge I felt tears gathering in my eyes before I'd made it halfway.

When I reached the spot where our car had been I found it completely covered in fresh snow without a tyre track to be seen. Again I wished that I'd thought to search for evidence of a third party when I'd come looking for Ethan yesterday. Now I'd never be sure if someone had pushed the car into the gulley or if it had rolled there by accident.

I carried on up the narrow way until I reached the main road where we'd turned off for Witwerberg. It looked as though no one had gone past since we'd driven that way. Or at least, not since the storm. I couldn't swear there'd been no tracks yesterday because I hadn't come this far. But certainly, not one single car or even a lone hiker had passed since the heavy snow I'd almost got lost in yesterday. So how long would it be until anyone came this way again?

Trying not to think of the futility of what I was doing, I uncapped my tube of 'Gilded Glamour'. With it I printed 'Broken Down in Witwerberg – Help' in thick red letters up the plank. Careful not to smudge my work I stood the plank up in the snow like a totem pole, close to a tree in case the wind tried to blow it down. Anyone driving from the opposite way to where Ethan and I had come from would see the plank and the splash of red in all that white.

After sweeping the snow off the road sign I used the rest of the lipstick to sketch a very wobbly arrow on it, visible from the opposite direction, and wrote 'Help' underneath. With the tube spent I tucked it into my pocket. Hopefully that would stand up to any snow. It was certainly noticeable. If anyone came by to notice. Though if it snowed like that again I'd have to come and dust the signs off. The one for Witwerberg had been absolutely plastered by flurries. To anyone driving past it would have looked like just another fallen tree covered in snowfall.

Away from town my unease subsided a bit. I was still scared, worried about what I was going to do and how I was going to survive, but I didn't feel so . . . cornered. The sense of being watched, of someone creeping along nearby, was almost gone entirely. Was it all in my head? Did I only feel creeped out because of the strange little village with its empty, sightless windows, not to mention the newly discovered hidden skeletons?

But if that was the case, and there was nothing wrong about the place, what had happened to Ethan? I hadn't imagined his disappearance. Neither could I write it off as an accident like with the car rolling away. It was the only thing that didn't hold up to logic. The fact that he'd vanished leaving no prints and with no reason to leave me. Something had to have happened to him, but what?

Every time I tried to rationalise what was going on I came up against the simple fact that my husband had evaporated into thin air. There was no explaining that. No matter if I could tell myself the car had rolled away on its own, that I was imagining the figure in the snow, Ethan's disappearance remained. I thought of that weird little hole in the wall. What had made it and why? Did it even matter or was I trying to find meaning in nothing, just some old knothole that had no more to do with Ethan's disappearance than I did?

As much as I wanted to I knew I couldn't stay by the road indefinitely. It might not have been snowing but it was still bitterly cold and standing still wasn't helping to keep my temperature up. I'd almost stopped shivering, which was a bad sign. Leaving the road behind felt like turning my back on the real world, the safe world. I was walking back into the unknown and my anxiety increased with every step. The eyes were back, following me. There were sounds in the trees as wildlife moved and snow settled, each one causing me to look up, searching for a human shape. There was never anyone there. Not even a rabbit or whatever other small animals were scurrying about.

On the way back I scooped up sticks and bits of wood. The sooner I could shut myself in the cabin, the better. None of what I'd gathered was dry, and the boards from the porch weren't either, but it would dry out inside. I just had to get a little more from inside one of the cabins to get a fire going.

I wondered what to do about the water situation. I didn't have any purification tablets or anti-bac wipes. I didn't really have much of anything. I couldn't sterilise the water but my throat was parched. I'd put it off for so long but there was no denying it. I would have to drink the snowmelt. I needed to do something to it first though; the idea of putting it in my mouth as is made me feel sick. Boiling was probably my only option. My water bottle was plastic so no good for boiling the water, but I had the drinks can. I felt a wave of hysterical impulse bubble up. I hated drinking from cans and now a can was my safest option. Ethan would love that when I told him.

I don't know what I expected to find when I got back to the little clearing with Witwerberg at its centre. Nothing seemed to have changed but there was a new sense of something amiss. Like walking into a room when you're half-packed to move house. Things missing or in odd places. But if something was missing or had moved, I couldn't tell what. The other cabins looked as they had that morning. The well was still covered, a thick cake of snow on top, and there were no other footprints in the snow but mine.

Though I didn't want to go back to the fallen cabin with the bodies beneath the porch, I didn't have much choice. It had the most accessible wood thanks to the collapsed roof. Standing over the hole I'd made earlier I looked down on the three bundled-up bodies. They looked smaller than when I'd first seen them. I suppose in thinking about them they'd kind of taken over the scene until I couldn't see anything else. Looking at them now made me feel less horror and more pity. This wasn't some horror film where the bodies could get up and come after me. They couldn't hurt me any more than they could tell me what had happened to them.

These were the remains of people who'd probably been forgotten for decades, or even over a hundred years. They'd never had proper graves, but just been hidden here, wrapped in what might have been their own bedding. Perhaps they'd died mid-winter when the ground was frozen and been put under the porch to preserve them? Maybe there was nothing sinister about them, no murder or other awful event. I was just looking at part of someone else's sad past.

I stepped carefully over the hole and pulled what fallen wood I could reach from inside the cabin towards me. With my arms full of splintered planks I headed back to my cabin and wedged the door shut once more. An immediate feeling of safety rushed over me, like the warmth of coming in from the cold. Only of course the whole cabin was freezing, the fire as good as dead in the grate.

I managed to coax the remaining embers to life. The warmth on my frozen fingers nearly made me cry. I needed to be more careful. I didn't want to lose my one heat source. What would I do if the lighter ran out of fuel? Best to keep the fire going and save the lighter for an emergency. From now on I'd make gathering wood a priority. Though I hoped I wouldn't be stuck in Witwerberg for too much longer. I glanced at my diminished heap of rations with a fresh sense of unease. Someone had to come soon, someone who'd see my sign and come to help.

With the fire going I assessed the drinks can. I could balance it in the flames to heat the water, but I needed to get the top off to get snow into it. Gathering snow in my bottle would only contaminate it. I checked my bag for anything useful, though I knew I didn't have any scissors with me. I did have a pin badge though. It was a little skeleton playing a guitar – so similar to

Ethan's tattoo that I had to buy it. Using the pin I set about puncturing the can all the way around the edge of the lid.

It was slow, tedious work but it was a distraction and I let my brain empty itself of worries. After a long, long time I had pierced the can all the way around the top. Holding the can between my legs, I carefully knocked the end in with a piece of wood. The edges were jagged, but I now had a topless can.

I stepped outside to scoop snow into my improvised pot. I'd been too amped up on pain and adrenaline to notice how hungry and thirsty I'd become but now that rest was in the offing I could feel my body making its needs known. I'd thrown up my small breakfast and hadn't had anything to drink since emptying the can. I'd been too scared of what was lurking in the snow. Even now I was worried about not being able to strain it, but I'd been wearing these clothes for days – they'd only make the water dirtier.

I packed the can with snow and emptied it to remove any leftover metal bits. Then filled it again. How much water would a can full of snow make? Not much. Snow was like ice, deceptively padded out with crystals and trapped air.

Standing there, holding the can, I suddenly realised what it was that had felt wrong when I arrived back in the clearing. The silence. All the way back I'd heard the movement of unseen animals and birds. But since coming into the village I'd heard nothing except the wind in the branches. Either there hadn't been any birds there to begin with, or something had already scared them away. Something like the presence of another person. Yet mine were the only footprints on the ground.

I swallowed, and turned to scan the treeline. Nothing, no one there, yet that weird stillness remained. It was like standing in a graveyard, which I guess I was. But still, it felt wrong, like something was out there that had scared every living thing but me away. Or maybe this was a place that every bird and animal was purposefully avoiding. Like it was . . . cursed.

I gave myself a mental shake and told myself firmly to stop it. There was enough about my situation to be scared of without inventing theories about a cursed village or a haunted cabin. Whatever was happening it had to have some kind of rational explanation. I just had no idea what it was, and couldn't keep my mind from conjuring up these bogeymen to explain what I could not.

Having gathered as much snow as I could I just wanted to get inside and shut myself in for the night. I was sure that once I had an instant coffee and a chocolate bar in me I'd feel more settled. Less shaky and overly sensitive. Perhaps this would be my last night in Witwerberg. My sign was up and someone out there had to pass by eventually, even if no one was searching for us yet. I hoped I was wrong about Jess writing me off. She cared about me, despite everything. She had to know that I wouldn't miss her wedding for the world. No matter what I'd done in the past. No matter what was said at Mum's funeral. I'd been trying to make up for it. She knew that. I hoped.

As I approached the cabin I took the lipstick from my pocket. On impulse I removed a glove and stuck a finger into the tube, scooping out the last chunk of product. The rough wood of the door scraped my finger as I marked an X on it. A red X that I hoped said, 'Here I am, come save me'. Though, as I shut the door, I couldn't help but think of the plagues of Egypt, a story from primary school. The blood on a lintel; a hope that death would pass by.

Chapter 11

Mum cried when they dropped me off at uni. Even Dad looked a little wet around the eyes. They unpacked most of my things and took me to Sainsbury's to fill my fridge and freezer shelves. Dad got us lunch in a pub nearby and pressed a fifty-pound note into my hand as they were leaving.

Once they were gone my room felt very quiet and empty. Even with all my things in there. I'd never been all alone before. I'd always had Jess just next door, Mum and Dad down the hall. Now I was on my own and without Mum bustling around, arranging things, I didn't know what to do with myself.

The last thing to unpack was my suitcase. All my new clothes for uni. Mum hadn't been thrilled about some of the things in there. She'd bought a lot of women's rugby shirts, blouses, blue jeans and even the university hoodie. But I'd taken my pocket money to the vintage shop, boot sales and charity shops and bought my own things; old tour t-shirts, holey jeans,

Converse high-tops and studded belts. My CDs were already up on a shelf. Some stuff of Dad's – The Stones, Queen and Pink Floyd – but a lot of it was my collection, mostly market finds and free CDs from Kerrang!

At the bottom of my suitcase I found a shoebox that I hadn't packed. It was taped shut, with an envelope stuck to the lid. I opened it and found a note from Jess. It said simply, 'Be who you want to be, Love Jess.'

I looked in the box and laughed. She'd packed me all the things Mum would never let me have: bleach and hair dye in rainbow colours, bold unnatural makeup, including a black lipstick, dangly earrings, a set of hair clippers and two books. More like thick leaflets really. The first on sex and sexuality, the second a guide for 'staying safe at gigs and festivals – everything you need to know'. Under the booklets I found a box of condoms, three wrapped 'dental dams' and a rape alarm.

I went to the mirror and examined my dark hair. I could finally do what I wanted with it. So, what did I want to look like on my first night at uni? Picking up the bleach and a set of plastic gloves, I got to work.

Two days after my transformation I met Ethan. I was at a student union party and he was outside having a smoke when I went out for some air. Well, air and a break from the awful music.

'Nice shirt,' was all he said, pointing at my Metallica top, which I'd cut into a crop to get rid of a nasty stain.

'Thanks.'

'Do you actually listen to them though?'

I rolled my eyes. 'Do you?'

'No,' he laughed, and I realised he was making fun of the kind of guy who'd ask questions like that, rather than actually getting at me. 'I mean, I've heard them but I like other stuff, you know?'

So we talked for a bit about Fleetwood Mac, Blondie, Black Sabbath and The Eagles. Going back and forth, swapping faves and least loved tracks. Until he threw his last cigarette into a bush and asked if I wanted to come back to his room.

I answered honestly, my belly fizzing with nerves and anticipation. 'Yeah, but I'm not going to.'

He looked confused for a moment, then laughed, like this was the best joke he'd ever heard. 'Oh really?'

I nodded. 'You're going to come back to mine.'

We had sex that first night. My first time. On the floral duvet set I would later tie dye to get rid of the twee print. After that we'd meet up a few times a week, usually at the union or sometimes at a grungy pub near the new Lidl. We'd drink and he'd chat with me then we'd go back to my room.

It wasn't true love or anything. Not at first. I was drunk on freedom and he was away from his mum and her shitty boyfriends. We were both just trying each other on, learning what we liked and didn't. Sharing our musical tastes and hanging around with each other because we didn't really know anyone else. Not like we were starting to know each other.

Then, almost without meaning to, I invited him home for Christmas. And just like that, we were serious.

Chapter 12

I woke up on my third day in Witwerberg and listened hard for the sound of an engine or voices. Any sign of imminent rescue. There was nothing. Not even the sound of birds in the woods. Just that same creepy silence.

I got up and ate a chocolate bar to stop my stomach squalling. Counting the unsweetened black coffee and chocolate bar from last night, I was down to my last bar after breakfast. With the waffles gone too that left only four packets of crisps, one sachet of coffee, two of sugar and milk and the random ketchup packet. I was scared at how quickly my rations were running down. The most calorie- dense food was mostly gone. Help had to come soon.

Sleeping on the floor and parcelling out rations of junk food was becoming increasingly wearing. Though the only thing worse than actually doing it was the fact that I was starting to get used to it. Like I was settling in to a long prison sentence with no chance of escape.

At least, that's how it felt when I was in the cabin. Outside my heart still began to race and my neck pricked at the feeling of something awful lurking just out of sight.

Neither sensation was pleasant, but I chose the lesser of the two evils and kept my trips outside short and perfunctory. Went to the loo behind the cabin, gathered snow out front and picked up firewood.

Once I had snow I boiled the can up over the fire. Using it last night had already caused the thin metal to warp, the bright colour of the packaging to be covered in soot. I'd burned my hands and singed my sleeves trying to fish it out of the fire but this time I was a bit better at it. There was nothing floating in the water at least.

To preserve some rations I made coffee with only half a sachet of instant Colombian, keeping the sugar and milk for later. Away from the dangers outside I felt monotony nibbling at the edge of my thoughts again. If I wasn't found soon I'd probably have to make myself a friend to stay sane.

I tried to tell myself I was OK for the moment. I had wood, enough food for the day, and had marked my door for rescuers. There was nothing I could do but stay in the warm and not expose myself to the anxiety that overcame me every time I stepped out into the village. Tomorrow's worries were for tomorrow. I hugged my knees to my chest and tried to chafe warmth into my arms. I wished more than anything that I had a sleeping bag.

I finished the weak coffee that tasted more of smoke than anything else. I'd poured it into the water bottle, the plastic of which was starting to turn cloudy from putting boiling water in it. At least I wasn't ill yet from the water. Boiling it was hopefully working. Though if I got out of this I was buying those purification tablets. When this was over I would also invest in a collapsible mug and not go anywhere without it. In fact I'd probably end up with a whole collection of handbag-size survival items: foil blanket, a penknife, portable urinal, first-aid kit, fire starter, freeze-dried meals. I would never take anything for granted ever again. I'd even get Ethan a matching kit so we'd be doubly prepared.

If I ever saw him again.

It was a horribly sobering thought, the idea that he might be lost for good. I'd not considered it before. So far I'd only thought of him as missing. That he was out there somewhere just as worried as I was. Trying to survive, to escape from whoever or whatever had taken him. But in that moment I felt the first very real fear that I might never see Ethan again. That even if I was found I would still have no idea where he was or how to find him.

Any attempt to try and find a distraction or make light of my situation crashed and burned with the knowledge that he might be lost for ever. Forget how he'd managed to vanish from right beside me without leaving a single footprint in the snow outside – where he was now had to be my main concern. Followed by why he'd been taken and by whom, or what.

My mind kept returning to those bodies under the porch. Something was wrong about this place. There was a danger here that I could feel but not explain. Every time I thought of Ethan I couldn't help but assume that his disappearance was the result of that . . . wrongness.

Witwerberg had clearly been deserted for some time. A ghost town on a mountain down a road so narrow our car never would have made it. I had no idea how old the place even was, a hundred, two hundred years? More? At what point had it been deserted? Did families leave one by one, abandoning the remote village for bigger towns? It was certainly possible, but there was something about the cabins. Each one almost identical. None of them had been modernised or added to over time by the people that remained. It looked as though they had been left all at once. No one had stuck around to make improvements or add on an extra room, board out the rafters for a sleep loft.

I lay on the floor by the fire and looked up at those rafters. If everyone had left around the same time there had to be a reason, surely? Some kind of event to drive them away. They had the Black Death in Germany, right? It was all over Europe, if I remembered my GCSE history lessons correctly. Which I didn't, as I'd mostly spent them painting my nails with Tippex. Was that why there were bodies under the porch? But, why would you bury plague victims under your front door? If not that then why was the village empty? Or was I over-thinking things and they really just had drifted away

108

naturally? Perhaps the people of Witwerberg just hadn't been as into DIY as their modern counterparts.

I sighed and clenched my hands into fists. My mind was running away with me again, trying to make sense out of things but making a mess in the process. All these unravelled threads tangling into a knot of frustration. I knew it was just my mind trying to distract me from Ethan, from the long wait for anyone to come and save me. As much as it sucked, I was stuck waiting. The only thing I could do was try to remain calm and be in the present.

It was then that I noticed the irregular shape of one of the beams above me. Something I hadn't noticed when looking around the room before. The rest were all straight but the thick one in the centre had a weird lump halfway across. Only it wasn't rounded like a natural part of the tree. It was pointed. Like a sharp corner.

I got up and stood on my toes to get a better look. From that angle it was easy to see that there was something on top of the rafter. Something with straight sides, man-made.

Having found the perfect distraction I wasted no time in getting my walking stick and trying to knock the thing down. It took a few tries; whatever it was had been there a long time. I could only imagine the kind of dirt and grime sticking it to the beam. It brought to mind the top of the kitchen cabinets when Ethan and I moved into our flat together. The thick coating of grease and dust that had to be scooped up with a wallpaper scraper.

Finally I managed to knock the thing off the beam. It fell too fast for me to catch and clattered across the floor. I winced as the wooden box, because that's what it was, burst open and its contents fell everywhere.

It became obvious pretty quickly that the box and everything in it was old. Very old. To me it looked like a box of random junk but to whoever had put everything together it had probably meant a lot. The things just had that kind of look to them; the kind of junk you'd only save for sentimental reasons, like my box of old Happy Meal toys, birthday cards and broken jewellery at home.

The box was like a cigar box, though the label had peeled off. Inside were bits of frayed ribbon, a glass ornament in the shape of a butterfly (now cracked from the fall) a champagne cork, a shell, a dried rosebud and a few bits of cross-stitch that had begun to fall apart with age. I gathered all the bits up and added a rusty bangle and a bent hairpin to the collection. Maybe this had been some girl's box of mementoes?

The glass butterfly was quite beautiful. I was annoyed at myself for breaking it. Unless it had been broken before it went into the box? That seemed unlikely once I found the bits of old newspaper it had been wrapped in. They were kind of moulded to the shape of its wings from being wrapped so long, brittle and ink-smeared. I smoothed them out, looking for a date out of mild curiosity. There it was in a sea of densely inked German – 1814. This place really was old. The paper might not even have been from when the cabins were first built.

I was about to re-wrap the butterfly when I noticed something else on the paper. A word I recognised, which was quite amazing since I'd taken French for my GCSEs and hadn't learned anything much except how to ask where the library was. I certainly couldn't speak a word of German beyond 'Auf Wiedersehen' but I recognised the word because it wasn't just any word, but a name on the page. The name carved into the well outside and the sign I'd cleared off only the day before. Witwerberg.

I frowned. Perhaps this paper wasn't just to protect the glass ornament but part of the keepsake box itself? Or just a handy scrap of paper that someone else had saved because it mentioned the village. It wasn't a big story with a headline, just a short chunk of text at the bottom of the page. The heading that had jumped out at me contained the name of the village, some short words that were probably something like 'in', 'and' or whatever, and *verschwunden*. What did that mean? *Versch* sounded like . . . first? 'First village' maybe? Or *Wunden* could be . . . wood? I had no idea. I wished I'd taken German instead of French, but to be honest I'd probably still be stumped. My D grades spoke for themselves.

It was frustrating to have a puzzle right in front of me which I could have solved with the internet in about four seconds. Another thing I'd never take for granted again: the ability to google things. Things like 'what does this word mean?' or 'how to purify water without chemical help'.

Though if I had been able to look that word up I'd have been bored again right away with nothing to focus

111

on but how hungry I was. So it was probably a blessing. I spent a long time reading over the words and trying to pronounce them, thinking of English terms that sounded similar, which obviously didn't help, and trying to work out what would be important enough to be in the paper. For all I knew it was a blurb about a local carpenter or a baking competition.

I intermittently fiddled with the rest of the box's contents. The newspaper was definitely the most interesting thing in there. Everything else was basically junk that someone, probably a child, had collected. The shell was probably from a visit to the beach, the butterfly maybe a present? The rose and the cork might have come from a special event like a wedding. The little bent hairpin had an enamel flower on it, and might have been part of a bridal outfit.

Maybe I was just thinking about weddings because Jess's was only a few days away. Somewhere up the mountain she was probably shaking imaginary creases out of her dress and thinking of the big day to come. My bridesmaid dress would be on a hanger in my empty room, if she hadn't already boxed it up. Like leftovers nobody wanted. The thought made my heart ache; Jess folding away my outfit and telling herself it didn't matter, that she was sure I wasn't doing this deliberately. Please God, let her forget all about the wake and realise I'd never do this to her on purpose.

'Come on, Jess,' I muttered to myself through chattering teeth. 'Please find me.'

But I knew it was pointless to hope she was already

looking. That she'd find this disappearance out of the ordinary. This was after all, what I did. I fucked up. Mostly, I fucked up Jess's milestones. Every time something great or important happened for her, I was there to pull focus and ruin it. I hadn't done it on purpose. Which was arguably worse. I'd been a thoughtless, selfish kid. Not even a kid – hadn't I completely bailed on clearing out the old house when Mum and Dad went into the home? I'd been manning our stall at a four-day music festival instead.

I felt a fresh wave of shame. I hadn't even tried to talk to her about what happened at the funeral. To attempt to mend that particular rift. Jess hadn't spoken about it either when we'd had to talk to arrange this trip. Like she was scared to open it all up again. Or too broken to try and salvage anything other than a facsimile of a relationship with me.

I'd had this one chance to try and make up for some of it, and it was passing me by. She would never have another wedding. I would never be able to make this right. I shuddered convulsively, with cold and suppressed misery.

Outside, the wind was blowing up. I peeped through the shutters and saw snow coming down heavily. Great, another few inches to wade through in the morning. More to keep me trapped in Witwerberg. I only hoped it didn't cover my signs, though there was slim enough chance of anyone seeing them. I flexed my foot and felt my swollen ankle pulse angrily. Could I make it back up there tomorrow, or was I in danger of ending up stuck between the road and the village, unable to walk another step? Just another horrifying possibility to consider.

Sitting back down by the fire I tried to distract myself. I thought of my own wedding. A happier memory. It was a small one, and we'd been determined to pay for it ourselves. Mum and Dad tried to 'gift' me things like the venue and a dress but I was stubborn. At the back of my mind I wasn't just thinking of Ethan's pride, because he hated accepting handouts, but also of Jess. I didn't want some mega wedding that she'd never be able to top. If I made ours a small event, maybe that would go some way to giving her a perfect day later on. The better wedding of the two.

Ethan and I wore vintage outfits, which smelled a tiny bit of mothballs even after a thorough cleaning. We made our vows at the register office with my parents and some of our friends as guests. Ethan's father dipped out when he was little and his mum emigrated to Spain as soon as he went to uni, so he wasn't too bothered about them. His mum did send him a cheque for fifty quid as a present, which we spent on a buffet lunch at ours. It was all very 1970s, complete with a frozen Black Forest Gateau in lieu of a wedding cake.

Mum and Dad sucked it up for the day and put on smiles. I could tell though that they disapproved. It was kind of the point, to do something that put myself in a bad light. Jess already shone so bright, yet they couldn't see her. She couldn't do any better than perfection, so I had to meet her in the middle by sacrificing some sparkle. It wasn't a total sacrifice on my part.

Ethan and I enjoyed the silly retro-ness of it all. My dress was a poufy nightmare and his suit was straight out of the original *Carrie* film – frilly shirt and bowtie, the lot. Even if I had all the money in the world I couldn't imagine a wedding that was more 'us'.

Jess was my one and only bridesmaid. She got to pick her dress, hair and makeup, at my insistence. I didn't want her in some 80s throwback feeling uncomfortable. She looked amazing. So much so that I felt a twinge of jealousy when Ethan complimented her on her dress, a wine-coloured sheath that made her hair look extra lustrous. But I swallowed my pride. I even got her and Pete to join us for a dance. It was the closest I'd ever felt to her, the two of us slow dancing with our guys in the living room. The best part was how happy she was for me. Or how happy she seemed, at the time. Since our argument at the funeral I'd been wondering how much of it was just her trying to mask her real feelings. But at least she tried. She made Ethan so welcome in the family and complimented us on every aspect of our wedding. Despite everything she wanted our day to be special.

I'd wanted to do that for her. To make her feel like everything she'd chosen, everything she planned, was wonderful. Because I don't think she'd ever felt that before; the total support of her family, their approval and attention. I was all the family she had left, and it was up to me to make up for some of what she'd missed out on. But I'd fucked that up too.

Just like I ruined everything else.

Chapter 13

'Amelia! What have you done to yourself?'

That was the first thing Mum said on opening the door to Ethan and me. For a second I actually thought she didn't recognise me. Then her eyes went wide and her mouth hung open.

In fairness I had changed a lot over that first term. She couldn't see the tattoos though, because one was on my lower back and the other on my leg, safely hidden. I had buzzed half my head though and the remaining hair was a faded turquoise. I'd also had a bar put in my eyebrow and a ring in my conch. Despite toning down my makeup for the trip home, I was still, I realised, wearing rather a lot. Certainly more than Mum had ever seen me with before. I also realised that perhaps I should have asked Ethan to remove his nail polish and forgo eyeliner for the trip. Somehow in the few months I'd been gone, I'd stopped thinking so much about what Mum and Dad found acceptable.

'Is Jess here already?' I asked, ignoring Mum's shocked outburst.

'Yes, she and Pete arrived ages ago,' Mum said. 'And is this the . . . guest you told us about?'

'This is Ethan, my . . .' I wavered. We weren't doing the boyfriend-girlfriend thing yet. I didn't want to scare him off. '. . . friend, from uni. He's doing a music course too, not my one but similar. Like I said his mum's in Spain so I thought he'd like to come here for Christmas.'

'It's nice to meet you,' Ethan said, 'you have a lovely home.'

I wanted to kick him for being so obviously sarcastic, because the outside of our house was about as heinous as you can get — down to the naff net curtains and literal white picket fence, but Mum ate it up. Just as Dad did when Ethan said hello and shook his hand, then offered to clear the drive of snow after lunch. He was doing really well with my parents. I'd enticed Ethan with promises of lavish Christmas food and plenty of booze, but it was still odd to watch him behave like one of Jess's boyfriends — all proper and polite.

Her new guy was no exception to this. Well, new in the sense that I hadn't met him yet. Pete, whom I'd only heard about from Jess, looked like a teacher. Very serious and neat with clothes that looked old and not in the vintage way. More in a 'I haven't gone shopping since my mum last took me' kind of way. Still, he was nice.

Jess looked amazing. She'd grown her hair even longer and plaited it in this insanely complicated style.

She had pearl earrings on and a sort of beige jumper that felt incredibly soft when she hugged me. Cashmere? She had to be raking it in at work.

'You look so different,' she gushed, ruffling my hair. 'I love it.'

'Thank you,' I preened. Though Mum's reaction had made me a bit self-conscious. 'I got this shirt at a kilo sale Ethan knows about.'

Jess turned her bright smile his way. 'This is the Ethan who's been taking you to all those amazing gigs?'

Ethan blushed for the first time since I'd met him, then nodded. 'It's no big deal. I know a lot of guys who do sound and light, that's all.'

'Well, you two are so cute together,' Jess said. 'I'm glad Mila has someone looking out for her at uni.'

'Jeeeeess,' I complained.

She laughed. 'Come and say hi to Pete, Ethan – he's a bit of a music nerd too. Though he's mostly only got ears for jazz.'

Ethan shot me a 'help' look as she towed him away towards her boyfriend. I waved him goodbye and helped myself to a glass of wine.

'Just the one glass, mind. Your mother's going to need some of that,' Dad said, sidling up to me. 'This new look of yours was a bit of a shock.'

'I don't know why, I always wanted to do something with my hair and get some more piercings. You guys just wouldn't let me,' I teased, half-serious.

'We're only trying to look out for you, Mila,' Dad sighed. 'In ten years you'll look back at pictures from *now and wonder how you ever went out dressed like that. Trust me. And where are you going to work looking like that?'*

I internally rolled my eyes. Jess hadn't gone through anything like this. She went to uni with the same kind of clothes she was wearing now. The same sorts of things Mum wore; neutral, classic, boring. Yet Mum had still got at her, always asking about boys and if she was drinking, how much she was spending.

'This boyfriend of yours seems nice though,' Dad said, begrudgingly, looking over to where Jess was standing with Pete and Ethan in a little huddle. She glanced over at me and smiled, her hand on Ethan's shoulder. 'Despite the fashion choices, he's a polite boy. Very nice.'

'He is,' I said, hoping that by the end of this visit, Ethan really would be my boyfriend. Officially. 'He really is.'

Chapter 14

I looked at my dwindling food supplies the next morning. The previous day I'd had crisps and the last of the coffee for dinner. My fourth day's breakfast was the final chocolate bar and a cup of hot sugared water. Things were looking dire. Despite carefully rationing my supplies I was now down to three packets of crisps, two long-life milks, one sugar and the ketchup packet. Enough for another meal today and perhaps breakfast tomorrow. The rationing was making me feel like my stomach had shrivelled up into a tight little ball that was intermittently numb but otherwise ached so badly I thought I'd be sick.

My strategy so far had been to keep myself full with coffee and hot water, but it was no good. I could maybe stretch this food for another day, two at the most, but after that, things would be very grim. I hadn't seen anything edible in the woods, not that I knew what I was looking for. Aside from pine trees the ground was a blanket of snow through which nothing seemed to grow. I found myself eyeing the green needles on the branches and wondering if I could stomach them, or if they'd poison me.

I divided my pathetic provisions into three piles: a pack of crisps per meal, with a cup of hot sugar water. That would make three meals. If I could call them that. I eyed the milk sachets and the ketchup packet. These were my wildcards. What could I do with them?

Hadn't I seen something once about homeless people making meals like this? They'd said something about making soup from free sauce packets and creamer. Whatever that was. Some American thing. Potentially another meal in the arsenal, one that wouldn't give me many calories but would at least ease the gnawing hunger.

What was I going to do once those meals ran out? Starve was the obvious answer. Unless I happened to find a dead animal or something to cook over my fire. Could I really eat some savaged rabbit, chewed up by a wolf and left to die? Not right now but in a day or two, who knew how desperate I'd be. I shuddered.

Adding to my worries was the cold. I felt it all the time now, like it had reached my bones and was refusing to let go. The lack of food meant I had nothing to chase it away with. Nothing to fuel my body's efforts to stay warm. Even the fire couldn't do much.

Still I had to keep going outside. I needed more water for one thing. I also needed the loo, which meant going into the woods behind the cabin. I'd been putting it off, that moment of vulnerability, but it was becoming increasingly urgent. If I'd had any kind of bucket I'd have thought nothing of using it inside. Something else to add to my growing list of survival kit I'd never travel without again.

Outside the smoky semi-darkness of the cabin, the village was blindingly white. The cold out here was like nothing else. No matter how many times I experienced it I was still left breathless. The whole area was blanketed in fresh snow. I scanned the ground for footprints but saw nothing. It had been quiet yesterday and my fear was as faded as the old newspaper I'd found. I was now merely anxious, rather than terrified, and pretty sure that I was alone in Witwerberg, for better or for worse.

I scraped a hole in the snow behind the cabin and afterwards kicked snow over the evidence of my morning routine. Then I picked my way back around the cabin. As I did so I caught a whiff of myself and grimaced. Another thing I'd never take for granted again; clean clothes. Specifically underwear. I smelled like an old gym bag, sweaty and stale. The idea that I had several complete outfits in a suitcase down the gulley was haunting me. Had my ankle felt stronger I'd have gone after them, but I couldn't risk it just for comfort. I looked down at myself and wrinkled my nose. My leggings actually had tide marks on them from continually getting soaked by snow and drying out. The sleeves of my hoodie were singed from being used as oven gloves to remove the drinks can from the edge of the fire.

I was pushing a low branch out of the way when I saw movement in the trees across the clearing. Freezing, I could hardly make myself breathe as a shadow moved between the trunks. Not just a shadow, *the* shadow. The same figure I'd seen in the snowstorm. I just knew it, even though I'd barely seen it then and only just caught it now. I could feel it. There was someone there, in the woods, and they were running away.

Maybe that was why I chased them. It's hard to be afraid of something that's fleeing. Or maybe it was because in the past day or so my fear of some kind of ghostly apparition had faded. I was more grounded and so when I saw that figure my mind was set on it being a person. Not a ghost or a demon or some kind of shadow creature. Just a person and one I thought I could fend off if I needed to.

I should have known by then that my mind wasn't to be trusted. It played tricks on me.

Still, based on whatever instinct I had, I dropped the empty can I'd been going to fill with snow and ran into the clearing. My ankle still gave twinges here and there but was mostly stable by now, at least on level ground. I ploughed through the village, kicking snow everywhere. I couldn't see the figure anymore but it had been there, I was certain of it. Just there, between the last two cabins. As I reached the treeline I slowed. The snow here was in small humps and hillocks because of fallen branches. The ground uneven. Still it was clear to me that there were no footprints there.

I stood and looked around me, thinking that maybe

the figure had been further to the left or right than I'd thought. But there were no tracks there either. Nothing to show that anyone had been there. Had whoever it was been further back in the trees? Where had they gone?

The familiar chill of fear washed over me. Just like that all my certainty was gone and I was back to questioning everything. I'd run towards what I thought was another person, yet there was no evidence of anyone being there. So either I'd not seen anything or whatever I'd run towards was somehow not leaving footprints.

I was sure that I'd seen something. This wasn't some hazy shadow through the falling snow. I had a seen a real, physical presence. No optical illusions this time. So that left me with the question of how someone I'd clearly seen running this way had left no tracks. A dozen possible explanations, each more ridiculous than the last, ran through my brain: snow shoes, a zip line, a puppet winched up into a tree. Somehow none of the more realistic ideas were as credible to me as the idea that it might have been a ghost or spirit. That this village was haunted by the people that had died here . . . or by whatever had led to the place being deserted.

I tried to dispel that idea but then another, potentially more worrying one occurred to me. What if I hadn't seen a person or a creature, but an animal? Something light enough to leave tiny impressions in the snow rather than great big dark prints. Something like a wolf threading its way through the tree trunks, prowling and catching the scent of easy prey.

The feeling of being watched was back and I looked around, scanning the trees. I was looking for anything then, a person, the glint of animal eyes or a cloud of hot, meat-scented breath. I heard a twig crack and jerked around to face where the sound appeared to come from. Nothing.

I could only hear my own desperate breathing, the blood roaring in my ears. I didn't know what to do: carry on and try to catch whatever it was, or run from it.

Suddenly, I saw a movement and without thinking I took off after it again. My decision made for me in a moment of blind instinct. I had no plan for what to do in any scenario. Man or animal, ghost or flesh, once I found it I was going to be equally unprepared for anything.

I hadn't gone more than a hundred yards when I tripped with my bad foot and fell headlong into the snow. The fall knocked the wind out of me, the snowy ground surprisingly hard. Spitting and shaking snowflakes from my face I looked up and found the trees ahead of me still and undisturbed. Whoever, whatever it was had vanished again.

Scrambling in the snow for purchase, I strained my ears for another sound. All I could hear were my own movements, the rustling of my coat and my breath sawing out of my lungs. Then my fingers brushed against something hard. Thinking it was a branch I pulled, hoping for a weapon in case the shadow suddenly rushed me. I wanted nothing more than to scurry back to my cabin and avoid the weird and unsettling woods. Then I looked down at what I'd lifted from the snow.

The scream that ripped out of my throat echoed through the trees until it hardly sounded human. My mind was shrieking at me to let go but my fingers were as frozen as the severed hand in my grip. I couldn't make my body obey. Finally, a full body shudder released my fingers and I clawed myself away from the grisly stump, scattering snow as I went.

Another shudder rolled through me, bending me to all fours in the snow. I think if my body hadn't already been in starvation mode I would have thrown up. As it was I couldn't stop shaking and recalling the feel of that hand in mine. For a good few minutes I thought I might come apart entirely. Only one thing brought me back to myself – the ring on the hand. A wedding ring, on what was, despite the mauling it had taken, clearly a man's hand.

I looked at it, the bluish-grey flesh and the jarringly red-brown marks that teeth had left in it. I would remember the way it felt in mine until the day I died. The wrongness of skin turned to stone by the icy conditions. The jagged peaks of bite marks frozen in place, rasping against my fingertips. I couldn't tell if it was Ethan's hand. It had been gnawed, frozen, until it could have been anyone's.

'Ethan?' It came out in a croaky hiss. I hadn't spoken

for ages. 'Ethan?' I said again as if the hand could answer.

Desperation took over from revulsion and I fell to my knees, raking up the snow with my hands. I'd not thought to wear gloves on what was meant to be a quick trip outside. My fingers were quickly red and raw from scrabbling in the snow but I hardly noticed. I was focused on uncovering whatever the snow had hidden from me. If that hand was here, what else was buried in the snow?

I quickly found the arm that the hand had been chewed from. I followed it, careful not to touch whilst brushing the snow away. I uncovered the shoulder, the neck and finally the face. The face of a complete stranger, contorted in pain. I barely looked at him before my eyes flew to the safety of the snow. I didn't want to see into those empty eye sockets, to look at the red tears and missing flesh left by something feeding on him.

It wasn't Ethan. Not even close. That was all I wanted to know.

I sat back on my heels in the snow and looked down at the dead man, carefully avoiding another glance at his face. I felt numb, all my emotions running together and overwhelming me until I couldn't pick them apart enough to actually feel them. It was almost like I was outside myself. Only the feeling of my breath sucking in and out of my lungs kept me grounded.

Slowly, I uncovered the rest of the body. I can't say what made me do it. A kind of morbid curiosity maybe?

Or perhaps I just couldn't take any more secrets, any more mysteries. I had to see, to know. Because this was not a skeleton in a hole. This was a person, with flesh and clothes and a face that I didn't dare look at. This body was a person who had been where I was now and died here. I had to know why and how. Had to know what this meant for me.

He was wearing a suit, that was the first thing that my mind seized on. A suit on a mountain. Not right. Not normal. Aside from the wedding ring, he was also wearing a very fancy watch on his other wrist. I couldn't quite bring myself to go through his pockets or actually touch his skin. That would have been too much, too awful. I just scraped the snow away so I could see him. So I could maybe start to work out what the hell I was living in the centre of. A haunted town with skeletons under a house and a whole human corpse in the woods. Only this was so much worse than some bones in the ground.

The skeletons under the porch had been shrouded and laid out, decayed down to bones despite the cold. They'd been there a long time, maybe since the 1800s, like the newspaper I'd found. But this guy . . . I looked at the watch again and swiped the face clear of snow. Ethan had a passion for ridiculous watches and would almost rip my arm off pulling us over to any jewellers' window. That watch was an Omega and looked incredibly new, with markings in blue and red. Bracing myself against the awfulness of what I was about to do, I reached over and carefully unclasped it. My fingers brushed his cold, stiff skin and I felt bile lace the back of my throat.

With the watch in hand I slid back from the body and looked at it. This was a safe thing to handle, all metal and glass. Nothing fleshy or bloodied.

I knew from looking at eye-watering prices that watches like this were not cheap. This one was five grand, easy. I turned it over, looking for an engraving. I was hoping for a date, but what I found was almost as good. It had the logo of the Beijing Winter Olympics on the back. I was probably holding a special edition watch from 2022. Which meant this man had been alive until very, very recently.

The watch slipped from my fingers and disappeared into the loose snow between the man's expensive shoes. I had so many questions. Who was I looking at and why was he here dressed like he was ready for a board meeting? How had he died, what had chewed him up and was it still around?

That last thought had me looking around me at the trees once more. Had I mistaken a wolf or a bear for someone prowling through the woods? Had my stupid ass pursued a literal predator back to its feeding spot?

Going back to the cabin suddenly felt very urgent. I couldn't be there anymore, I needed to get away, to get as far from that corpse as I could. I didn't want to be around when whatever had gnawed on him came back for seconds. I also couldn't stand to be near him, to feel those eyes on me. Or at least, to feel the stare from the bloody sockets where his eyes once were.

I stuck my hand into the snow to get the watch as I stood up. It was reflexive, picking up something that I'd dropped. I had no use for it, after all.

My fingers sank into the snow and two things happened at once that had my body seizing up and my mind cracking down the centre. The first was that my eyes fell on the man's face and I registered for the first time the utter terror that had contorted it, along with the pain.

The second thing was my fingers closing around the watch. As they did so they brushed the lips and nose of a face, buried between those shiny loafers.

Chapter 15

I snatched my hand back as if the icy flesh had burned me. Then scrambled backwards and looked down. There, newly uncovered by my groping hand, was the face of a woman. Her eyes were shut, her mouth lolling open, packed with snow.

This time I did throw up, into the snow a foot or so away. My body was trembling so hard that I could hardly wipe my mouth. How much of it was cold and how much was revulsion I couldn't tell. Afterwards, my head pounding, I covered my ears with icy hands and tried to stop the roaring of my own terrified pulse. I felt as if the trees were closing in around me, like the air was being sucked out of me by the cold. Even the ground underneath me seemed to be tilting, like it wanted to throw me off entirely.

After long moments I came back to myself. I was kneeling in the snow, facing away from the bodies. I'd hunched over, my forehead against the clean snow. Cold sweat stuck my hair to my neck and my mouth was bitter with bile. Slowly, I straightened up and looked back at the face in the snow. A woman, maybe my age or younger. Why was she here? What the hell had happened to her?

What was going to happen to me?

My hands were still shaking as I reached for the snow around her face and began to dig. Slowly I uncovered her ears, throat and the collar of a multi-coloured outdoor jacket. As I dug, her long black hair matted around my fingers like seaweed. The touch of it made me flinch. A sense of unreality was rising up over me, my body acting on its own as I watched from somewhere far away. That safe numbness claiming me now that the shock was over.

One of the woman's arms was folded up on her chest, like she'd been trying to shield herself. Her fingers were shrivelled from the cold but her rings hadn't fallen off; a gold band with a sparkling diamond. There were diamond studs in her ears too. Between the two of them there had to be over ten thousand pounds' worth of jewellery just sitting here. Either they'd been left there by someone who wasn't out to rob them, or there'd been no one around to loot their bodies.

Or, they'd been killed by something that didn't care about money at all.

I shook myself, trying to chase those thoughts of the supernatural away, but they clung on stubbornly. Even out here in the woods, away from the village, I felt eyes on me. I could sense something around me in the trees, watching me.

Looking at the two bodies in front of me I wondered if perhaps it was them. Some kind of spirit or echo of these people reaching out to me. Were they haunting this place like the people whose skeletons I'd lived beside for days now? How many more bodies were there in this place? How many before I couldn't deny anymore that there was something incredibly wrong with Witwerberg that nothing rational could explain? Something that brought death with it, to whoever strayed into the village.

I realised then that I had about as much of an idea of what had killed these two as I did the skeletons. Not that I could see much of them, fully dressed as they were. The woman's bulky coat and the man on top of her meant I couldn't really see much of her torso. Just her raised arm, head and shoulders. The man's dark suit made spotting any kind of blood or wound impossible. I could only see his extremities, which had been gnawed on. But that might have been long after he was dead.

What had killed them and when? Had they died together, or had the woman under the man's body perished first? Had they even been together on the mountain, or were they complete strangers who'd ended up dead in the same place? If so, how and why?

From the looks of both of them I doubted they'd come to Witwerberg together. He with his suit and fancy watch, her in her outdoor gear. There was an age gap too, though I wasn't going to look at the man's face again to gauge how much of one. His hair had been greying though and she looked barely twenty. He was dressed like he'd been headed for a business meeting, she for a hike. No, they had to have been separate people, here for different reasons.

How had they not been found? She had an engagement ring; surely her fiancé had noticed she was missing? They were under days' worth of snow. Maybe even weeks'. Even if the cold had kept them . . . fresh, there was no way they'd only just died. What about the man's work colleagues? He looked important, rich at least. Was no one looking for them, or was Witwerberg just that well hidden?

Unbidden thoughts of the Bermuda Triangle began to surface. A place it was all too easy to end up in but impossible to escape. Perhaps that's what Witwerberg was; a village many found themselves stranded in, but never left. Maybe no one had found me yet because no one was ever going to. Like these people I might just slowly die here and be buried under the snow.

What if whatever it was had already claimed Ethan? Was his body out here somewhere, under all that snow? Had I stepped over it without knowing? I let out an involuntary whimper at the thought, looking around me as if his frozen face might appear between the mounds of snow.

I couldn't face that possibility, or the sight of the bodies that had sparked this new fear. I had to go, now. I had to get somewhere safe. I turned and slowly walked back to the cabin, as if in a daze. On the way I scanned the ground beneath my feet, terrified that I'd see eyes looking up at me through the dense, white, blanket. Or hands reaching between the tree roots. My own hands, red-raw from digging in the snow, were throbbing and itching with cold.

When I re-entered the semi-circle of cabins I paused, a new fear taking hold. There, to the right of my cabin, was the collapsed building I'd found the three skeletons under. My eyes moved from cabin to cabin, porch to porch. There were six cabins including mine. Three bodies, now five, given what I'd just discovered. But . . . what if there were more. What if I'd only just begun to find out what was hidden, quite literally, under the surface?

Suddenly I couldn't bear the idea of not knowing, of things being hidden from me. I'd been drowning in uncertainty, devastated by waves of awareness ripping the rug from under me at every turn. I needed to take control and seek out the truth before it was sprung on me when I was least prepared.

There was a rock by the second cabin, about the size of one of my boots. It was heavy and I struggled to lift it even to my knees, but it would work for what I had in mind. I went to the third cabin, to the right of where I'd torn up one porch already. Bracing my legs against the weight of the rock I brought it down on the wood.

The planks cracked on the first blow, but it took two more to splinter a board enough to break. With burning fingers I prised up the broken bits and then, slowly leaned over and put my face to the narrow gap.

In the gloom, I could just about make out some shapes on the packed dirt beneath the porch. Shapes both horribly familiar and terribly alien; the outlines of a human pelvis and the smooth dome of a skull.

I have no idea what came over me but I started ripping at those planks. The rusty nails screamed as I dragged them out and threw them to one side. I knew it had to be hurting my hands, my fingers, to be prising up boards like that, but I couldn't feel it. Even when I saw in my periphery the bright red blood smeared on my skin. My eyes were glued to the ragged hole I was making, to the bones I was exposing.

These ones weren't wrapped neatly in sheets or blankets. Whoever had put these bodies here to shrivel and rot down to the bone hadn't taken much care at all. It was hard to tell how many bodies I was looking at because the bones were mixed up, like they'd been moved since the connective flesh withered away. I guessed, from the number of skulls, that four people had been laid under the porch. Though one skull was way back in the shadows and I almost missed it. Two of them were smaller, and it took a moment for me to realise that these were the bones of children. Two children and possibly their parents.

I covered my mouth with my forearm, tears springing to my eyes. Children, left to rot under a porch in the middle of nowhere. Who had done this? Who had shoved them under this floor without even bothering to wrap them or do anything to stop the jumbling of their bones as decay took hold?

With more light from the wider hole I could see marks on the bones nearest to me. At first I thought maybe they were crumbling to bits and the surface was just worn away. Then I saw deeper marks towards the ends of the long bone I was looking at. These weren't signs of wear, no. They were teethmarks. Hundreds and hundreds of tiny teethmarks all over the bones, where tiny mouths had feasted. I was looking at the remains of a family that had been dumped under a porch and left for the rats to eat.

Turning my head away I looked at the rest of the cabins in the row. What were the odds that they had skeletons under them as well? Two out of six wasn't a coincidence. It was a pattern. What if even my cabin had bodies under it? Why hadn't that occurred to me before? Probably because I'd wanted to believe that the first skeletons were an aberration and not part of a chain of deaths associated with this place.

As much as I wanted to know, my strength was spent. My sweat was freezing to my skin. Even in the middle of that horror, my stomach wailed for something, anything, to eat. Survival was, for the moment at least, more important than my impulse to dive into the unknown.

I stood up and began to walk towards my cabin. I felt like I was walking through water; every sound was deadened and every movement took extraordinary effort.

Once I reached the cabin I climbed the step, trying not to picture what might be under it. The cold had well and truly got me in its grip and I could barely open the door with my stiff fingers. With it shut I leant against it, then slowly sank to the hard floor, trembling. My thoughts of getting water seemed a lifetime ago. I felt hollowed out and empty. My leggings were soaked once again in snowmelt. The cold was seeping in under the door, reaching out for me. A roaring sound swelled in my ears and I stared at the log wall opposite me, unblinking.

Images of the bodies I'd found filled my mind. It was like I'd looked too long at a bright screen with those awful pictures on it. They were floating like flash spots in front of my eyes. The man, the buried woman, the three shrouded skeletons under the porch, the gnawed bones. A string of corpses parading through my head. I was surrounded by them. Surrounded by death.

Eventually, as if in a dream, I stripped off my leggings and laid them out by the fire to dry. With my coat wrapped around my legs like a skirt to keep warm, I sat by the grate with my hands over the glowing embers and tried to make any kind of sense out of what I'd just gone through. I still felt numb, like all that horror had blown a fuse in me. But I could sense the full impact of what I'd seen waiting for me. Like a wave gathering itself to destroy a fragile sandcastle.

As for what I'd seen; there were two bodies, partly buried in the snow. One on top of the other. Like they'd been tossed into a hole big enough for only one. Who they were I had no idea. I had even less of a notion as to why they were this far up in the Alps, the man in particular as he wasn't dressed for a walk in the frozen forest.

Had they perhaps broken down as well? On their way to or from a resort just like Ethan and I were? Or maybe she had hiked here? Perhaps they had both stumbled into Witwerberg looking for shelter or directions. Maybe, just like we had, they'd found only empty cabins and a creeping dread of being followed.

I'd now found at least nine bodies tied to this place. Skeletons and fresh corpses. So much death for such a small place, a nothing dot on the map. That besides everything else had me more on edge than ever. What even was this place? What was doing this and was it the same thing responsible for Ethan's disappearance?

It had to be. There was no way the two weren't connected. Disappearances and deaths, the unexplained vanishing of my husband, and the appearance of skeletons and new corpses. The odds of them being the work of separate things were insurmountable.

Things. I felt a chill overtake me. I kept doing that, slipping into thoughts of 'something' or 'whatever' not 'someone' or 'whoever'. Logic and sense were in as short supply as food. I was fast running out of ways to put what was going on down to a person. What person could do all this? What human being could somehow spirit Ethan away without leaving a footprint, then lure me to the buried bodies without disturbing the snow around them? What could lurk in the woods, watching me, without me ever really catching a glimpse of it?

No matter how I tried to look at the situation I kept coming back to there being no earthly explanation. I could reason out individual parts of it, like the car rolling because we hadn't put the brake on or the figure in the woods being a passing animal. But I couldn't make all those individual rationalisations fit together into a neat picture. The only thing that explained it all was something that was in itself unexplainable – a spirit, a ghost, a monster. Something not bound by the laws of nature. The laws that said a foot leaves a footprint and a man cannot vanish without a sound or sign.

I was on the edge of both believing and finding the whole thing ridiculous. My mind was going around in circles. I wanted to find some kind of rational way of looking at things but every time I tried, I ended up in the grip of another panic over whatever might be out there.

I hugged myself and tried to keep my thoughts in check. I couldn't lose my grip, not when my survival hinged on being practical. I needed to keep from spiralling into another horror story, especially one that would keep me from taking care of myself. If I truly believed in monsters roaming the woods, I would just sit in the cabin and starve rather than face them. If I ever wanted to get out of Witwerberg, if I ever wanted to see Jess or Ethan again, I had to keep my head out of the clouds and focus on what was real.

The only problem was, it was getting harder to know the difference.

Chapter 16

I told myself to put the bodies out of my mind. I of course couldn't. They might as well have been in the cabin with me, propped up like dolls. The bones a litter across the floor. I was surrounded by death and could think of nothing else for hours, even after it grew dark outside and exhaustion began to tug at my eyelids.

Eventually, though, it began to snow. Through a crack in the shutters I watched the fat flakes falling down and slowly erasing my tracks from the day. Soon, if it kept coming down like that, the bodies I'd seen would be covered over. It was as if nature was finally cutting me a break. I watched until the ground was freshly crisp and featureless. The awful vision of that man's savaged face might still be printed on my brain, but in reality he was out of sight once again, if not out of mind. I didn't have to worry about stumbling across him again.

Yet thoughts of Ethan's body, frozen beneath the snow, weren't so easy to let go of. I kept telling myself that he was alive. That whatever had taken him wouldn't just kill him. But I had a hard time convincing myself. Little by little I was starting to doubt that I'd ever see him again. That doubt was like a stone in my stomach.

When my leggings finally dried I put them back on, glad of the extra warmth. Chasing phantoms and digging in the snow, never mind the successive panic attacks, had sapped me of energy and I was fighting a losing battle trying to keep myself warm. When I briefly went outside to find the can I'd dropped, my temperature only plummeted further. I had to make myself eat, though my stomach rebelled against the thought. It was getting harder and harder to predict when I'd be craving food and when my body wouldn't accept it. Which worried me.

I ended up making 'soup' from ketchup and water, mixed with the UHT milk for good measure. I also caved and wolfed down one of my bags of crisps. The 'soup' was revolting but it created a ball of heat in my stomach that I was grateful for. I only hoped I'd be able to keep it down.

I tried to get to sleep by the fire, curled up like an animal against the chill of the outside world. After a few days I was getting better at sleeping on the floor, though not as good as that first night when I'd crashed out completely. The night Ethan was taken from my side without waking me.

Even with some distance from the bodies in the woods, the new fear that he might be out there somewhere amongst them refused to leave my mind. That doubt inside me warred with the soup for space in my gut. Lying on the hard floor I told myself over and over that Ethan was still alive. That he was fighting his own battle for survival and that soon we'd find one another again. I wanted so desperately for it to be true that I dreamed of him. A hazy, weirdly paced dream where Ethan appeared in a helicopter and landed right outside. We hugged and he wrapped me in a blanket. Inside the helicopter it was warm, so warm I could hardly stand it after the freezing woods.

When I woke up that warmth didn't go away. For the first time since leaving the car I felt completely warmed through from head to toe. I stretched and sighed, completely, blissfully, comfortable after days of shivering, of numb extremities and freezing down to my bones. Then I sucked in a lungful of smoke and jolted awake within seconds.

The cabin was on fire.

The dark ceiling above my head was laced through with lines of light, glinting between the boards. I sat bolt upright and shielded my eyes from the bright flames that had engulfed the far wall. Pushing myself backwards with my heels I felt the heat baking my skin, my eyes streaming in the smoke. The logs were crackling and spitting as the fire got its jaws into the wood. Already they were charred and black, the fierce heat searing the air dry. I could hear it, the crackling and popping of wood, clattering debris falling as the overhead beams caught. It was deafening. The sound of it tapped into something deeply instinctive in me – the animal terror of fire.

I twisted onto my front and flung myself across the floor. My hands found the wall and I dragged myself upright, turned to find a way out. But the door was behind a curtain of fire, leaping from the wall to the floor. Trapped, I coughed, my eyes streaming from the thick smoke. The window behind me was my only hope.

Unable to see I felt my way to the latch on the shuttered window and fumbled it open. As soon as I did the fire behind me roared forwards and I felt the heat of it on my back like a physical hand clawing at my clothes. I'd given it oxygen and now it was coming for me. With a hoarse scream I threw myself over the windowsill and kicked my legs until I fell forward into the snow. I rolled back and forth in a panic that my clothes were on fire. The sudden shock of ice on my scorched skin was like balm on a sunburn.

Twisting, I looked back and watched as flames flickered at the window, cheated by my escape. They lapped greedily at the window frame and the wood there began to spit and catch.

A coughing fit took over and I hacked up phlegm onto the snow. Even with my limited experience of fire, I could tell it wasn't just wood burning in there. This was nothing like the smell of the log fires I'd been making. The tang of chemicals filled my mouth and nose. A thick stink that made me choke. Where was it coming from? The building wasn't full of plastic and synthetics, it was mostly wood. Yet it smelled like an overheating engine, rank with oil.

My eyes were so full of tears it took me a moment to notice that aside from the glare of the fire, it was still night and deathly cold, even with the flames at my back. After spitting on the snow I staggered to my feet, trying to get my fuzzy brain around the past twenty seconds of pure adrenaline. I was slowly realising that if I'd delayed even a second longer I might have found myself burning to death. My trainers, even damp as they were, had scorch marks where the fire had caressed them. I'd very nearly burned in my sleep because of my own carelessness with the fire.

That was when I realised that everything, aside from the clothes I was wearing, was still in the cabin. The little food I had, the water bottle and Ethan's lighter. All of it was in there, burning.

In a panic I turned to the window – maybe I could climb back in and salvage some of it? As if to mock me, a piece of the roof crashed down and I heard the fire snickering as it began to consume it. The window frame was already ringed in fire, and smoke belched from the opening up into the night sky. There was no way I could get back inside without risking my life. Not to mention my things were probably already gone, melted and destroyed in the fire that was raging out of control. Having a fire in the grate for a few days had apparently dried the place out enough to become the perfect bonfire.

Tears that had nothing to do with smoke filled my

eyes and I curled my fingers into frustrated fists. All that time spent hungry, saving food, when I should have eaten it all before falling asleep. Now it was gone for ever. No use to me at all. I cursed myself for letting the fire burn whilst I slept, even if the alternative would have been to freeze to the floorboards.

A fire in the grate for a few days. I blinked, forgetting for a moment the terrible unfairness of losing the last of my supplies. The words circled my mind as I tried to work out what bothered me about them. I'd been making my fires in the fireplace in the cabin. Clearly I'd neglected it tonight, let it get out of control whilst I slept. In the midst of all the uncertainty I'd forgotten that the fire wasn't my friend, only a tool I had limited control over. I'd been careless and almost burned alive as it spread. So what was so weird about that sentence?

Then it clicked. The fire was in the grate at the back of the cabin. I'd been sleeping on my back and had seen the opposite wall ablaze. Not the wall to my left as would have been the case if my fire had spread. The flames couldn't have jumped to another surface without leaving an even greater blaze behind them. If the fire in the grate was to blame, I'd have burned before that wall even smouldered, surely?

But if that was the case, what had started the fire on the wall?

Intent on seeing the outside of the wall I circled the cabin, mindful of the dark and the uneven hillocks of snow that the wind had driven against the cabin walls.

But once I reached the front of the building, all thoughts of finding the source of the fire quickly evaporated. The clearing was bathed in a livid orange glow which the cabin had shielded me from. Out in the open however, waves of hot air swept at me from all sides and the garish light threw chaotic shadows across the ground.

My cabin was not the only one ablaze. Every single building in the village was on fire.

I turned in place and looked around at the semi-circle of cabins. Although none was burning as brightly as mine, every single one had tongues of flame at the windows, roaring into the night air as if from a blow-torch. Fire so hot it wasn't even orange in places but palest yellow, almost white. All around me damp wood smoked, spat and hissed but succumbed to the blaze. I heard things falling as if, inside, each cabin was coming apart, ready to collapse.

How? How was this happening? Struggling through the deep snow I found my way to the gap between my cabin and the next. The virgin snow was melting at the edges, fizzling into steam as the fire reached up to the sky and belched out enough heat to make my hair float on the current of it. But there were no footprints in the snow.

I staggered to the next cabin. No prints. Every cabin was ablaze, yet there was no evidence of anyone going between them to set the fires. I was certain now that my fire was not to blame, because how could it have spread between the cabins so quickly? Yet it did seem like mine had caught first. Even as I stood there watching the flames convulse, I heard a great cracking creaking sound. A rush of hot air, sparks and ash hurtled towards me from behind and I turned to see that my cabin's roof had fallen in.

Edging away from the buildings in case any sparks caught my clothes, I looked around and realised that every single cabin seemed to be burning from the inside out. The flames reaching from the windows and licking upwards towards the roof. Yet my cabin, despite its collapse, was burning from the side closest to its neighbour. From the outside, if I was remembering that awful moment of realisation correctly. The light coming through the logs, spreading inwards rather than escaping. I had no idea what it meant. Looking at the ground there were no prints, though the snow was pitted with dripping ice melt, scarred from falling sparks and hot shards of wood.

Standing there in the snow I felt like I was going mad. My brain couldn't take it all in; the danger, the fear, the loss of all my supplies and now this . . . impossibility on top of all that. It was too much.

Only then did I think of the skeletons I'd found under the porches. The same porches that were even now being taken over by the fire. The bodies would burn, the worn shrouds going up like tissue paper around the brittle, mummified bones. I was breathing in the smoke from them. The thought sickened me and I had to fight not to throw up, already nauseous from the smoke and its odd chemical stink. Where was that smell even coming from when every building was made out of wood from top to bottom?

A biting wind at my back swept that question away. It was still absolutely freezing outside. Even this close to the blazing fires the cold was making its presence felt, like a wolf prowling at the boundary fence. It could snow again at any time and I needed some shelter. I looked back at the burning wreck of the cabin that had been my safety net for the past few days. The lighter was in there, burned up to nothing by now. I had no way of lighting my own fire. But if I stayed by the burning remains of my shelter – the only source of heat – I'd be out in the open, visible to anyone or anything prowling in the woods.

I stood there a moment, scared and unsure what to do. My gaze flicked around into the darkness, afraid I'd see eyes reflecting the flames. The glinting eyes of wolves or a bear . . . or a man. Whatever had been watching me, following me, had taken Ethan and was now trying to burn me alive as I slept. If I was right and the fire hadn't come from my grate. That meant it had been started on purpose. How else? Whatever was going on had just escalated beyond giving me the creeps. Whoever, whatever was out there had just tried to kill me. Though how I had no idea.

I gave myself a mental shake. Was I really thinking that some kind of shadow creature or ghost had come after me in the night to burn my shelter and all the supplies in it? A man, possibly, but a ghost with matches? Some kind of curse that had been following me since I arrived and could cause spontaneous fire? No. It was ridiculous. It was just my mind making things up in this desolate, creepy place. Just like in those stupid films Ethan loved so much – *The Shining* and the rest of them. Your mind could do weird things in a place this lonely, this empty.

Only . . . In that movie, it wasn't the evil spirits of the hotel that got you in the end, was it? It was the man with the axe. A very real, very pissed off man. Turned as crazy as I was getting in that place.

Fear was zipping up and down my spine. Fear of what I didn't know. Of what was out there. Whatever it was. In that state I couldn't stand the thought of leaving the light of the fire behind, never mind the heat. I'd have to stay in the village and keep my eyes open for any sign of my mystery stalker.

Thankfully, in my first bit of good luck, I'd gone to sleep in my gloves. That made using my hands to shape a windbreak out of snow less unpleasant than it might otherwise have been. I heaped more snow up around the sides, making a sort of burrow facing the well. From it I could see every cabin in the village. I wasn't sure it was going to work, but it at least gave me the feeling of being safely enclosed. Even if anything out there could knock it down like a kid's snowman.

Finally I used my foot to drag some partly burning planks out of the inferno of the cabin and used them to make a campfire a bit closer to my shelter. Though the cabins were blazing well enough that even as far back as I was, it was still reasonably comfortable. I had to save some of the fire that had nearly killed me. It was all I'd have to keep me warm come morning. If it went out, I was as good as dead.

Without food, though, wasn't I already dead?

I sat down on my heels and folded my arms around myself to keep the heat in. Curled up like that I anxiously scanned the row of cabins from end to end, over and over, like it was a line in a book I was struggling to read. Every time my frightened mind turned a tree trunk into a human figure, my heart skipped a beat. But every time I calmed myself, until the next false alarm.

In the morning I'd have to try and work out what to do, but I wasn't moving another inch until the sun came up. Anything to give me the slightest sliver of safety. Not that I thought daylight would keep whatever had done this at bay. I couldn't convince myself, no matter how hard I tried, that this was the work of a random person. Even after my stern words to myself on the subject of horror movies, I still felt a wrongness to everything I was experiencing. Some kind of evil that wasn't bound by the natural laws of that place. Maybe I just couldn't fathom another human being hating me enough to do all this. It was inhumane and therefore had to be the act of something other than human. Or else I had to face the idea that somewhere out there was a person who'd been watching me suffer for days now and who, far from trying to help me, had tried to murder me.

In the end the cause didn't matter. Man or monster,

I was still in danger and keeping both eyes open for any sign of attack, from anything. Even if I was looking for a ghost, I'd see the mad axe killer coming. Being alert to everything was my best hope of survival now.

I didn't dare sleep, so I sat there, all night, watching the only safe place I'd found on the mountain burn.

Chapter 17

'Three more boxes, then I'm off to A&E for a hernia repair,' Ethan groused, dumping a crate of records on the counter.

Behind him my sister's boyfriend, Pete, was wrestling with a tangle of cables to get the speaker system working. Our move from the market to a proper shop wasn't one we took lightly, but I was relieved that it was going this well.

Jess came in behind Ethan, carrying a black binbag of wall hangings. The usual psychedelic, mushroom, hemp leaf and flaming skull stuff.

'Where do you want these?' she asked.

'I'll show you.' Ethan darted away and led her into the back room. It would eventually become our office. Right now though it was a dumping ground for stuff we hadn't quite got space for at the moment.

'Do you need a hand, Pete?' I asked, watching him struggle to secure a wall bracket.

'Yes, please,' he puffed.

I went over and helped him to hold the speaker bracket stable whilst he drilled into the wall. I heard Jess laugh from the back room.

'Thanks for helping out,' I said. 'I know it's not the most relaxing way to spend the weekend.'

'No worries,' Pete said, brushing plaster dust off his glasses. 'Plenty of practice for when we do our house up.'

'Are you asking Jess to move in?' I asked, delighted. They were really taking their time over it. Ethan and I started sharing a house in our second year of uni and had lived together ever since. Even before we got married, much to Mum and Dad's quiet disapproval. Though they had eventually come around to Ethan and our marriage had smoothed things over.

'Not quite yet,' Pete muttered, turning pink around the ears. 'But, eventually, you know, when . . . we've been talking about it maybe being time to think about getting married.'

I almost smiled. He was so anxious, thinking about thinking about things. But then Jess was sort of the same. Cautious.

'Well, I think Jess would be over the moon to marry you,' I said. 'Whenever you think is the right time. I promise to act surprised – can't wait to hear the news.'

'What news?' Ethan came up behind me, arms circling my waist.

'Oh . . .' I floundered, not wanting to put Pete on the spot. 'Pete was just telling me there's going to be some kind of . . . jazz festival in town next year. Do

you *think we should have a stall there if it goes
ahead?'*

'Not *really our scene, is it, babes? No offence,'* Ethan
said to Pete.

'It's *not for everyone,'* Pete said, *shooting me a
grateful look. 'I think I'll go help Jess with the rest of
the stuff in the van.'*

Pete *shot off like a whippet and Ethan watched him
go with an odd look on his face. Then he looked up
at the newly installed bracket.*

'Man *of mystery, that Pete – you wouldn't think
he'd be much cop with DIY.'*

'He's *a surveyor,'* I *pointed out.*

'Yeah, *but they don't like . . . build stuff, do they?'*
Ethan *reached up and wobbled the bracket, which
almost immediately fell off the wall.*

'Case *in point,'* I *laughed.*

'Pass *me the drill,'* Ethan said. 'He *need never know.'*

Chapter 18

The day of Jess's wedding dawned bright and crisp, stinking of smoke.

I awoke from a slight doze with a jolt, convinced I'd felt a breath on the back of my neck. The sense of someone right behind me. But it was only the cold wind against my skin. Still I couldn't shake the sense that whatever was out there with me was the closest it had ever been.

At some point in that seemingly endless night, it had begun to snow again. It settled across my shoulders and on my hat and hair. By the time it was light enough that I felt able to move, my body didn't want to unfold itself from the crouch I'd adopted to stay warm. It was like my legs had been replaced with sticks and I stumbled around in circles trying to get my circulation going.

I didn't feel safe. A feeling I was almost starting to forget. I'd expected to feel better once the sun was up, chasing away the thoughts of ghosts and demons. But although the lack of flames and madly dancing shadows made things a little less intense, I was no less afraid of what might have caused the inferno now that it had died down. The only real difference to me was that in the daylight I might see an attack coming a fraction of a moment before I'd spot it in the dark. It wasn't much of an advantage but I was clinging to it.

Once I'd shaken some feeling back into my limbs I began to search the wreckage of Witwerberg. I had no idea how long those cabins had stood on that spot. How many years they'd been occupied before that newspaper clipping was printed. Maybe a century or more. But now all six had been reduced to charred logs and cinders. The furthest one from mine was the most complete. I guessed the fire had reached it last. About a foot of its walls remained and some of the timbers from the roof had fallen after the flames died, so they were barely singed.

Mindful of the lost lighter I quickly gathered some charred pieces of wood to feed my fire. If it went out I had no way of starting another. That done, I looked for answers.

If I'd expected to find more evidence of human involvement once the sun was up, I'd have been disappointed. As it was I hadn't expected to see anything at all and so the complete lack of footprints besides my own wasn't much of a surprise. As far as I could see no one had moved between the cabins. Each one of the six buildings had, it seemed, spontaneously erupted in flames. From what I could remember of the shocking sight, mine had been burning brightest when I'd made it outside. Which to me suggested that it had been burning the longest. So a fire had started with my shelter and then somehow spread to five other buildings, each several feet from the next.

More pressing than being confronted with yet another impossible series of events was my complete lack of supplies. Everything I had, and there hadn't been much, was now burned to ash. The bit of food I'd been eking out, the can I'd used to boil water and the bottle I'd kept it in, all gone. Worst of all, the lighter, my one means of creating a fire to stay warm, was gone. I had no shelter and no way to keep the cold at bay. Which meant that I was pretty much fucked. I was going to freeze to death before I even got a chance to starve.

After a thorough search of the wreckage I'd found nothing to help me. Each cabin had been as empty as mine. Not that much could have survived the fire. The only things that had made it out of the blaze with me were in my coat pockets. This included the stupid news-paper cutting. I found it whilst trying to keep my hands warm. I must have put it in there after keeping myself occupied with it one evening. Just what I needed. Fantastic.

My mouth was dry and the taste of smoke coated my tongue and throat. I was burning for a drink, but my only method of boiling water was gone. For several long moments I hovered in indecision, warring with myself. Then I slowly walked to a patch of clean-looking snow, scooped some up and looked at it. I had to do this. I could make myself do it. After a few seconds I took a mouthful of snow and chewed it down to water, swallowing quickly. I kept going until the taste of smoke was gone. Then I started to feel sick so I stopped and took deep breaths. I felt so stupid for still being worried about germs at a time like this, but I couldn't control it. I had to try though. With no food and no shelter, the least I could do was keep myself from dying of thirst.

It was then that I remembered the car. It was still sitting at the bottom of the gulley as far as I knew. I hadn't wanted to chance my ankle for clean clothes, but shelter was far more important. My ankle was healed enough that I felt confident I could reach it without falling or getting stuck at the bottom of the slope. Or else I was more confident in my ankle than my odds of surviving in the open.

The car wasn't much compared to a cabin with space for a fire but at least it would provide me with some shelter. A way to keep the snow off and my heat in. All I wanted was to be out of Witwerberg and to have a door I could shut against the night. The car would do nicely.

What to do about the fire though, that was the question. I couldn't have one burning in the car obviously, but neither did I trust the idea of making a campfire beside a vehicle full of fuel. I'd only just escaped one fiery death-trap, I wasn't going to help someone make another one for me.

I stood by the newly fed fire and tried to think of a

compromise. A way to keep the fire without putting it too near my one remaining source of shelter. Because once this fire was gone, there wouldn't be another. After a long time, however, I had to admit to myself that I had no idea how to keep the fire going whilst maintaining its distance from the car. And, although I'd miss its warmth, the danger was too great.

I kicked snow over my only source of heat and watched the glowing embers sizzle into blackness. There was no going back now. Fireless, the car was my only option for keeping warm. Suddenly gripped by a fear that it wouldn't be there when I reached the gulley, I left the village quickly.

The walk up towards the road took longer than it had even when I was injured. It had snowed a lot in the past few days and the way was thick with it. There was an icy crust on the surface which broke against my shins as I waded through the drifts. My leggings were no barrier to the cold or the wet and soon they were soaked and freezing from the knees down. Likewise my trainers were so poorly suited to the snow that I couldn't tell if my feet were wet because they were simply too cold for me to feel. I realised with a surge of despair that I had no way to get my things dry without a fire. Still, I reminded myself, the car had our bags in it. I'd at least be able to get a change of clothes.

I was about halfway to the spot the car went over, when I decided to take the extra few hundred metres and check on my sign. I'd been so caught up in the awful discoveries in Witwerberg that I hadn't thought to maintain it. Though I'd had so little food that hiking all that way wouldn't have done much for my odds of survival. Sign or no sign.

I was, though, a bit worried that the heavy snowfall had covered the sign. That, or the accompanying winds had blown it over. Not that I suspected many people had driven past given the weather of the last few days. That sign was the only thing guiding people to my location. The only thing that would tell passers-by that I needed help. If any ever came. So I had to check it now, especially when I was passing so close to it.

I reached the road before realising that I should have gone to the car first. My suitcase had more makeup inside which I could use to edit the sign. It needed to tell people that I was in the car now, not the village. I'd made a stupid spur-of-the-moment decision and now I'd have to get to the car, come back up out of the gulley and then go back. Wasted effort meant wasted calories and I had no way to replace them. I'd have to make smarter choices or I was going to end up dead even faster than I'd imagined.

In the end though it didn't matter. When I reached the place where the plank sign had stood, it was gone. I kneeled and rifled in the snow in case it had fallen and become buried. Even as I did so I knew, deep down, that I wouldn't find it. Someone or something had taken the board I'd written my SOS on and got rid of it. Not only that but, when I cleared the snow that had once again covered the sign for Witwerberg, the red arrow I'd drawn and my message were both gone. Erased. Only a faint scarlet smudge could be seen.

I ran my fingers over the place my arrow had been. My fingers came away slightly tinted with red. The remains of 'Gilded Glamour' where it had stained the wood. Something in me snapped and I slapped my palm against the sign. My hand stung despite my gloves. I hit it again and again, then grabbed at the solid wood in an attempt to shake it loose. I kicked the post it stood on and screamed until my throat was raw, only stopping when I was blinded by tears.

At last I leant against the sign for Witwerberg, the smoking ruin I'd left behind me, and sobbed until my lungs burned for air. Without the sign to lean on I'd have fallen right into the snow and probably stayed there. Everything I'd been through in the past few days, everything I'd done to try and keep myself together, keep myself alive. All of it for nothing. It had been taken away from me in one move. How could I protect myself now? How could I fight against something I couldn't even see? Something that was always there just behind me, erasing my efforts and tearing down my defences?

Even then, in the middle of a frustrated breakdown, I could feel the eyes on me. I was being watched even now. Something had followed me from the village. Something that I never caught sight of no matter how many times I turned around or glanced to the side. Not so much as a glimpse.

'What do you want?' I screamed, my own voice

sending a bolt of fear through me as it echoed back. 'Why are you doing this?'

It came out as a whine, like a child that doesn't understand why they're being punished. How their parents could be so mean. But I wasn't being punished, was I? I hadn't done anything to deserve this.

Unbidden, thoughts of Jess filled my mind. Of all the times I'd been put over her by our parents, all the times I'd taken it for granted that they'd be there for me instead of her. I wasn't blameless. I did have something to be punished for. But how could this possibly be related to that? And why like this? Why now? I folded my arms around myself, suddenly trembling. Why was this happening to me? To Ethan? He hadn't done anything . . . Maybe that's why he'd vanished. This was a private purgatory just for me.

Completely drained, I traipsed back to where I thought the car had gone over and looked down into the gulley. There it was, covered in snow, the shape of it standing out against the smaller snowdrifts. I just had to reach it. I needed to hide away, to escape for a while.

Getting down into the gulley wasn't easy. The sides were steep and I almost slid most of the way, grabbing at the branches of dead bushes and the trunks of trees. A few times my feet caught in holes under the snow and I felt my ankle twinge. Thankfully it was nowhere near as bad as the pothole I'd caught it in on the way to Witwerberg with Ethan. By the time I staggered into the side of the car I was exhausted and bruised, but thankfully in one piece.

The keys for the car had been in my bag when we'd broken down, but I'd shoved them into the pocket of my leggings on the day I'd gone back to look for Ethan. Luckily, when I'd taken my bottoms off to dry them, I'd moved the key to an inner pocket of my coat. Otherwise I'd have had to break a window to get in. I swept the snow off the rear passenger door, unlocked it manually and crawled inside.

Inside the car it was about as cold as it had been outside. Like slithering into a fridge. It was at least dry though and I hoped it would keep my body heat in and slowly warm up a bit. It was odd to be back in the car, which smelled of air freshener and Ethan's aftershave. Normal, commonplace smells that didn't match the unfamiliar environment of that place. After so long in the woods and the village of old cabins, being back in a car felt wrong. Like I'd travelled in time, suddenly and against my will.

I leaned over the seats and looked through the front of the car. The first things I laid my hands on were the rental company folder and some paperwork. I shoved those under the seat with the stupid traitorous satnav. Other than those there wasn't much; a pine tree air freshener, rubber floor mats, the crumpled paper covers that had been on the seats. Finally I fiddled with the central console and lifted up the padded armrest to reveal a rack for CDs. Empty and defunct, naturally, in the age of smart phones. Someone had stashed a handy pack of tissues and a tin of car sweets in there. Probably someone who'd used the car before us and their stuff had been missed by the detailers. I didn't care. I immediately prised open the sticky tin and stuffed two sweets into my mouth. They were coated in icing sugar that had crystallised with age. I sucked on them and could almost feel energy returning to my body.

Returning to the back of the car I hunted for a lever or release for the boot hatch. I really didn't want to go outside and dig the back of the car out of a snow drift to reach my suitcase. Luckily the car had a small access hatch. I was able to reach through and pull my cabin bag out. A hard shell thing with very scratched sides, covered in stickers from music festivals. Ethan's holdall was in much better shape and I pulled that through next. Seeing it sent a knife of grief through my stomach. He'd packed that bag himself, not knowing that he wouldn't get to wear any of the clothes inside. That he'd end up trapped in a cabin before being taken God knows where by God knew what.

I slowly unzipped the bag and was met with a waft of his aftershave. I could remember him spritzing it into the bag so he didn't have to pack the bottle. He'd given me a twinkly look, proud of his 'life hack'. I'd rolled my eyes and reminded him to pack his toothbrush, because he always forgot it and we had six spares he'd had to buy at various airports over the years. I let out a shaky laugh when I found his wash bag and saw he'd once again forgotten to bring one.

Under the wash bag I found his clothes and slowly unfolded a jumper. It was one of the vintage ones he'd found at a kilo sale. Every single one had a weird stain or a hole or an obvious repair. I was convinced he picked those ones on purpose, the unloved items that wouldn't appeal to anyone else. The one in my hands was a very bold Argyle pattern in greens and mustard yellow. The old wool was scratchy at the cuffs and there were loose threads from Ethan's endless fidgeting. I rubbed the wool against my cheek and took a shaky breath, then removed my coat and put the jumper on underneath. Ethan's scent clung to everything, a mix of Pears soap and lemony aftershave.

I kicked off my wet trainers and shuffled out of the soaked leggings. With clean, dry socks on my feet and a pair of Ethan's jeans on, I felt the most human I'd been since arriving in Witwerberg.

My bag was packed with makeup and hair stuff for the wedding. I'd brought fancy lingerie for the week, figuring that Ethan and I would get a chance to enjoy our luxurious resort accommodation. I filtered through the items I'd brought, the tangle of chargers and jewellery, tights, belts and shoes I'd brought along just in case. Not much of any use to me now. Though I'd layer on the tights when I had the energy.

Underneath it all I came across a box wreathed in bubble wrap. I carefully peeled back the layers until the ivory cardboard was exposed. The lid was decorated with a cluster of dried white roses and tied with satin ribbon. My wedding present to Jess. Well, our wedding present technically, because it was Ethan who'd spotted it at one of our regular vintage shops. The place was a maze of antiques, vintage, repro and retro finds. Everything from Victorian furniture to nineties toys all under one roof in case after case and box after box. A great place to get boxes of unsorted and ungraded records from sellers who didn't have the time or inclination to deal with them.

I slowly undid the ribbon and opened the box to check on the contents. Given that the car had crashed down a gulley, I'd expected to find a mess inside, but I was surprised. The box was lined with satin over a kind of cushion, so that was probably what kept the tiara from being shaken around. It was part of a set: tiara, drop earrings and choker. They sparkled intensely even in the dim interior of the car. Each piece was made of silver and set with marcasite, sapphire chips and pale blue topaz. It was vintage, obviously, and in a baroque style featuring tiny stars.

We'd been looking for a wedding present and Ethan had been the first one to spot it, pinned onto a polystyrene mannequin head. I'd immediately decided Jess had to have it. Not only was her birthstone a sapphire, not only would it be her something old, something new and something blue; it was almost the same tiara as our mum had worn in her wedding picture. She'd not had the set but I remembered the tiara vividly. It was one of the pieces of jewellery she'd sold to pay for my first car. The piece Jess had always wanted for her wedding.

Despite the price tag, which was a lot for us to manage given I hadn't yet received my inheritance, I had to get it. It was the perfect way to give something back to Jess. Something I had literally taken away from her, albeit without meaning to.

I carefully straightened the earrings and necklace, then put the lid back on the box and retied the ribbon. Jess's wedding was already underway, if not over already and she'd never get a chance to wear the tiara set. Even if I did manage to escape this place and get it to her, it wouldn't matter. I'd have missed her wedding and she'd never want to see me again, or give me the chance to explain, never mind accept a gift from me.

After stowing the box safely under the passenger seat I made myself a nest of my and Ethan's clothes. The inside of the car was freezing cold and my breath was already creating ice on the inside of the windows and the cracked windscreen. Surrounded by the comforting scent of my missing husband's clothes, I cried myself to sleep.

Chapter 19

After that virtually sleepless night and the long trek out to the car I slept like the dead. When I woke, contorted on the back seat of the car, it was light, but not the same light it had been before. Peering through a gap in the snow crust on the car I could see lengthy shadows and knew darkness was creeping in. I'd slept the day away. Despite the cramped conditions it was easily the most comfortable sleep I'd had in days. Mostly thanks to the lockable doors rather than the padded seat.

My eyes were sticky with dried tears and my nose was raw from the cold. I didn't want to move but as I was lying there, I had an idea.

A pretty awful idea.

Lying in the cold I thought about the village and the bodies I'd found in the woods. The newer ones. Specifically I was thinking about the woman I'd partially uncovered and the coat she was wearing. I wasn't yet desperate enough to wear the clothes off of a corpse's back, but I was desperate enough to wonder what she had in her pockets.

The coat I'd pegged as an outdoor brand and it suggested she was a hiker or something similar. Someone who wouldn't have come out into the Alps unprepared. She'd have things in her many coat pockets, maybe even a rucksack with her; hopefully a map to help me reach the resort, maybe even some food. Car sweets were not going to sustain me for ever. I was already dangerously underfed for the cold. I could feel my body getting weaker. I needed something, anything, to change the odds in my favour. Because right now I had nothing. Without food I would just lie down and not have the strength to get up ever again.

I wondered if, wherever Ethan was, he had food and a roof over his head. I'd had our snacks but he'd vanished in only the clothes he was wearing. Was whoever had taken him keeping him fed and alive? I hoped so. I really did. Maybe he'd have the strength to escape from them and get help.

I lay on my back to layer up some clothes. After taking off Ethan's jeans I put on a pair of tights, a new pair of leggings and some thick socks over the ones I already had on. Then with the jeans belted on over the top I flexed my legs, checking for manoeuvrability. A bit stiff but I would be fine once I got going.

My trainers were still wet inside, whatever water-proofing they'd ever had giving out after all my snow hiking, but I had nothing to replace them with. Unless I wanted to head back to Witwerberg in satin stilettos.

Not exactly practical but at least my footprints wouldn't give me away as much. I put my feet into the trainers and tied them up, hoping the layered socks would keep my feet dry.

This time I wasn't making the mistake of leaving anything useful behind. I ate two more sweets then put the tin in my pocket and slung Ethan's holdall across my back. Inside I had two more jumpers and some of the more useful things from our washbags – tweezers, clean flannels and a tube of antiseptic. If whoever, whatever, had torched the village decided to burn the car, at least I wouldn't lose everything. Just the last roof over my head. I didn't want to think about my odds of survival without it.

After a moment's indecision I also slid the wedding tiara set into the bag. It was added weight I probably should have left behind but I couldn't bear the idea of losing it. Besides, if my frozen body was one day discovered in this horrible place, Jess would at least know that I'd tried to make things right with her.

Getting out of the gulley was a bit of a nightmare. It was too steep to go up where I'd come down. Trying to climb made me feel dizzy. I had to walk parallel to the road a way and eventually found a fallen tree trunk that acted like a banister. I used it to pull myself up the slope and reach the road. I was already breathing heavily, my energy levels plummeting.

At that point what I was doing began to feel more real. I was spending my last bits of strength on going to dig up a body and search it. The idea of seeing those dead people again, let alone touching them, filled me with dread and made me shiver inside my layers. I didn't want to do it, but I knew that I had to. This was my only chance.

It took a while to find them again. The snow that I'd been grateful for, because it covered over the horrors I'd found, was suddenly my biggest enemy. I'd been running through the woods when I'd come across them before and not taking much notice of my surroundings. The snow made finding my way back almost impossible. However, once I got within shouting distance of the right area, they were impossible to miss. Not because I recognised a given tree or heap of snow, but because someone had dug them up.

I stood about a foot away from the very edge of all that churned-up mud and tried not to vomit at the sight in front of me. The two bodies had been dragged out of the snow and piled up, then set alight. I refused to believe a human being could burn up so easily, so something must have helped it along. Something either chemical or unnatural in a more abnormal way. The bodies were burned to blackened husks, like mannequins. It was only when I got closer that I could see the cracks in that black coating and the oozing red beneath.

I turned away and looked at the forest, partly because looking at the bodies made me feel sick, partly because I could feel something watching me. The fire must have been huge and incredibly intense; even the trees around the grave were scorched from leaping flames. The snow was completely melted, and ash mixed with mud had frozen into a dark blotch around the remains.

At the edge of the scorched area I could see the hole where the two had been buried. It was dug mostly in snow, but with some disturbed dirt at the bottom. Like the original grave was too shallow for two people and only the snow had covered them over completely.

There was a roaring in my ears, a new wave of shock cresting over me. I raised both hands to the back of my neck and squeezed down, my cheeks pressed to my forearms as I closed my eyes. Leaning back I opened them again to look at the dark branches and the stark white sky. More snow on the way, I guessed. It had that weirdly still feeling in the air and the sky was like TV static, fuzzy with dark edging in. Spots appeared across my vision and I stumbled slightly, looking down too quick. Dizziness overcame me and I locked my legs in place, desperate to remain upright. If I fell into the snow I didn't think I'd be able to get up again.

I let out a breath, took another, tried to stay in control. Whatever that poor woman had in her pockets, it was gone now. Burned up with her clothes. With her skin and hair. I tried not to think of human flesh roasting in the fire, of spitting fat and bursting eyeballs, but the thoughts came anyway. Along with the knowledge that if I'd woken even ten seconds later, I too would have been burned up. Alive.

My aching stomach turned over and over. I tried to distract myself by thinking of other things. The fire here must have been at the same time as the one in the village. I'd have noticed, surely, if there was smoke pouring out of the woods after the first fire. I'd have smelled it. *God, don't think about the smell, Mila.* No, only the fire at Witwerberg could have masked this one. Whatever had caused those twin blazes had been very busy that night.

I'd found no prints in town and here the ground was so churned up and melted around the bodies that I couldn't work out if there were any prints. Even the unmelted snow was pitted with drips and pockmarks from what had to be sparks from the fire. Snow had fallen from the trees and added to the general confusion. Though I suspected the lack of prints wasn't because they'd been erased, but because they'd never been there to begin with.

Something had attacked me, tried to burn me. It had burned every building I might have been able to shelter in. How had it known I'd come back to check these bodies for supplies? What if it had brought its mysterious fire here to make sure I couldn't get my hands on anything to save myself with? At every turn I was being hemmed in, kept defenceless and starving. Something was doing this to me on purpose.

I wanted to see the idea as ridiculous, but I couldn't rationalise it any other way. Maybe the only reason the car was still in one piece was because it was off the road. Somehow out of reach of whatever had a grip on Witwerberg. Otherwise the cabins, the bodies at the outskirts, even the town sign, were all within the influence of whatever I could feel, watching me, whenever I was in town. Anything connected to Witwerberg was tainted. This place was under the control of something and I was standing in it as night closed its jaws around me.

That thought was enough to make me turn, ready to run back to the comparative safety of the car. As I turned though I saw something in the empty grave. Something that wasn't the brown of mud or the white of snow; something bright orange, though dulled with dirt. It was just a tiny scrap of fabric, but it caught my eye.

Feeling like I was pushing my luck, I kneeled down and grabbed it. As soon as I started pulling I realised it wasn't something small. It was something that had been mostly buried and which hadn't been dug up for the improvised funeral pyre. Something that had been forgotten by whatever force had done all this.

I pulled, the frozen ground resisted, but eventually the fabric broke free. I fell backwards, clutching a backpack encrusted with earth. With difficulty I managed to get to my feet, though my legs were shaking. Surrounded by the sensation of being watched, of something closing in, I forced myself into a stumbling run. I had to get away from that place, back to where I was safe. Even the ache in my ankle wasn't enough to make me slow down. Only the black spots in my vision and the tang of bile in my throat slowed me to a walk, and I was clear of Witwerberg by then.

Night had fallen and the temperature was dropping fast. I'd spent most of my energy and had to drag myself along through force of will alone. With every step I felt the world around me twist and tip.

It wasn't until I'd slithered down the gulley slope and shut myself back in the car that I felt secure enough to stop and go through the bag. I propped myself up on the door, too exhausted even to sit up. My hands were shaking as I opened the stiff zip, trying not to think about what might have soaked into the fabric as it lay under two bodies.

The first thing I found was an ID. It was tucked into a plastic sheath in the top of the bag. I had to hold it almost to my nose to see in the darkness. It was all in French and the picture looked like the woman I'd found. In the way that a doll modelled on a celebrity looks like them, only stiff and lifeless. Her name was Jaqueline and judging by the date on the ID she was about twenty. Or nineteen, depending on when she'd been killed, I realised, as her birthday was only the month before.

I couldn't read most of the ID card but guessed it was for a college or university based on the crest in the corner and the date of expiry, four years from the issue day.

The rest of the bag had her wallet, passport and travel tickets neatly zipped into a plastic case, some energy bars – one of which I immediately crammed into my mouth – a first-aid kit, GPS unit (completely dead), a mostly empty plastic bottle of water and a phone. The phone was out of battery, not that I expected much else.

According to the date on the ticket she had arrived

four months ago, but there was no return date. She must have been planning to buy a ticket later, or get home some other way, by train maybe. Had she been lying in a hole in Witwerberg for four months? Or had she only ended up here recently? I didn't know and it drove me crazy. Surely if she'd been missing a while someone had to come here looking for her eventually? Someone who could help me?

I finished up the energy bar and forced myself not to reach for another. There were only two more and one pouch of something that had frozen solid. In the dark I read the tiny print on the side, 'Peanut Protein Pack'. Probably some kind of special hiking food, peanut butter mixed with something else to give you a bit of added energy. From the feel of it there was maybe enough for two good meals, or three snacks. I tucked it inside my jumper to thaw out. I needed to get my strength back and that meant using some of this precious food right away.

Whilst I waited for the pouch to thaw I thought about the bag's owner. Jaqueline hadn't brought much with her so maybe she wasn't planning to be out long? Just a short hike. But where to and where from? Was I near somewhere that had actual people in it, or had she been killed somewhere else and brought to Witwerberg? It was frustrating to have such an incomplete picture of where I was and what was happening. I wished she'd brought an old-school map with her. I was beginning to really resent gadgetry of all kinds: phones, GPS, cars and especially satnavs.

I was about to stuff the bag under a seat when I felt something shift in the heavy base of it. I turned it upside-down and realised that what I'd thought was a chunky bottom to the bag was actually a compartment with something heavy inside. I had to rip the fabric to get at it because the zip was so seized up with dirt. I was hoping for more energy bars or maybe the map I needed; instead I found a guidebook and an English-German dictionary.

I held both for a moment, confused. Why would a French girl need to translate English to German? Then I rolled my eyes at myself. I was seeing mysteries everywhere. She might not be French, just studying there. Maybe she spoke French and English and this dictionary was cheaper – who cared? It wasn't going to help me anyway. I didn't even have a lighter to use it as kindling.

Bundling myself back up in my nest of clothes, I flicked through the guidebook, squinting in the dark. It was in English and looked like a pretty specific guide to the region for hikers. No usable maps though; clearly they were relying on you buying those separately. Lots of info on what sort of gear to bring, advice Jaqueline seemed not to have followed. Where was her emergency blanket, her fire lighting kit? Maybe the expensive coat was just for show and she was a novice? Was that how she'd ended up in Witwerberg; she'd got lost and had to look for shelter?

Thinking of Witwerberg I checked the index and found it listed, mentioned on a single page. I flipped through and found it. The paragraph was quite short, but still managed to bring my train of thought to a complete halt:

There are many abandoned settlements in this area, some dating as far back as the 14th and 15th century, when the black plague spread across Europe. This route will take you past at least four (five if you are doing the added loop to make this a two-day trip). This fifth settlement, Witwerberg, is the most recently abandoned. It was populated until 1816 – the infamous 'year without summer', caused by the eruption of Mount Tambora in Indonesia. The resulting cold, wet growing season, caused by debris in the atmosphere, led to crop failure and starvation across Europe. Witwerberg is not unusual in this regard as many villages failed during this period, which was followed by the coldest winter in 250 years. What makes Witwerberg worth a visit is its history of mysterious disappearances and ghost sightings. Though many stories appear exaggerated or entirely fabricated as with many legends, at least eleven people are confirmed to have vanished from the area, without a trace.

Chapter 20

At least eleven people.

There followed a link to a website, encouraging the guidebook owner to 'read more!'. But I couldn't read more. I was stuck with that one frustrating little paragraph of information. The words 'without a trace' ringing through my brain as a new and brutal wind began to howl outside. Without a trace. Eleven people. That they knew of.

How many other stories were there that the guidebook classified as 'legends'? Ten? Twenty? How many people like me, like Jaqueline and the unnamed businessman had 'disappeared' here, since the book was printed?

How were people still allowed to come here? Why was there no warning? No giant chain-link fence across the road to Witwerberg that said 'Keep Out – Bermuda Triangle of The Alps Ahead'? Why was the village still standing and not demolished to keep people away? Or to find the bodies of the ones who had apparently never been found?

Holding that guidebook I wondered if each and every one of those eleven confirmed missing persons had gone through what I had. If perhaps I had found their skeletons under the cabins. Had they seen the mysterious figure, the shadow with no footprints, things being taken or destroyed, signals for outside help tampered with or taken away? How long had each person endured the ordeal? Was there a pattern, a time limit? Was I unknowingly reaching the end of a series of events that would culminate in my body being buried in the snow?

My breath was shallow, thin white clouds puffing out as I tried to fight my rising panic. What if there was no escape? I was already too far into whatever was happening here to be found. Perhaps in some sort of parallel world where no one could reach me even if they tried. It sounded mad even to me but every horror movie I'd ever seen was flickering in my mind. Maybe Ethan was still in the real world, looking for me. Only I was in this weird twilight zone and he had no idea.

'Come on, Mila, get a grip,' I said to myself, but even to my own ears I sounded unsure and shaky. Every day in that place reality felt further and further away. My sense of what was and wasn't possible cracking like ice under the weight of everything I'd seen.

I wanted to know what those people had gone through. What their disappearances had been like. Was it the same thing as me? I'd never wanted access to the internet more. Any hint would have been better than sitting there, not knowing.

Then I remembered the cutting. The German newspaper from 1814, two years before the 'year of no summer' mentioned in the guidebook. Two years before the inhabitants of Witwerberg were subjected to a fruitless summer and a harsh winter. Was that where the skeletons were from? Were they missing people or simply the unfortunate residents of this tiny village? Maybe a lot of the villagers had starved to death or died of cold and been put under the porches whilst the ground was hard as iron. Then their remaining relatives had fled the prospect of a similar death and never returned.

Maybe. Or maybe they were the first victims of whatever was wrong with this place. Because there was something deeply wrong with Witwerberg and I'd felt it from the moment we arrived. That sense of being watched, a place too quiet and too untouched by the outside world, like it existed somewhere else altogether.

I pulled the crumpled cutting from my pocket. When I'd found it I'd assumed it was a harmless keepsake. The one time this place was mentioned in print, so someone had carefully clipped it out and kept it. Perhaps to send to a relative in the big city. If they even had 'big cities' back then and not just other small towns. History, like every other subject, was not my speciality. Now though, looking at it, I began to wonder if perhaps it had been kept not out of nostalgia but out of something else entirely. Fear. What if it was the story of someone's missing child? Or of a young wife whose husband went out to kill a deer and never came home?

I slowly flicked the pages of the German dictionary until I came to the unfamiliar word in the headline: *verschwunden*. A word I'd guessed meant something to do with wood, carpentry perhaps. Just based on how it sounded to me. As it turned out, it was nothing to do with woodwork or bake sales or anything cutesy that'd land you in the local paper and that your auntie might clip out and save. No, *verschwunden*, according to the dictionary in my cold hands, was the past tense of a word meaning 'to vanish'.

Someone, or something, had vanished in Witwerberg and this newspaper had reported on it. Before the year of no summer, there had been a disappearance.

Was this one of the disappearances that the guide-book writers knew about? I had no idea. How long had this been going on? What had started it? If someone had disappeared even before the town was hit by a tragic winter, did that mean it was somehow . . . cursed? That whatever was causing the things that had happened to me, whatever had made those people disappear, had also brought on the terrible events of that year?

I tried to get a grip on myself. It wasn't just Witwerberg that had suffered a bad winter. If it was caused by a volcano all the way over in Indonesia the effects had to have spread pretty far. The guidebook said this happened all over Europe, possibly even other continents.

Thinking about it in as coldly rational terms as I could manage, I told myself that people probably went missing in the Alps every year. They were mountains after all, dangerous and covered in snow and forests. Prowled by wolves and who knew what else, especially back then. A hundred years ago if someone bashed you on the head and buried you in the woods, you were never found. Even now it wasn't unlikely that the odd hiker, ski enthusiast or ill-prepared tourist might have an accident or wildlife encounter and drop dead somewhere no one would happen upon them.

But if that was the case, why was Witwerberg worth commenting on specifically? If people disappeared annually throughout the mountain range, why was this place significant? It had to be because of the sheer number of people. Somehow, Witwerberg had more disappearances than anywhere else nearby. A cluster of occurrences that made it stand out against the rest of the Alps. This place was a hotspot for that kind of thing. Why though? That was the question which made my neck prickle. I couldn't explain that. But maybe the article could.

I rummaged in my case for my makeup and found an eyeliner. With a blank page torn from the back of the dictionary I began to translate the newspaper clipping. Despite my awful language skills and complete lack of German knowledge, I was determined to work out what it said. I was surprised just how quickly I could work when properly motivated. Knowing that this scrap of newspaper might hold the secret to Witwerberg had me flipping pages and scribbling words with intensity.

At the end of the piece I had a smudgy, not terribly grammatical translation. Most of it was guesswork, just filling in connectives where they made sense and joining verbs and nouns to try and form sentences that matched up. Not every word was in the pocket dictionary either. I guessed because it was such an old paper and some words had either slipped out of common use or were the names of places or things that didn't exist anymore. But I had the basics of it down in my own, Mad Libs style way.

Heir Vanishes in Witwerberg

Heir to Köhler mining fortune still missing after several weeks of searching. Friederich Köhler became separated from the hunters touring the mountain forest. Friends said they heard shouting in the distance but arrived to find only Köhler's hat on the ground. A search found no further sign of the man or that an accident had occurred. The village residents too heard the shout but saw nothing. They have aided in the search.

Fernand Köhler has offered a priceless reward for his son's return.

I went over it several times, checking and rechecking the words. Nothing about footprints or a figure in the trees. It was annoyingly vague, but I guessed words were at a premium back then. No time for editorialising or recounting every last detail. Still, any detail at all would have been useful.

One thing the paper clipping did prove was that Witwerberg had been making people disappear for a long time. Since before the winter of 1816, before the town was apparently abandoned. I wanted to know more; had they ever found this Köhler guy? Was he just dragged off by a wolf and eaten or had he actually vanished, like Ethan had? And why had someone from Witwerberg cut out this story and kept it? As a souvenir of a crime they'd committed? Or out of civic pride for their involvement in the search? Hell, maybe they'd been interested in this 'name your price' reward.

The lack of information was so frustrating, and the article so vague, that I ended up imagining my own version of events, adding in what I knew about Witwerberg and the weird stuff that happened there. I could imagine the search party finding his hat in the snow, puzzling over the way his footprints just stopped, as if he'd been plucked from the ground. But I couldn't know for sure what had actually happened. It was just my mind creating creepy scenarios to match my experiences.

I shoved the page of smudgy scribbles into the back of the guidebook. This wasn't helping me. I needed to keep warm and fed and somehow attract rescue. Nothing about reading old papers and speculating on a centuries-old mystery was going to help me. I extracted the protein pack from my jumper and squeezed a third of it into my mouth, chewing the too-sweet peanut butter as I went to put the book away.

As I closed the guidebook however, I caught a glimpse of the inside of the back cover. Someone had written there, maybe Jaqueline herself. The top of the page had a list of eleven names and some dates. Friederich Köhler was on that list, dated 1814, the same as the newspaper. The only name before his was a 'Baumann?' as if part of their name had gone unrecorded. Not unsurprising given that the date was simply '17th C'.

These had to be the names of the people whom the guidebook mentioned. The confirmed disappearances in Witwerberg. I touched the looping biro scrawl and wondered if Jaqueline's name would one day appear on a similar list. Would mine?

At the bottom of the page were some other notes, some which looked to be in French, others in English. Bilingual show-off. But I could tell some of it was names, maybe the unconfirmed disappearances? Perhaps Jaqueline had come to this place for a reason, not just on a whim. She was interested in Witwerberg's mysterious history.

I could almost see her hunched over her guidebook on the plane, making notes from memory, trying to work it out like a puzzle in a video game. Ethan was always leaving scraps of paper with maps or riddles half completed on them around the laptop in the office at home. He liked all those indie games with murders to solve and puzzles to beat. I half smiled at the thought that he'd have worked this whole thing out days ago if he was here. Just like the time we went to an escape room and he bounded from lock to dial to keyhole in a frenzy of discovery. I think my contribution that day was limited to driving us there.

Scanning over the notes, one word jumped out at me; footprints. A word that had been on my mind a lot lately. The maddening lack of them had been a constant itch in my brain, a crack in every rational explanation.

What Jaqueline had written was: '1976 – *The Bianchis – shelter in cabin, evidence of campfire – footprints in not out? No other prints?? How – where to?*'

Assuming 'The Bianchis' were people, perhaps a couple, it looked like they had disappeared from a cabin in Witwerberg whilst taking shelter. More importantly – if I was reading the stream of thoughts she'd hastily scribbled correctly – they had left prints going into the cabin, but not coming out. Nothing else had gone in or out either. They had disappeared in exactly the same way Ethan had. In more or less the same place, depending on which cabin it was. I had a weird feeling though, that it *was* our cabin. It was all too eerily similar.

Judging by their presence on that list, they had also never been found.

It wasn't only that which stilled my thoughts and made my heart skip a beat however. The idea that I might never see my husband again was smashed apart by the sudden realisation that I knew how he'd been taken.

Chapter 21

I opened the car door and immediately felt the drop in temperature. It was cold enough during the day, but at night it felt as if the air would stop my heart if I let it. The moonlight was all that cast a glow over the woods, intermittently blocked out by dense cloud. The storm that had been blowing up wasn't that heavy yet though and I couldn't stand waiting. With all my things stashed in Ethan's bag across my shoulders and some food in my belly, I hurried along the gulley.

As I climbed up to the road, fear started to erode my sense of purpose. The shifting of branches in the wind sounded a lot like footsteps, or a prowling animal. But I swallowed the whimper of fear that scratched at my throat. If I was right there was nothing ghostly about Ethan's disappearance. Ghosts don't need trap-doors.

It had come to me out of nowhere, reading those sparse notes. Every time I'd thought of the footprints I'd been stuck in a loop of terror and paranoia. I'd not been able to let go of my dread of something out there, watching me, out to get me. That superstitious fear had kept me from looking at it in terms of straight facts. If no one had come out of the door, but the cabin was empty, there had to be another way out. Not the window as I'd briefly considered, not a zip line to the trees. But a trapdoor to a cellar or something under the cabin.

I still had no idea who had done this, or why, but I was utterly convinced that I now knew how. The rest I was hoping to find out when I got through that trapdoor.

Still as I got closer and closer to Witwerberg's ashy ruins, my steps became smaller and slower. Was I really about to jump feet first into a hidden cellar? What if it was a serial killer's lair or the den of some kind of creature? No matter how much I wanted to shut out thoughts of supernatural monsters, they came anyway. I didn't have a weapon or even a torch to light the way. That had vanished along with Ethan.

What choice did I have though, in the end? I had nowhere to go and no one to save me. If I cowered in the car I might live long enough to starve to death. Unless whoever was out there decided to finish me off first. By doing this I wasn't just taking control of the situation, I might also be able to surprise them. So far I'd just run around like a scared little girl; like they probably expected me to. This was different. I was acting unpredictably and there was a chance they wouldn't be ready for me.

As I approached the remains of my cabin I wondered if Ethan was somewhere underneath it and had been the whole time. Tied up, gagged, listening to my footsteps overhead. Hearing me sob in terror and talk to myself, feeling the heat from the flames. Tears welled up in my eyes at the idea of him being helpless, hearing me but unable to get to me. I grabbed at a charred log and lifted it, letting it crash to the ground. I would find a way in. I had to.

It was hard work to clear the debris, some of which was just whole logs with char on the outside. As I lifted them or rolled them away, I tried to imagine the floor of the cabin as it had been. I'd gone over every inch when Ethan vanished, hadn't I? Searched each wall and the floor for any sign of him. That was how I'd found that weird hole in the wall, like a woodpecker's bore.

The floor had that weird matting on it, like burlap worn down to threads and gummed to the floorboards. No trapdoor could open through that. I faltered, a shower of charcoal falling from my hands. Was I making a big mistake? Had the idea of a trapdoor just been a stupid guess and I'd put myself out here, in the open, at night, for nothing?

But that covering on the floor – when I'd looked at it I'd seen thin places. Parts of it where the threads were worn away, almost invisible. Invisible, or cut through, to line a well-fitted trapdoor that had become hidden under dirt and dust.

I was here now. I had to know, one way or the other. Eventually I found the plank floor. The fire had started outside and must have run out of steam by the time it reached the boards. Though cracked and warped, none of them had burned completely. But, as the heat twisted and shrank them, it had revealed a very clear pattern to the boards. A rectangular piece, where planks had been cut through. The door I was looking for, which had been disguised by a century of filth.

I braced myself, wondering what I was about to uncover. Was there someone down there right now, listening to me rifle through the charred cabin? Were they tensed and ready for me, or soundly asleep? Was Ethan looking up, hoping against hope that it was me he was hearing?

The planks crumbled as I pulled them up. The whole piece was like the lid of a box, not hinged in any way but resting on a lip. I tossed it aside and looked down into the dark hole below. I could see pale ashes from the fire which had fallen through the cracks. Nothing else stood out in the dark. No sound and no movement. I released my breath and swallowed a trace of disappointment and relief. There was no attacker coiled in the dark, but no Ethan either.

With one hand on either side of the hole I lowered my head and peered into the cellar. Even though I'd not had access to any electric light for days and had walked there in the cloudy night, I still couldn't see anything. My night vision wasn't good enough to penetrate the shadows.

The smart thing to do would be to wait for daylight.

With some sun coming in through the trapdoor I'd be able to see anything, or anyone, that might be down there. Only I've never been accused of being smart, and I was done waiting for the next attack.

I sat up, dropped both legs into the hole and lowered myself down. Ash crunched under my butt and showered into the hole around my legs. I was surprised when my feet touched the floor and I was still holding the edge of the hatch with my shoulders sticking out. The cellar wasn't that deep; the cabin's residents must have been able to kneel on the floor and place things down there. I snatched up a lump of wood to use as a weapon, hoping I wouldn't need it, then ducked down under the floor.

My feet crunched on the floor of the cellar. It felt like leaves and sticks that must have fallen in when the trapdoor was last opened. Though that meant it must have been used since the cabins were abandoned. My mind however instantly jumped to the conclusion that I was standing on bones. A cold sweat sprang up on my neck and I gritted my teeth, willing the thought away. I was hunched down, semi-crouched to fit under the floor above. I was level with the porch I realised. If there were skeletons beneath it, they were only a few inches away, walled off by a little soil.

Stretching out an arm I felt my way around the space. It was about the size of the cabin above and the walls were not dirt as I'd expected, but planked. I could feel roots that had snaked in between the boards and the crumbling texture of wood slowly decaying. My fingers brushed a cold bit of metal and I jumped, but it was just a hook. There were more beside it, one with a loop of string still around it. Somewhere to hang bags of grain or sausages, whatever people ate a hundred years before Deliveroo. Overhead I felt thick beams supporting the floor above.

I crunched along the floor in tiny heel-toe steps as I searched. Eventually I took a step that made no sound. The floor there was covered in a soft layer of earth. I felt the wall down low and my fingers found a jagged edge. Someone had chopped a hole in the planks and earth had fallen in. No, I realised, feeling around, the earth had been scraped out. I stretched my arm into the hole and couldn't feel anything on the other side. It went straight into what had to be the cellar of the next cabin. Someone had dug a tunnel.

Feeling a chill at the thought of crawling through the narrow tunnel, I pushed my bag through and crawled after it. I could just about make it on my hands and knees, though my back brushed the roof of the tunnel. Why was it there? Maybe at some point the two houses had been shared by a single family? They might have dug through to create a shared cellar?

The second cellar was somehow darker than the first. I guessed some light had to have been getting in from the hatch after all. I felt around and found nothing on the walls or floor. It was as empty as the first. But there was another tunnel on the opposite side. Three cabins were connected?

I followed the tunnels from one cabin to the next,

counting houses. Each tunnel curved slightly, following the semi-circle layout of the cabins. When I reached the cellar of the final cabin I felt above me for a hatch and pushed it open in a cascade of ash and charred sticks. Peering out into the greyish pre-dawn I found myself where I expected to be; opposite the cabin I'd started in. Every single cabin in the village was connected by a tunnel.

It seemed really unlikely that they'd been built like that originally. Apart from anything else, the cabins were meticulously put together. As tightly joined as an antique puzzle box. The people who spent time and effort boarding their cellar were not going to put up with a dirt hole in the wall. Yet not even one tunnel was finished differently to the rest. It looked like a giant insect had bored from one to the next all at once. Someone had made those tunnels after the cabins were empty, I was certain of it. The only question was why.

After throwing my bag out through the trapdoor I pulled myself out. On the way up something scraped my hand and I hissed in pain. Sitting on the ashy ground I had a look at it and was relieved it wasn't bleeding. Just a graze. I looked for whatever had scratched me and saw a large splinter sticking out from the rim of the trapdoor. Caught on it was a tuft of what looked like Clingfilm.

I reached out and fingered the scrap of plastic. It was thicker than it looked, but still felt like part of a sandwich bag or something similar. It wasn't from anything I had on me, that was for sure. Had it been there before the fire or was it more recent? This last cabin was the least affected so it wasn't impossible that the plastic had survived the flames. What was it from? A plastic sheet or bag? More importantly, how had it ended up inside the tunnels, which I'd only just discovered? Who else had used them and why? Obviously someone who didn't want to be seen, or who just didn't fancy braving the cold every time they needed to move between cabins. Perhaps both.

Sitting there, I wondered if maybe Jaqueline or the man buried with her had found the same tunnel I'd just crawled through. Who knew how long they'd been in Witwerberg before they met their deaths? For that matter there might be other people buried in the woods who had spent time in the town. Any one of them might have left that scrap of plastic behind by accident.

Plastic aside, I was fairly certain I now knew how Ethan had disappeared. He'd been taken through the tunnels. The only thing bothering me about that was how I'd not heard anything. He was right next to me that night. The trapdoor only inches from where I was sleeping. How had I slept right through the removal and replacement of the hefty wooden hatch? Never mind that if he had been taken, as I assumed, there ought to have been a struggle.

Maybe we'd both been drugged somehow? I'd slept through the noise and Ethan had been unconscious and unable to defend himself, so there'd been no fight to hear. I tried to think about that night, what we'd done and how we'd been incapacitated. We'd brought the food with us, it was all pre-packed. I'd lit a fire – was that it? Had there been something hidden in the grate that let out a vapour? Or had someone simply crept in and pressed a rag over our mouths, doused in a drug?

Now that Ethan's disappearance wasn't so ethereal, I felt more certain that I was dealing with a person. Obviously I'd told myself that a ghost or monster was ridiculous, but now I actually believed it. Even deep down inside the part of me that was still a bit scared of the dark, the part that made me walk faster through graveyards and knock wood when I worried about someone I loved dying.

Knowing about the tunnel, though, wasn't much help in knowing where Ethan was now. Whoever it was, serial killers, mountain cannibals or organ harvesters, they could have carried him off to a car and gone anywhere by now. The high of my discovery was fading and I felt more lost and alone than ever. Helpless in the face of so many unknowns and so little information.

I glanced down into the cellar, where the cold light of another sunrise had just crept in. Despite my discovery I was no closer to knowing who had dug this tunnel or why and what it had to do with the bodies I'd found. I thought of poor Jaqueline who'd apparently come here to solve this mystery. I wondered how far she'd got before her death. How much had she discovered and was I even close to knowing half of it?

That's when I noticed the shadow on the back wall of the cellar. When I'd crawled out of the last tunnel I'd felt the opposite wall and found no further way forward. I'd been counting the cabins and knew I was in the last one, so it had made sense to me that I'd also reached the end of the tunnel. But now I saw that there was a second tunnel, not carrying on in the same direction, but striking out away from the village centre.

The cabins were not simply connected by a tunnel, they led to a way out of the village. One that I realised might explain the mysterious comings and goings of the figure I'd seen in the dark.

After glancing around the clearing to check that nothing was about to creep in after me, I slid back into the cellar. I would find out where this tunnel went, and if it led me to the person responsible for all this, I would face them. At least then I wouldn't be waiting for them to come and get me.

Chapter 22

It was my first time visiting Pete's home and yet it was exactly as I'd imagined. The whole living room could have been airlifted straight from the nearest IKEA. A variety of highly modern lamps cast a golden glow over the leather chairs and brown cord sofa. A selection of industry magazines were fanned out on the table alongside a neat line of remotes. I wondered if the magazines meant he met clients here or if that was just how he kept them. It was oddly endearing to think of Pete rearranging them every time he dusted.

There were only eight of us there for the party: Pete and Jess, Ethan and I and two couples who were university friends of my sister and her boyfriend. Fiancé as of tonight. Pete was pink with the pleasure of landing a catch like Jess and she was bubbling over like the bottles of champagne. Both of them so happy I couldn't stop smiling when I looked at them. Finally – finally! – Pete had proposed. He and Jess were two of a kind, methodical and slow-moving. Hell, they weren't even living together yet. Pete probably spent two years just researching the ring that now glittered on Jess's finger.

'This is amazing,' I said to Jess as she refilled my glass. 'That ring though! You're going to have arm ache.'

She laughed, self-consciously adjusting it and then fiddling with her dark braid. 'Pete helped to design it. The setting's meant to look like a snowflake, because when we met it was snowing and all the trains were cancelled. The stone's been passed down from his great-grandmother. New ring, same diamond.'

'Very eco-friendly that – recycling,' Ethan said. I could feel a tiny dig in those words and wanted to nudge him. He was a bit funny around people with more money than us.

Jess nodded earnestly, either not getting or choosing to ignore the jab. 'If you'd read the things we have about the diamond trade,' she shuddered, 'you did the right thing with yours, Mils.'

My own ring, a vintage silver piece, felt very cheap in that moment, but I tried to take her compliment as it was intended. I was glad she hadn't taken Ethan's comment as a dig. Or if she had she was covering it well.

'Ethan picked it.' I threaded my arm through his so he'd know I loved it as much as I loved him. 'Amethyst is my birth stone and Ethan's is aquamarine.'

Ethan muttered something about the bathroom and left my side, almost knocking the bottle of champagne off the nearby table. I watched him go, hoping he didn't feel as out of place as I did with Jess's friends. They were all as well off as Pete and Jess themselves. Professionals with careers and goals leagues ahead of us.

'I wish Mum and Dad were here,' I said, trying to cover the awkwardness of his departure.

'Hmmm,' Jess said, but didn't meet my eye.

Both our parents were in care homes now. Originally together but since Dad's stroke he'd had to move to a more intensive facility where they could handle his needs. Mum didn't seem to know what to do without him. Not that the dementia was helping in that regard. Sometimes she didn't even recognise me and the last time Jess and I visited together, Mum threw a cup at her and called her a homewrecker. God knows who she thought she was talking to.

It occurred to me that Jess was probably glad they weren't there. Not in a mean way, but in the sense that if they were here she'd be on edge, trying to make sure everything was perfect. Then looking more and more deflated as the night went on and all the little pricks of disapproval started to build up.

I could imagine what they'd be saying if they were here. Dad, or the dad that now existed only in my memory, would be quizzing Pete about his career, noting his soft hands and owlish glasses. Dad thought office work wasn't 'real work'. Odd considering he thought Jess had a 'man's job' and she did mostly the same things as Pete. He liked Ethan well enough — running a shop was something Dad understood. Like vinyl records. Something old-fashioned and analogue he could wrap his head around.

Mum would be repeating her usual line on Pete: 'He's very . . . clean'. Which was either the nicest thing she could think of or a sly suggestion that my sister's long-term boyfriend was gay. Which was Mum's reasoning for the lack of a ring up until now. Then she'd move on to the champagne; if cheap she'd say it tasted 'funny', if expensive, 'why did you go and spend all that on it!' Then after a deviation into Jess's outfit ('frumpy' if professional, 'common' if the least bit sexy) and weight ('no more of those, I think' or 'you're skin and bones, do you still not know how to cook?'), she'd start quizzing her on children and tipsily remind her that by Jess's age she'd already been married for half a decade.

All in all I couldn't blame my sister for being the tiniest bit relieved they weren't there. But I could see a sort of sadness in her too. That on this, the night of her long-awaited engagement, she didn't have them here to witness it.

'They'd be really proud of you,' I said.

Jess smiled a tiny, sad smile, and both of us pretended to believe it.

Chapter 23

The second tunnel was much, much longer and slightly larger than the first. The small passages between cabins had been low and only a few feet long. This one was tall enough for me to crawl with my arms fully extended and the bag on my back. Width-wise there was space on either side of me, though not enough for me to turn round. It also went on for ever; I'd been crawling so long that my knees and hands hurt but still there was only darkness ahead of me. I began to feel faint at one point and had to eat one of my remaining two precious energy bars. My body still wasn't back to full strength and I was in danger of overexerting myself.

Long thin roots dangled from the ceiling like hair, trailing over my face and neck. Loose dirt showered down as I brushed past and the floor was damp and crawling with tiny creatures. I felt worms thrash under my hands and beetles zip away over my questing fingers. Each time I snatched my hand back and stifled a cry of disgust. I didn't want whoever was at the other end of the tunnel to hear me coming.

I was increasingly certain that there would be someone there. As I crawled I decided that whoever had been stalking me, whoever had taken Ethan and burned the cabins, had to be holed up nearby. Yet I'd never seen them. So, it made sense that they were literally 'holed' up, underground where they were safe from prying eyes. They'd been using the tunnels to get around without leaving footprints, popping up wherever they wanted and vanishing again just as quickly.

On the night of the fire I'd thought it looked like the fire in my cabin started first and from outside. That the other cabins in the row had gone up one by one, but from within. I guessed now that this was down to someone using the tunnels to go door-to-door, lighting fire after fire, before they escaped down the tunnel I was currently in. It was just a theory but I could almost see my mystery figure at the window of the cabin next door, throwing petrol on my roof and lighting it before repeating the process inside the other cabins. The last one probably didn't burn as well because he was scared of being trapped in the blaze and half-arsed the fuel to give himself time to escape.

I was shaking a little at the thought of confronting the person behind this. I still had my chunk of wood but that wouldn't do much against a knife or a gun. I wasn't sure about the laws in Germany but this seemed like the kind of area with a lot of hunters. A wickedly sharp knife was all it would take for whoever it was to get the upper hand. If they couldn't manage that with just brute strength.

The only thing keeping me going was the thought that I might find Ethan. That together we would get out of here. He'd know how to find the resort, how to get help. As long as he was OK I could face anything.

Finally, I looked up and saw a sliver of light. It was hard to tell how far away it was in all that darkness, but I thought it was quite close. A few metres perhaps. I crept forward slowly, trying to minimise the noise I was making, straining to hear any sign of another person. I couldn't hear anything. More than that, the place had the feel of an empty house. The dead quiet stillness that said no one was home. There was a faint smell of stale bedding and old food, mixed with a chemical toilet reek that reminded me of festivals.

The tunnel broadened into a kind of burrow. I felt my way through it and towards the light, bumping various objects that clattered, rustled and scraped. The tiny amount of sunlight was coming in around a piece of white plastic sheeting. I pushed it aside, feeling bold now I knew no one was in the burrow. It exposed a hole up through the dirt and snow. I saw trees above and knew I was out in the woods somewhere, far from the village.

In the brighter light I looked around the place. There wasn't much and what there was looked like junk. I'd bumped into a pot caked with the remains of someone's dinner and overturned some empty tins. In one corner there was a white plastic camping toilet. Or at least, it had once been white, but now the plastic had a beige tinge like it had been there a while. That explained the smell. A pile of blankets and a sweat-stained sleeping bag were shoved to one side, the yellow lining mottled with mould. It looked like the field on the last day of a festival, when people just abandoned their trash. Someone had been here, but it seemed as if they'd left in a hurry. Then again, maybe they were just a massive slob.

Looking around I saw grooves in the dirt floor like there had been heavy objects there at some point. But whatever had been there was gone now. Tanks of petrol maybe, that had been used in the fire? Or boxes of tinned food to keep this weird hermit going? Judging from the gouged earth around the exit hole, someone had crammed something large in and out that way. But why? Who would want to live like this out here? What was the point?

The more I looked around the more it seemed as if the place had been abandoned. I was just looking at the rubbish they hadn't bothered to take away. Still, I hoped there might be something worth finding. A clue as to who had done this to me and why, or at least some food that was still edible.

I scuffled through old snack packets, a German magazine that looked like a lad's rag – all tits and cars, some cigarette packets and a few screwed-up bits of paper. I flattened one out and found notes on it in German, which I obviously couldn't read. But I didn't need to understand it to feel a sudden chill in my gut.

My name was on the page, with Ethan's. His had a question mark by it and mine was spelled 'Meela' like it had been written by someone who overheard it. There were also some times, written in the twenty-four hour clock. A record of our movements, my movements? From someone watching me, keeping track of where I went and what I was doing? What other explanation could there be for the times?

I put the paper in my pocket. It was all the evidence I had of what was going on in Witwerberg. Having gone through the rubbish I flapped the sleeping bag to see if anything fell out and glimpsed the dark shine of a screen underneath. A phone! I dropped the stinking bag and snatched it up. Maybe this one would have signal? Or at least some battery, maybe a downloaded map. But my excitement dimmed as I got a better look. It wasn't just any phone, it was my phone. The one I'd dropped in the snow whilst trying to find wood in that first storm. The night I'd seen the figure. He clearly saw me drop it and took it. Maybe to stop me using it or to spook me. I'd never even thought to look for the useless thing.

With my phone and the paper in my pocket I realised I'd found all there was to find. Unless I wanted to crack open the chemical toilet, but if it was being used as a hiding place, whatever was there could stay hidden. My heart sank. I'd been hoping for a map of the area, a torch, some food or a way to start a fire. But there was nothing I could use. Nothing to help me get out of Witwerberg. Nothing that told me who had been here and why they'd been making my life hell.

I felt drained, all the adrenaline and determination fading away. I'd been expecting a confrontation, finally. To meet my tormentor face to face and be able to lash out against them. Instead I was left with their rubbish and a frustrated kind of relief. Frustration that I couldn't look them in the eye and know them the way they'd come to know me. Relief that I'd been spared the violence of a confrontation.

Unwilling to crawl back down the long tunnel, defeated, I pushed back the plastic sheet and climbed out. The hole let out in the woods and I knew the vague direction of Witwerberg. I just had to follow the way the tunnel went.

I began to walk, my defeat heavy on my shoulders. I had one energy bar and two thirds of a protein pack, no way to call help or to find my way in the wilderness. If I tried to reach the resort or any kind of civilisation, I'd probably end up even more lost. Or else I'd be savaged by a wolf, freeze to death or just break my leg on the uneven ground. Even my ghostly enemy had run off now. I was truly alone.

Was I going to die here? It had occurred to me a few times as I struggled to survive, but now it was all I could think about. Ethan was still missing and I would never see Jess again, but that felt like a concern from another life. A life that I would never return to. Now all I could think about was my slow, painful death. How long would it take? To starve or freeze. Was I better off stripping down and lying on the snow or waiting for the food to run out? Which would hurt less?

I stumbled, tears stinging in my eyes. I wanted my sister. I wanted Ethan. I wanted my parents, which right then felt just as likely as ever seeing anyone else again. I tripped my way through the trees, snivelling, cold and hungry. I hated the person who'd abandoned their little hideout; not because they'd terrified me, watched me, tried to burn me alive, but because they'd left me here. The kindest thing would have been to strangle me in my sleep.

A hysterical laugh escaped me and a bubble of snot burst on my nose. I didn't care. I was going to die here. Who cared about what I looked like, for fuck's sake? Keening sobs followed the laugh and I slumped against a tree as my legs began to shake.

For a long time I just leant against the tree, hysterically sobbing, the wind freezing my tears. I couldn't find the strength to move away, to walk on. What was the point? If I stayed or went back to the car the result would be the same. I was going to die in Witwerberg.

'Are you . . . all right?'

I was so startled that I lost my grip on the trunk and fell into the snow. Gazing up, I found myself looking into the face of a woman in a thick down parka. Her hair was shiny and blow-dried under her knitted hat. Her face wrinkled in concern, eyes wide. A camera swung on a strap around her neck.

For a moment I couldn't find any words. I was so

unprepared for the sight of another person that if I'd had the strength I might have tried to run away. As it was all I could do was lie there, staring.

'Josh!' She half-turned her head, like I was a dangerous animal she wanted to keep in view at all times. 'Josh – I need some help!'

A guy in a similar jacket came crunching over the snow in a hurry. His cheeks were pink from the cold, but he paled when he saw me. He looked at the woman and she looked back, both of them helpless.

'What do we do?' she whispered.

'I . . . uh . . .' He looked at me, then squatted and wet his lips. 'Are you lost? Do you need us to take you somewhere? Hospital? Do you speak English?'

I swallowed and nodded, still not daring to blink in case they vanished.

'I need to get to my sister's wedding.'

Chapter 24

Of course I'd already missed the wedding. It was just
the shock talking. Shock that only began to wear off
after Josh and Allison guided me through the woods
to their car. I'd somehow managed to lose my way and
gone off into the forest. Stumbling around in a near
catatonic state will do that to you. I'd ended up closer
to the main road instead of walking in a straight line
towards Witwerberg. If I hadn't, Allison wouldn't have
heard me crying. They'd only just pulled over to get
some pictures of the woods.

'I thought you were a ghost,' she said, only half
laughing, her eyes still wide as she bundled me into
the backseat.

I felt like a ghost. Even after they piled their coats on
me and gave me coffee from a thermos. It was like I was
frozen all the way through. Even my mind was slowed
down, barely ticking over, like a cold engine trying
desperately to fire. I could only just give them the name
of the resort, it felt like trying to talk in slow motion.

The two of them talked, maybe to me or to each other. I wasn't sure. They might as well have been in a different car for all I understood. The car swept smoothly over the snowy roads and I leant my head against the cold window, looking out at the trees. Only a short while ago I'd been out there amongst them, now I was sealed in a neat box of glass and metal. Separated from nature again, though I'd never feel safe from it again. I knew now how little it took to be at its mercy. A broken-down car, snow a shade too deep, a road too far from a cell tower, and suddenly it was the dark ages. Witwerberg in the 1800s, snowbound and empty.

As the knowledge that I was finally out of that place sank in, I thought of Ethan. I still had no idea where he was or what was happening to him. Looking to the front of that car I wondered if I ought to tell my rescuers that there was someone else in those woods who needed help. But what was I going to say? That Ethan could be anywhere? That I hadn't seen him in, how long now . . . This was the seventh day since our car had broken down. So much time in which Ethan could have been taken anywhere. Hopelessness filled the pit in my stomach. How was I ever going to find him?

I watched the trees go by and gradually lost the ability to grasp my thoughts. I just let them slip by in a wave. I didn't sleep but was almost hypnotised by the whir of the heating vents and the swish of wipers against the fresh snow. It was almost like being back in the car with Ethan on that first day. Just before everything went wrong. Time drifted past and I was only lifted out of my trance when we passed the resort sign.

The resort almost reminded me of Witwerberg's cabins, only grown to an enormous size. It was the same kind of wood chalet with a wide, shallow pitched roof. Only this place swarmed with life. The windows were glittering in the sun and smoke rose from several chimneys. The doors constantly opened and closed as people went in and out. Couples on skis glided past, glancing at the car without much interest. The sheer number of people made me feel suddenly very exposed and frightened.

Josh left the car and Allison peered through the seats at me with a nervous smile. I couldn't marshal my face into one in return. My eyelids were starting to sag and I realised just how on alert I'd been in the last few days. Even though I'd slept, there had never been a moment of true rest. Exhaustion was quickly catching up to me.

I wasn't sure how long Josh was gone but a shriek made my head jerk up. It was Jess. I watched as she came flying down the wooden steps of the porch and ran through the snow. She was wearing a white satin robe, part of a bridal set I thought, over some flannel pyjamas. She was only wearing slippers and they slipped and skidded on the icy ground. She ripped open the car door and threw herself at me, hugging me so tightly that I felt my bones grind together.

I gripped her back just as tightly and started to cry, like I was a kid again. Jess was crying too, sniffing and hiccupping against my neck. She kept saying my name, over and over. I only held on to her tighter and sobbed until I couldn't breathe, the numbness finally giving way to hysteria.

After several long moments Jess manoeuvred me out of the car. She didn't let go of me for a moment. Her hands came up and framed my face and I saw for the first time how tired she looked. Her bloodshot eyes were surrounded by dark bags and her skin was peppered with tiny breakouts. Her lips were peeling and pitted from being bitten and she had rings of red-raw skin around her nose. She looked like she hadn't slept or eaten properly in days, whilst crying continuously.

'Look at you,' she said, her eyes filling with fresh tears. 'God, Mils, you look awful. What happened, where were you? We've been looking everywhere.' Her voice cracked. 'Come on, we need to get you inside. We'll get you warm and into some clean clothes and then sort out some breakfast. You'll need a doctor, I don't know if there's one here . . .'

She was babbling and only let go of me to grab Allison's hands when she got out of the car. She kept telling her and Josh 'thank you' whilse they shuffled and said it was nothing and looked confused. I caught Allison's eye and whispered my own thank you. It was hard to put words together without dissolving into tears. I was just so glad to have been found. To be with my sister, who was glad to see me, even after everything.

The scene was broken up by Pete's arrival. My sister's fiancé came skidding down the front steps and put his arms around both of us. Jess was sobbing again and he shushed against her hair. He was wearing clothes rather than pyjamas, but they looked hastily flung on. He was in just as bad a state as Jess; tired and pinched-looking like he'd been waiting in a hospital for bad news.

'I can't believe it's really you,' he said, touching my hair like he expected his hand to go right through it, eyes round and bulging in shock. 'We had people out looking, we searched everywhere and we didn't find anything. For days.'

Despite my mixed feelings about Pete and the disgusting pictures I'd seen on his phone, I was almost as happy to see him as I was Jess. To see anyone familiar at all when only an hour ago I thought I would die alone and undiscovered.

In the middle of that hug I tried to tell them about Ethan, but I was half sobbing, my teeth chattering too. I only managed to get out, 'He's gone.' My voice was muffled against Jess's shoulder, my tears soaking into her robe. I don't think she even heard me.

The three of us clung to each other in a bizarre group hug that only ended when Pete glanced over my shoulder and muttered, 'Oh . . .'

I felt Jess stiffen and she looked over as well, her tear-streaked face twisted in a mixture of happiness and humiliation.

'I'm so sorry,' she said. 'I shouldn't have said . . . I'm sorry.'

I turned and followed her gaze, then froze. On the steps, looking down at us, stood Ethan. I sucked in a breath so sharply that it made a sound, a high-pitched whine. My grip on Jess tightened in shock and my whole body stiffened as if I'd been electrocuted.

It was like seeing a ghost. I opened my mouth but couldn't form a single word. For a second I thought I was hallucinating. He was just . . . there, after all those days of uncertainty and fear. Standing right in front of me and wearing unfamiliar clothes that had to belong to Pete.

'. . . Ethan?' I whispered, taking a few steps away from Jess. I reached out, terrified that if I blinked he'd vanish again. That I'd wake up on the ground in a clearing with some trees around me, going fully mad. Oh God was I . . . dying? Was this all just a hallucination?

But then Ethan ran down the steps and scooped me up. I held on to as much of him as possible, straining my arms across his back and turning my face to his cheek. I could smell him underneath an unfamiliar soap, feel the scratch of his stubble against my face. He was real and he was really here. I sobbed against his neck and he squeezed me tighter.

'Mils . . . Oh, Mils, I thought . . .' He couldn't finish the sentence, his voice choked off. I felt wetness on his cheek, though if they were my tears or his I had no idea. Both of us were a mess. I felt his chest heaving as he struggled to breathe.

'Mila . . . Oh thank God,' he murmured, finally pulling back and looking at me, his breath warm against my cheek. His eyes were red and he looked exhausted. 'I thought . . . It doesn't matter now. I'm so glad you're OK.'

Looking behind me he spoke to Jess and Pete, his voice cracking. 'Do you believe me now? I told you – so many times – but, you wouldn't listen, you wouldn't believe . . .'

I grabbed his hand and squeezed it, scared he was going to hyperventilate.

When I looked around at Jess she was blushing furiously and nodding without a word. I could tell something had gone on whilst I was missing. Clearly she'd said something to Ethan, something about me and what had happened. But that didn't matter now. Not when I was here and so was he. I squeezed him tighter and he held me so close that I could feel his heart beating under Pete's ridiculous salmon-coloured shirt.

'I'm never going to leave you again,' he mumbled against my hair. 'Never. I was so scared. What happened to you – where did you go?'

'Where . . .' I looked up at him, disbelief and shock stilling my tongue. 'What happened to *you*?'

Chapter 25

Ethan pulled back and he and I stared at each other mutely. Both of us wanting answers to the same question. Neither of us sure what to say.

'We should get you inside,' Jess said. 'It's cold and Mila looks like she could do with a drink and something to eat. Come on, we'll go to our room.'

I didn't want to let go of Ethan and he didn't seem to want to let go of me either. We went hand in hand through the foyer and up the stairs of the lodge. I could barely take in my surroundings, only that it was warm and bright. I could smell frying bacon and rich coffee. My stomach howled and I began to shake, my limited energy running out.

In Jess and Pete's room I dropped my bag and Ethan helped me out of my coat, barely wrinkling his nose at the smell of it. He put me in a huge armchair and Jess tucked about a thousand blankets around me. I didn't realise Pete wasn't with us until he swept into the room with a tray of hot coffees and a plate piled with rolls, ham, cheese and fried potatoes. He hadn't even put it down before I snatched up a buttery roll and ripped into it, stuffing it into my mouth too fast to taste.

I was halfway through a second roll before I looked up and found the three of them looking at me in shock. Ethan perched on the edge of my chair and put his arm around me. Wordlessly, Jess filled another roll with meat and cheese before handing it to me. I took it and tried to eat slowly. The burning hunger in me had only dimmed a bit. I could have demolished the plate and still been ravenous. Pete stirred five sugars into a coffee and put it on the table beside me, looking at me the way you'd watch a starved dog – with pity but also wariness.

Ethan's hand rubbed circles on my back. When I swallowed the last of the second roll I looked up at him, the third roll still in my lap.

'Where did you go?' I asked. 'That first night . . . you vanished.'

'I was gonna ask you the same thing,' he said gently. 'Not just you but that whole damn place disappeared. It was like once I was out of that village I couldn't find it again. We looked for days and didn't even find the sign we passed that day.'

'It got covered in snow,' I said, 'but that's not what I mean. You disappeared that first night. I woke up and you were just gone and there were no footprints. None at all.'

I realised I'd nearly shouted that last part and winced. Ethan stroked my arm gently. Soothing me.

'I'm so sorry . . . I didn't think about how it must've looked to you. How scared you must be. I just couldn't get to sleep on that floor. I was lying there, awake, looking at the planks and realised there was this . . . hatch and guessed it might be warmer if we got in the cellar or whatever was down there. You were so exhausted you didn't even wake up when I opened it. Only then I saw this tunnel. I didn't want to wake you but I was curious and desperate for anything that might help us. So I followed it.' Ethan looked at Jess and then back at me. 'I shouldn't have left you, that was stupid. You have no idea how much I've been kicking myself about it. Worrying about what happened to you. If you were OK. This is all my fault.'

'I don't understand why you didn't come back to me,' I said, still reeling at the idea of him leaving me voluntarily. 'You weren't there when I woke up.'

Ethan came around the chair and crouched in front of me, looking pained. 'I tried to come back. The tunnel ended out in the woods and I thought I heard a car on a road nearby. I went running off to try and flag it down but when I got there I didn't even see any tracks. I decided to wait by the road in case the car was further off and I'd heard it coming instead of passing us. The whole time I was worried you'd wake up and panic if I wasn't there but I thought if I could get us out of there, it would be worth it.'

He swallowed and I watched regret pinch his features. He was angry at himself and I wanted nothing more than to tell him it was all right. Only I didn't think I could, not just then.

Ethan took a breath. 'I was there so long it started to snow, then it got really dark and the snow came down hard. I tried to find my way back in it but I ended up getting all turned around. Eventually I nearly ran into some skiers and they brought me here.'

'We tried retracing Ethan's route but it got covered in the storm,' Pete said. 'He couldn't remember the name of the place you'd ended up and so we drove around looking for your car, but it was gone.'

'I was looking for the sign too, I remembered there was one. But I guess you're right – it got covered in the storm,' Ethan said. 'I was . . . If I could've traded places with you, I would have. I felt awful. I still feel awful, Mils . . . I'm sorry.'

I took his hands in mine. 'I'm glad you're OK. I was really worried about you. I thought . . . I had no idea what happened, it was so scary.'

What he'd said settled into the gaps in my knowledge like fresh snow. I thought about how I'd uncovered the sign, only for more snow to fall. Had it really just been chance that they hadn't come by when it was clear? Thinking back to the morning Ethan disappeared, I remembered how I'd run from cabin to cabin yelling for him, then tried to find him by the car. Only the car had been at the bottom of a gulley. Then the storm had sent me running for shelter. He must have been too far away to hear me by then. To think we'd missed each other by that much made me feel sick. All that fear, all that paranoia, and it meant nothing. Just an awful mistake.

'What happened to the car, Mils?' Ethan asked. 'We never saw it, the rental company were no help – turns out they don't track their shittier models.'

'It's in a trench,' I said. 'The morning after we got stuck I went up there. I thought you were maybe trying to fix it. But it was gone.'

There was a short silence whilst the three of them processed this.

'I must've left the fucking handbrake off,' Ethan groaned. 'I was in such a state that night. Jesus, I'm so sorry. This was all my fault. I never should have gone exploring like a fucking asshole.'

A glance at Jess's face told me she was thinking the same thing. I could only imagine the hard time she'd been giving Ethan over this. I was just happy he was alive and OK. I said as much and he hugged me tightly.

'What happened to you, Mila?' Jess asked me gently.

'I don't know, it was all so . . . I don't really know what was real and what I imagined. I had this feeling like I was being watched, being followed? Stuff kept going wrong. Ethan disappearing, then the car. The fire.'

'Fire?' Jess asked sharply. 'Someone said they saw like, orange light a few nights ago while they were up the mountain. Like the northern lights or something. Was that a fire?'

I nodded. 'The cabins burned down. All six of them. I camped out in the car and then I realised about the trapdoor. I thought that was how Ethan . . . how you'd been taken.'

'Taken?' Pete gave me an odd look.

'I didn't know what had happened. He was just gone.' I felt defensive and stupid now that I heard it out loud. 'So . . . anyway I went down the tunnels and I found this camp there. Did you see it?'

Ethan shook his head slowly. 'No, there was just the tunnel and this like . . . wider part. Like a burrow. You say someone made a camp there? After I left? Why?'

I nodded. 'I think I saw them a few times, in the snowstorm and then again running in the woods. I found . . .' I couldn't find a way to say it. Having to explain it for them made me feel like I was nuts. Like trying to recount a nightmare that made no sense in the light of day.

'I found notes. Like someone was watching me.'

The silence that followed was so heavy, I could feel it pressing down on me. I could tell from their faces that they didn't believe me.

'What do you mean . . . watching you?' Pete asked, eventually.

'Mila . . . I think maybe you need some rest,' Jess said. 'It's been a stressful few days and I have no idea what that must have been like for you, but—'

I picked up the sweet coffee with shaking hands and took a gulp. 'I didn't imagine it, Jess. I might have been freaking out and thinking that Ethan was kidnapped, but I know what I saw.'

'Mila . . . you have to admit this sounds incredible.

Someone was following you? –Ethan said he didn't see any camp,' Pete said.

'Hey, if she said she saw something, she saw it,' Ethan cut in, fierce in my defence.

'In my coat pocket, there's a page of notes they made on me. In German,' I said. 'I don't know what was going on or what it all means but I'm not crazy. I might have assumed some things, but I didn't imagine it all.'

Ethan took the paper out of my discarded coat and frowned. Pete took it from him and I remembered that he worked with foreign companies and knew a fair few languages.

'What does it say?' Ethan asked.

'It does seem to be a record of Mila's movements,' Pete said, clearly reluctant to confirm my story. 'This looks like it was written the day you left, Ethan. It says they didn't see you go, but they were waiting to see if you'd come back. Watching Mila.'

'You see!' I said, nearly slopping coffee over myself. 'There was someone there. I couldn't write that. You know I couldn't, Jess. I can barely write in English.'

Jess's smile was wobbly, but there. I could tell though that she was still freaked out. It was only as I watched her twist one hand with the other that I realised she only had her engagement ring on.

'Jess . . . where's your ring?'

She blinked as if surprised by the sudden change of subject. I couldn't blame her; from secret stalkers to her jewellery, if my mind wasn't such a jumble I'd have whiplash too. As it was I had almost become used to my thoughts falling all over one another in a tangle of emotions and realisations.

'I'm wearing . . . oh, you mean the wedding ring?' She looked at me like I'd asked her why she wasn't currently on the moon. 'We postponed the wedding. The minute Ethan showed up and said you were missing.'

'We were determined to find you,' Ethan said, hand on my shoulder. 'That was the only thing that mattered.' Jess nodded and even Pete seemed to agree.

'No!' I almost shouted, making myself jump. 'Oh Jess, you shouldn't have.'

'Don't be silly, we couldn't do it without you. It wasn't even a question.'

'That's right,' Pete confirmed. 'And management has been really good about it. They even said they'd give us a discount if we rebook. Though there's a long waiting list so we might have to look for something closer to home.'

'Rebook? Closer to . . .' I echoed. 'No, this is your wedding trip. You've been talking about this wedding for ages, about being here and how this was the first holiday you took together. You . . . you're here for another day, right?'

Jess glanced at Pete uncertainly. That same 'Mila's gone nuts' look coming back.

'Yeah, we're not leaving until tomorrow afternoon,' Pete said.

'OK, great, then, get married. Please. It's not too late to do it here, like you planned, if that's what you want,' I said, all in a rush.

'But, Mils, we need to go to the police over what happened. You're right, this note is evidence that someone was watching you. Someone who didn't try to help you and who might have had something to do with the fire you told us about,' Jess said. 'It's not a big deal if we delay the wedding and have it somewhere else. What happened to you is more important.'

'She's right, Mila,' Ethan said gently. 'I know how you feel about . . . I know this is important to you, but come on – we're talking about a crime here. This has to take precedence.'

Frustrated tears filled my eyes. How many times had Jess heard those words growing up? That this was 'more important'. Always something of mine, a mess I'd made or an event our parents had to be at for me. A trip or present she wouldn't get because I needed braces, a prom dress, driving lessons. This was her wedding and she was still waving it off like she'd have five more next year. If she didn't get married here, now, she'd never get the chance to come back. I could see that beneath Pete's rueful tone. This was their one chance at their dream venue. The first place they'd visited as a couple. I was not going to let her sacrifice it for me.

'Jess, it can wait. Whoever was there, they were long gone by the time I found that camp. They might have just been like . . . a wildlife spotter or something. Some kind of paranoid hermit. They probably got scared of me. God, I mean, I thought Ethan had been kidnapped and he'd just got lost. It could be a misunderstanding, or just some anti-social weirdo who got scared off when I found his tunnel.'

Of course, even if I believed that, which I didn't, it wouldn't explain the bodies. Those two fresh corpses in the woods. Not historical famine victims but modern people. I still had no idea how they'd died. Had they been trapped in the town like I had, slowly freezing or starving? Or had something else happened to them?

But I couldn't tell Jess that now. What difference would a day make? The bodies were already burned beyond recognition. The cabins reduced to ash, likely taking the skeletons with them. I didn't really have much proof of my story and I doubted the police would get far trying to investigate. Even if they believed me, which wasn't likely. Even I was having trouble making sense out of my story. The longer I was back in the real world the less likely it sounded.

Under that was the dread of going back there. The police would want me to show them the car, the cabin wreckage, the site where the bodies were burned. I didn't ever want to set foot in Witwerberg again. I just wanted to see Jess get married, and go home with Ethan, where it was safe and familiar.

I owed Jess this day. Just this one day for it to be all about her. After that I'd see her off on her honeymoon and then deal with the nasty business of going to the authorities.

'Well . . .' Jess looked at Pete. 'I'm not sure . . .'

'You've been through a lot, Mils,' Ethan pointed out, reaching out and taking my hand in his. 'Wouldn't it be best to just have a good night's sleep and fly home tomorrow? Put this behind us?'

'No,' I insisted. 'Jess, if you want to go on your honeymoon tomorrow without getting married – if that's what you really want, that's fine. But don't do it for me, OK? Whatever you want, I will do it.'

The unspoken 'I owe you that much' hung between us like a bad smell. Unacknowledged but undeniable. This was, I realised now that I had my wits about me, the first time we were meeting face to face since the funeral. Her eyes met mine and I knew she was thinking the same thing. Remembering that day and everything that had happened since. Everything left unsaid. Her face softened from confusion to understanding. I watched as she reached for Pete's hand.

'How about it? Still want to get married?'

Pete's whole face lit up like she'd just told him Christmas wasn't cancelled after all.

'Of course I do.'

They kissed and Ethan's hand tightened on mine. I looked up at him and he smiled, but there were still signs of stress in his tense forehead and thin lips.

'I'm OK, I promise,' I whispered.

He squeezed my hand. 'I will make this OK, Mila. I promise. I will make it up to you.'

I could only imagine what the past few days had been like for him. The searching and the worry that they'd never find me again. Hadn't I felt the same way? But we were both safe now and the wedding was going ahead. Which reminded me.

'I've still got your present,' I said. 'I had it with me ever since the fire, just in case anything happened to it.'

Jess actually laughed, tears making her eyes shine, then swept me into a tight hug.

'This is the only present I wanted – I'm just glad nothing happened to you.'

I held on to her tightly, closing my eyes so she wouldn't see me cry.

Chapter 26

Of all the most unforgivable things, being late to your own mother's funeral is right up there. Possibly one of the worst. I really had tried but a last-minute meltdown triggered by a zip breaking, but which had very little to do with the zip itself, meant I was a few minutes behind.

Everyone was already inside the crematorium. The same one where we'd been for Dad's funeral. It created a weird sense of déjà vu. The flowers were even the same, as if everyone who'd sent them for Dad had gone to their 'recently purchased' tab and just reordered them. I was late then too, though that was due to traffic. That time Ethan was with me. Today he had to open the shop. We were too behind this month to close unexpectedly.

I crept in the back and sat down in an empty row, cursing my rubber-soled boots, which squealed on the wet linoleum. Jess twisted round in the front row, red-eyed and pale. The look she sent my way made my insides turn cold. I sank down in my seat and tried to keep fresh tears from falling.

It was a pre-arranged ceremony. Mum and Dad had their funerals all planned and paid for. We just had to show up, and one of their daughters had managed to be on time for both. The ceremony swept over me in a long mumble of words and songs. I stood when everyone else did and sat when each song was over. Then, as people filed out, I watched the coffin sink and the mechanised curtain close around it.

Just as it had at Dad's funeral, a weird feeling came over me. The feeling that I couldn't just leave my mum here, alone in this place. Only Jess's hissed instruction to 'come on' got me out of my seat. I followed everyone else out and got into one of the two cars that were taking us to the wake. Jess was in the other car with Pete and a selection of distant cousins and family friends. I was stuck with two of Dad's old colleagues and their wives.

When we reached the church hall where the buffet had already been laid out, I couldn't see Jess anywhere. Pete was on the door greeting people and accepting condolences. He looked uncomfortable and seized on me as soon as I came in.

'Jess is in the ladies,' he whispered. 'Can you check on her?'

Of course Pete would never go into the ladies' toilets himself, even if his fiancée was in there. Another weird little quirk of his; even in an emergency he wouldn't break that taboo.

I went to the loos, an echoey bleach-scented cupboard with only two stalls and sticky tiles on the floor. It reminded me of school. They even had the green paper towels. I grabbed a handful as improvised tissues.

'Jess?' I asked, spotting her heels under the door. 'Are you all right?'

A bitter laugh bounced around the tiled space. I shut my eyes for a moment.

'That was stupid, I know you're not . . . but do you need anything? A tissue, a . . . hug?'

The door slammed open so suddenly I nearly twisted my ankle as I leapt backwards. When I regained my balance and looked at Jess, I saw that she was trembling, face red and tear-streaked. Her normally sleek hair was, this close, clearly in need of a wash.

'I don't want a hug,' she rasped. Her face contorted with a suppressed sob and she covered her eyes with her hands. 'I want . . . I want . . .' she hiccoughed uncontrollably.

'I know,' I said, reaching for her arms and stroking the black sleeves of her dress.

But it was the wrong thing to say. Jess twitched away from me and uncovered her face. Her red eyes were sharp and furious and I felt suddenly very afraid. Not of what she might do, but about what she might say.

'You don't know,' she said, scornfully. 'How could you possibly know how this feels? You had a mother and father – I didn't!' She started to cry, gulping sobs that made her whole body quiver. When I tried to reach out she pushed me away, hard. I stumbled and fell into a row of coat pegs, dropping onto a wooden bench.

'You had perfect parents,' Jess repeated, clearly struggling to contain her sobs and sucking in harsh breaths between each gritted out sentence. 'They loved you, they were proud of you . . . You had a mum and dad. She treated me like nothing. They gave me nothing.'

'Jess . . . I . . . I didn't know,' I stammered. 'We only got the letter this morning. I swear I had no idea.'

If I thought that would help to calm things down, I was mistaken. It only seemed to make her angrier. Jess's whole face scrunched up in disgust.

'This isn't about the will. About fucking . . . money,' she spat. 'You have no idea, do you? Just get away from me. Get. Away. From. Me.'

'Jess,' I said, realising what a stupid mistake I'd made. Of course this wasn't about the split of the inheritance. This was about the deeper, unspoken, issue with our family. The lack of balance that went far beyond money. Not unspoken anymore though. It was out there, hanging between us in the air.

'They're gone. She's gone. It's done,' Jess snapped, stepping around me and swiping tears from her cheeks. 'We're done. I never want to see you again.' Her bloodshot eyes met mine in the rust-speckled mirror. 'We're not sisters anymore.'

Chapter 27

Reluctantly, Jess and I went our separate ways. She and Pete had a wedding to reschedule and I needed a serious bath and some rest in a real bed. Not to mention enough food to embarrass a small family.

Fortunately, as far as wedding prep went, the guest list was fairly small. Jess and I weren't close to our extended family and Pete even less so. The wedding was limited to his parents and step-brother, Ethan and me, plus twenty or so friends from work, university and their board game group. Everyone was still at the hotel and apparently the cake and all the raw ingredients for their catering were still on site as well, waiting to be picked up. The only thing they had to do was get the room set up, wrangle some new flowers and get the officiant back.

I did offer to help but Jess waved me off. She did it gently, but I still felt bad about it.

'You're falling asleep on your feet. Besides, this is what I live for,' she said, waving a notebook fringed with many coloured sticky tabs. 'Get some rest and tomorrow you can put in a full day of maid-of-honour duties.'

I flushed when she said that. She'd never asked me to be her maid-of-honour. I was just one of her three bridesmaids, and, to be honest, I'd been surprised when she asked me to do that. This 'promotion' felt like an olive branch. An acknowledgement of the efforts I'd made to put her first. I almost started crying again right then and there. I was just so glad to have her back. To be there for my sister.

When she opened the slightly battered tiara box I did cry. We both did. She touched the tiara like she didn't believe it could be real.

'It's just like . . .'

'Mum's,' I finished. 'I know you always wanted to wear it . . . Now you can.'

Jess hugged me so tightly I thought my bones would break. My last glimpse of her as I left their room was her holding the box to her chest, tears drying on her cheeks.

Ethan showed me to our room and closed the door soundlessly behind us. The place was lusciously decorated, lots of sheepskins, polished copper and plush rugs. I removed my trainers and socks, wincing at the blistered and prune-like state of my toes against the posh carpet. A smell of stale sweat and stagnant water rose up and I wrinkled my nose. God only knew how bad I stank under my clothes.

Ethan took the shoes and quickly quarantined them

in a cupboard. For the first time I took in the full outfit he had on. They were definitely Pete's things – too long for Ethan in sleeve and leg. The salmon shirt was too preppy for him and the less said about the chinos the better. He caught my look and rolled his eyes.

'Very me, don't you think?'

I snuffled a laugh.

'When I got here they lent me some stuff – what with all our clothes being in the car. Though thanks to you my jeans made it back to me.' He gestured at my legs, then turned and rummaged in a drawer. He came up with a pair of pyjamas, still wrapped in plastic. 'Jess sent out for these . . . for when we found you.'

I swallowed. When. Not if. Jess hadn't given up on me, even after days of searching. None of them had. I wondered what she would have done when it came time to check out and head off on her honeymoon. Something told me she wouldn't have gone. That would have been another sacrifice for me. One I was glad she didn't have to make now.

Ethan crossed the room and put his arms around me, burying his face against the top of my head. I knew my hair was matted and dirty, but he didn't seem to care.

'I'm so glad you found your way out of there.'

'I just kept asking myself what you'd do,' I said.

He held me like that for a while, the two of us rocking slightly. We didn't need to speak, just feeling each other there was enough. I was finally back where I belonged.

Eventually he kissed my cheek and said he'd get more food sent up whilst I had a wash. I took the pyjamas into the bathroom, shut the door and looked at my reflection for the first time in days.

If it was possible to die from shame, I'd have been laid out on the floor. My hair was indeed matted, and some parts were singed from the fire. There were smudges of ash, dirt and char on my face and hands. My clothes were stained and marked all over with dirt from the tunnel. The less said about the state of my nails the better. What shocked me most was my face. In only the week I'd spent in Witwerberg I'd acquired an almost ghostly look. My eyes looked too big and my cheeks were gaunt. Even my lips looked thin and pinched. I looked like I'd started to shrink in on myself. As if fear had somehow begun to mummify me.

I turned my back on the mirror and stripped off my clothes. At least I'd changed them once whilst living in that place. Though from the smell that wafted out of them you wouldn't have thought so. It was the musty, slightly feral smell of an old gym bag left to marinate in a hot car boot. The rodenty reek of old underwear and sweat.

I kicked the clothes into a ball and wrapped them in a bag from the bathroom bin. Then, with tiny gold-topped bottles of toiletries in my filthy claws, I stepped into the shower.

I stayed in the shower for so long that Ethan had to knock on the door. The heat of it drove back the cold in my bones and I never wanted to leave. The water, which had started off brownish grey, now swirled down the drain as clear as it came from the showerhead. The smell of pine and juniper dripped from my hair and skin.

Towelled off and in the clean pyjamas, I stepped back into the bedroom to be greeted by a tray of food. All of it steaming and most of it fried. Ethan had ordered a hot toddy and the combination of brandy and honey lit a fire in my belly, preparing it for a heap of chicken schnitzel and fries.

I snuggled up with Ethan, propped up against him and the headboard. He put some random film on the TV and let me eat in peace, only intermittently kissing the top of my head or stealing a fry. At last, when the final remnants of slaw were mopped up with a roll, I settled back with a sigh. I'd almost forgotten what it was like to be full. Not only full, but warm and safe.

My eyelids began to droop then and I found myself struggling to stay awake. My body grew limp and I stretched slowly, like a cat. Just before I fell asleep, Ethan cuddled me close.

'I love you so much,' he whispered against my hair.

'Promise you'll be here when I wake up?' I murmured.

'Every day for the rest of your life.'

I think I slept with a smile on my lips.

As it turned out, Jess wasn't kidding about me putting in a full day on her wedding. I woke up to a knock at the door and as soon as Ethan opened it she swept in with my dress and shoes in hand. Her hair was already in curlers and she was followed by a uniformed porter carrying a breakfast tray.

'You look so much better,' Jess cooed, a relieved smile on her face. 'Ethan's taking good care of you then?'

'Only the best for my girl,' he smiled, pouring coffee for the three of us.

I could tell he was trying to make up for leaving me behind. I didn't blame him for it. How could he have known what was going to happen? I was just glad he was OK and that I had made it back to civilisation. Still, the pampering didn't suck. I was probably going to let that go on at least until we got home. Maybe longer if the bins needed emptying.

First though I had to touch up Jess's manicure as her makeup artist had left for another job. Then I had a look over her reference pictures and tried to get her makeup right. She seemed happy with the result. I thought she looked gorgeous.

'You were always so good at this stuff,' she grinned, fluttering her false lashes.

I took the praise, though it wasn't really deserved. She looked amazing with a naked face, I was just gilding the proverbial lily. Then I had to arrange actual lilies for the bouquets.

'Let me help,' Ethan said.

'Don't overdo it,' Jess warned, 'I mean it. If you need a rest, take one.'

But oddly I found that I didn't need one. I was focused on the wedding tasks and barely felt my aches and pains. It was shocking what a good sleep and some food could do. That and a steady supply of caffeine and paracetamol.

Finally I helped Jess into her wedding gown and arranged her veil for her. The tiara sparkled and the matching jewellery looked amazing against her skin. Her eyes were shining with tears when she saw herself in the mirror. Only when I looked closer I realised she wasn't admiring herself, but watching me.

'I was so scared I'd never see you again,' she almost whispered.

'I'm here now,' I said, worried one of the tears clinging to her lashes would smear her liner. 'And I am so, so, happy for you. For both of you.'

She turned in a rustle of stiff fabric and tulle. Her hands found my elbows and she held me there, her face creasing with emotion.

'I wanted to say . . . I'm sorry.'

'For what?' I was genuinely taken aback. We hadn't spoken about what she'd said. I thought there was a sort of unspoken agreement that we weren't going to mention it.

'For what happened at the funeral,' Jess said as if reading my mind. 'And for thinking what I did, the day you were meant to arrive, the day you didn't show . . .' She sniffed. 'You were a few hours late then and I . . . I thought to myself that it was because of that day, that maybe it was a good thing, that you weren't coming . . . that maybe it would be better if . . .' She struggled. 'That maybe without you or Mum and Dad here, I wouldn't feel so . . . broken.'

I swallowed. I knew this was how she must feel, had told myself this a million times. But to hear it from her, now, was something else. I wanted to say something, to apologise, but Jess cut me off.

'I will never, ever, think that again. I know things haven't always been . . . well, they haven't always been even between us. But that's not your fault and it's not mine. And I am so lucky to have you as my sister. I never want you to think that I'd be glad if you weren't here. Because when you weren't . . . I couldn't stand it.'

'I couldn't stand not being here either,' I said.

The tear that had been threatening to fall slipped down her cheek in an inky trail. I carefully dabbed it away with a tissue and put my arms around her. We stood there, rustling in our expensive gowns, remembering what it was to be sisters.

When Ethan arrived to break us up and escort me to the event space, I gave her a final squeeze. She smiled, feverishly blinking the rest of her tears away.

'Break a leg,' I whispered.

'That would be the icing on it, wouldn't it?' she laughed, taking her bouquet from the table.

'It'll all go fine,' I promised. 'See you on the other side.'

Ethan and I walked to the event room and he gave me a kiss on the cheek before taking his seat. The music started and I walked slowly up the aisle with the other bridesmaids. Once we took our places at the altar they gave me a series of sympathetic but morbidly curious glances. I focused on the door at the back of the room. My sister was about to walk through it, dressed to the nines. This was her day. I made myself a promise that if anyone asked about what happened to me once the wedding was over, I'd only say, 'Doesn't Jess look lovely?' She deserved to be the focus.

The Wedding March began to play from hidden speakers and I exchanged a nervous smile with Pete. He was very dashing in his suit, elevated from average-looking to downright handsome. He looked so excited to see Jess that I couldn't help liking him, despite the phone incident. I'd put that behind me, I decided. He was allowed one mistake. God only knew I'd made more.

The doors opened and Jess stepped through. Despite seeing her a moment or two before I still gasped with the rest of them. She looked amazing. Happiness radiated out of her and when she saw Pete she smiled like the sun coming out. I remembered that kind of joy from my own wedding. Glancing at the guests I tried to catch Ethan's eye, but like everyone else he was looking at Jess.

I took a deep breath, held tightly to my bouquet and watched my sister as she entered the happiest moment of her life.

Chapter 28

The reception, like most gatherings of celebratory English people, quickly devolved into drunken chaos. We only had a few hours before we had to leave and people were trying to cram in as much dancing and as many glasses of free champagne as possible.

'Brown Eyed Girl' played as Jess and Pete took their first dance together and before too long the dancefloor was swarmed, fascinators left on tables and heels kicked off. All the staples were there: hammered bridesmaids, crumbled cake, spilled champagne and a litter of confetti. We were only missing the birdie song and a cat fight.

All this much needed traditional revelry had to be squeezed into a three-hour period in the mid-afternoon. That was when everyone had to check out and head to the airport. On the one hand I felt bad for Jess, having her reception foreshortened. On the other, I was glad to be going home.

Well, home eventually. Before we caught our evening flight I still had to speak to the police. I was hoping they'd let me leave once I'd given them my statement. But the worry that I'd have to stay on in an airport hotel for a night, maybe even longer, had me feeling sick all through the party. I couldn't stomach even a sip of the expensive champagne.

At last the moment came for Jess and Pete to leave. We crowded around outside in the freezing cold to watch them climb into a taxi. I waved to Jess so hard that my arm began to ache. I kept going until their car was out of sight and most of the other guests had filtered back inside. They'd be changing into their airport outfits, stuffing away their party clothes and all the mini-toiletries they could find.

Finally only Ethan and I stood outside. He shrugged off his suit jacket and draped it around my shoulders. Then put his arm around me and kissed the top of my head.

'You were right, they pulled it off,' he said. 'Though I could do with a week in Barcelona to get over this cold. Lucky bastards.'

'How about a nine euro hot chocolate at the airport?' I offered, nerves already jangling at the prospect of telling him we might not be home safe yet.

'Mmm, sounds just as good,' Ethan said, squeezing me. 'I'll just be happy to be home again, with all this just a bad memory.'

Unable to take it anymore, I turned to face him. 'Ethan . . . There's something I need to tell you.'

He quirked a brow. 'Sounds very serious. Do you not have nine euro?'

'I mean it. I . . . There's stuff I didn't want to tell Jess about what happened in Witwerberg. Stuff that might mean we can't up and leave yet.'

He seemed to sober immediately. 'Like . . . what?'

'Like, when I was there I found some . . . remains under two of the cabins. Human remains.'

His eyebrows shot upwards. 'You mean like . . . skeletons? Or . . .'

'Skeletons under the cabins. From ages ago, like, when the village was still inhabited.'

'Oh, well, that's not such a big deal, right?' he said, shoulders losing their tension. 'I guess we have to report it though. Not sure to who – a museum or something?'

'It wasn't just skeletons though,' I said, determined to get it all out there. 'I found two bodies in the woods. Fresh bodies. Modern clothes, a watch commemorating the Olympics . . . I'm not sure where they came from or what happened to them but I need to contact the police before we can go anywhere. And, we might not be able to leave today if they won't allow it.'

Ethan was quiet for a long moment, then rubbed a hand over his face and shook his head. 'Jesus, Mils, why didn't you say anything yesterday? We could have had this all dealt with by now.'

'I know! I was going to but then, I just thought it could wait a day. Until Jess left on her honeymoon.'

'Until . . .' He looked at me like he couldn't believe what I was saying. 'Mila, you have been so weird about this wedding from day one, but come on. Some things are more important. Jess isn't a silly little girl, she'd understand that potential murder kind of trumps a party.'

I winced when he said 'silly little girl'. It was something I'd called myself before, in my head, so many times. Silly little Mila with her stupid little problems. The baby of the family. Hearing it from him was worse. But he was right. Jess would have done the right thing if I'd told her yesterday. She always did. I was the one who never knew what to do, who only made things worse.

'I should call them now,' I said, so quietly I could hardly hear myself.

'Yeah, I think you should.' Ethan looked up at the hotel. 'I'll go ask if they can accommodate us for another night. Just in case. God knows how much that's going to cost.'

'I'll go make the call and get changed.' I gathered up the skirt of my bridesmaid's dress and hurried up the stairs, feeling like a child who'd just been chewed out at a birthday party. Being there in that fancy dress was making me feel ridiculous.

Upstairs in our room I rang down to reception and asked for a non-emergency police number. Then I called it and waited for someone to answer. All the while my heart was pumping hard, feeling like it was stuck in my throat.

A man answered in German, then switched to English when I introduced myself. I explained who I was and where I was calling from, then lapsed into silence when it was time to explain myself. How could I even begin?

'Miss?' the man on the phone prompted. 'Are you all right?'

'Yes, I just . . . I'm not sure where to start? I was stuck in a village, an abandoned village, near here and I found someone. Two people, um . . . dead people.'

There was a long, steely silence. I began to panic, sweating in my layers of satin. He wasn't going to believe me. I'd said it too clumsily, too stilted. He was going to call me a timewaster or ask a billion questions that I couldn't answer. Starting with, where is this village?

'Let me take the address of where you are staying. Someone will come immediately.'

After hanging up I quickly changed into some of Jess's clothes. She'd left me a bag of stuff from her luggage. Although she was a little thinner than me and slightly taller, at least I wouldn't be wearing a full-length gown. The clothes felt wrong on me, not uncomfortable, just strange. Like I was wearing a costume.

Ethan let himself into the room and stopped short, looking at me. 'You look . . . different.'

'They're Jess's things,' I said. 'I don't know how she looks so chic in them, I feel like someone's mum.'

Ethan pulled a face. 'Anyway I asked about booking another night but if we stay here it's going to cost us. I mean, really cost us.' He scrubbed a hand through his hair. 'I don't know that we can afford another night on top of new tickets home. Even the tickets might be too much, I'll have to check coaches or the train.'

'Fuck.'

'Yeah.'

'I'm so sorry for not saying anything sooner. I'll try and explain that we need to leave, like, today. Hopefully I can give them everything they need and just hand over our home contact details for anything else. I mean it's not like we don't have a million ways for them to contact us.'

'Do you want me with you, when they get here?' Ethan asked. 'Or I can give you some space if you need it?'

'I'd like you there, please. Especially if they want to take me back there, I don't think I want to be alone with strangers. Even if they are the police.'

Ethan nodded and went to change out of his suit. I packed the little stuff we had. If we did end up returning to Witwerberg I hoped we could get our luggage back. I wanted my own things and my phone charger – I could really do with a soothing audiobook, today of all days.

We had to vacate the room before too long and remove ourselves to the lobby. The hotel staff were still being quite nice and respectful but I could feel our welcome wearing thin. They had new guests coming and our personal circumstances weren't going to grant us much more leeway. Especially now the people paying for our room were safely checked out and on their way to Barcelona.

The state police arrived in a marked BMW. Two men approached the hotel, one in a uniform and one in a grey

258

suit and oversize black coat. The uniform looked similar to the ones in American TV shows – blue and with a flat hat. Yet it was weirdly uncanny, like the off-brand costumes they sell at supermarkets. Both had guns, which I also wasn't used to seeing. Their belts were heavy with those, a holstered can of pepper spray and a baton.

I was so anxious at the sight of real and actual guns, which always gave me a chill when going through an airport, that I completely missed the introductions. Ethan shook both their hands and they exchanged names in a deluge of titles and locations.

Eventually the older of the two police officers took Ethan's vacant chair. He looked about forty and had a smattering of premature grey in his stubble. His hair was also greying at the temples, which I supposed was due to stress. He looked like a very rumpled, over-worked sort of person.

'Mrs Swift? I am Karl Voigt, a detective with the Kriminalpolizei. I understand you made a call to a local station about finding remains in the forest? What more can you tell me about that?'

His voice was soft and heavily accented. Sitting next to me he seemed to fill the foyer. Like a bear in a suit. The uniformed officer with him, on the other hand, looked about twelve and like a fencepost had sprouted legs.

'Our car broke down on the road near a village called Witwerberg, and we hiked into the village and decided to shelter there. Only my husband and I got separated in a storm the next day. I was trying to keep going there, waiting for someone to come. Then I found these . . . skeletons underneath two of the houses and more recent um . . . corpses in the woods. Two of them.'

Detective Voigt nodded, steely eyes flicking to the fencepost, who was writing this down, a crease between his reddish brows. Ethan was looking at his shoes, probably feeling awful all over again about leaving me whilst he explored.

'These skeletons, how were they put there, would you say?' Voigt asked.

'How . . . ?'

'In . . . um . . .' He waved a hand, reaching for a word. 'In boxes? In bags? Just with the bones on the floor?'

'Oh, right. They were different. The first ones were three people wrapped up in sheets, blankets. Like, bedding. The second group were just bones. Like they'd been piled in there and not laid out. In a hurry.'

He nodded thoughtfully and said something in German to the uniformed officer, who nodded and scribbled faster.

I cleared my throat. 'I found a guidebook on one of the bodies. With her ID, that said she was called Jaqueline. The book said that Witwerberg was probably abandoned in 1816? The "year without summer"? That crops failed all over Europe and people starved in the winter. I thought maybe that's why the skeletons were there,' I said, feeling awkward and foolish, but the detective nodded as if thinking the same thing.

'It could be this, yes,' the detective said. 'Or we have

villages that were wiped out with disease, or people just leaving for the city. But if it was this, there wouldn't be bodies left, and if it was disease they probably would not have kept the bodies so close. So—' He made a gesture as if to say, 'What do I know?' 'For now we'll say these people starved like your book says. I'm more interested in the two others. The bodies.'

I nodded. 'It was a man and a woman. The woman had the guidebook. She was wearing outdoor clothes, like a hiker? I think she was interested in the history of that village. Her book had notes in it about the disappearances there.'

'Disappearances?' Voigt repeated.

'You don't know about Witwerberg?' I asked, surprised. I'd thought it was famous, like the ghost in the Tower of London.

'I'm sure you don't know the name and stories of every old village in England,' the detective said, sounding amused.

He had a point. 'There have been people who vanished there. She had their names in the book. I can give it to you.'

'Good, and the other body, the man?'

'That was weird because he was in a suit. A business suit. He had on those stupid impractical loafers? The shiny ones that can't grip anything other than pavements.' I glanced down and was embarrassed to find a cheaper pair of such shoes on the detective's feet. He smiled, so I continued. 'Anyway, he had a very expensive watch on. An Omega that was designed to commemorate the Olympics in Beijing. It's like . . . five thousand pounds.'

The fencepost whistled, earning him a raised eyebrow from his superior. He went back to scribbling, his cheeks turning pink.

'It must have been disturbing to find them, but it sounds like you took a long look,' the detective said lightly.

I felt the back of my neck go hot at the hint of suspicion in his voice, as good-humoured as it was.

'It was really frightening, and awful. But I was desperate to know what was going on, who they were, how they got there. I thought maybe whatever I could feel watching me had somehow been responsible for their deaths. That knowing what happened to them might help me avoid the same death.'

The humorous twinkle in Detective Voigt's eyes was replaced by a flinty interest.

'Something watching you?'

My mouth felt suddenly dry. 'Yes . . . I felt like there was someone there. Someone who tried to kill me by burning my cabin and the rest of the village down whilst I slept. I have notes they made about me – I wasn't imagining it.'

'I don't believe you were imagining it,' he said.

We looked each other in the eye for a long moment. For the first time since I tried to tell my story to Jess and the others, I felt like someone was taking me seriously. Like he was reading the truth of what I'd been through directly off the surface of my brain.

'I'd like you to show me this place, if you are able to go back?' he said.

I nodded, just slightly, and his eyes warmed with approval. I could do this. I could be strong. 'I'm not sure if I can remember the way we drove?'

'With the name of this place we can find it on the map. It's not a problem.'

'We have a flight this evening,' Ethan said, making me jump. 'I know it sounds stupid but we can't really afford another flight if we miss this one.'

Detective Voigt turned a much less approving gaze on Ethan. 'I'll do what I can, but two people are dead, so that flight may need to wait.'

Chapter 29

The drive back to Witwerberg felt like it took for ever, yet I never wanted it to end. Once it did, I'd be back in the nightmare I'd so recently escaped. Sitting in the back of the police car with Ethan's hand holding on tightly to mine, I thought about being in that village again and shuddered. It wasn't that I was afraid that something was waiting there. Or maybe I was. But the most pressing feeling was of tempting fate. Of begging the universe to come back and finish what it had started when it trapped me there.

Once, when Jess and I were really little, I locked myself in our room by accident. When we moved in our door was the only one with a lock. This great big stiff latch in the handle. Even the door was thicker and heavier than all the other internal doors. They were a mismatched lot someone had fitted years before we moved in. Mum made us promise not to play with the lock, because we didn't have a key for it.

Obviously, I ignored her and played with it. I got

locked in and couldn't turn the stiff handle to unlatch the door. I remembered that we had no key. The door could only be opened from my side. I panicked and turned that knob until my hand was red and the skin was burning from the textured metal. Finally, finally, I got it open. I was so relieved that I had not only escaped the room, but avoided a catastrophic scolding from my parents. I felt like I'd won a contest against myself.

But I tried my luck, confident that I could open the door now. I locked it again to scare Jess when she was in there with me. Only this time we couldn't get it open. Dad had to try and break down the door and then climb up a ladder to the bedroom window when that didn't work. That was the only time they were really furious with us. Jess got the worst of it because she was the oldest. She was meant to stop me. Though she'd been reading at the time and obviously didn't see what I was up to. Mum insisted we have the door taken down. We lived without one for two months.

Going back to Witwerberg felt a lot like turning that lock for the second time. I'd escaped once, now I was going back there, full of confidence that these two policemen and my husband could protect me. That they could drive me in and out of the village as easily as they might take a trip to the supermarket. All it took was one breakdown and we'd be trapped.

I was also astounded that knowing the name of the village was all it took to locate it with GPS. All you had to do was look up a map and there it was, on an unnamed road. If Ethan had retained that information he could have told Jess where I was and they could have found me straightaway. It was such a cruel irony that I'd had that information. That if I'd been the one to get out on that first night, Ethan would have been safe and sound the next day. I couldn't blame him for not knowing though, as much as I blamed the situation. We'd both been through a lot that day.

When we passed the sign, lightly powdered with snow, my stomach flipped. I could still remember seeing it for the first time when we were lost, and the shock of seeing my arrow erased, my sign gone. It felt like a bad omen.

Halfway down the road it became too narrow for the car and we had to get out and walk. I'd put my newly dried trainers on and Ethan had his walking boots but the two policemen weren't really dressed for it. I saw the skinny uniformed officer suppress a smile as his superior slithered over the frozen ground. He saw me looking and blushed to the roots of his hair. He was carrying a plastic case, which I assumed contained some kind of evidence kit.

'Jesus,' Ethan murmured, when we came into view of the ashy remains of Witwerberg. 'You weren't kidding about the fire – it's all gone.'

'Yeah,' I said, my mouth dry. 'I barely got out.'

The detective nodded, thoughtful. 'Can you show us where the skeletons were?'

I led him to the site of the cabin where I'd found the first three shrouded skeletons. Both he and the uniformed cop pulled up debris from the burned porch.

The dry remains had clearly burned well. There wasn't a scrap of sheet left, only some blackened bits that might have been sticks, or bones, and some pale ash.

'Fire,' the detective said, sucking his teeth in disapproval. 'Always makes things interesting.'

It was the same at the other cabin, where I'd found the second lot of bones. Only charred fragments remained.

'Get pictures of these, and the others,' the detective told our uniformed shadow. He nodded and took out a digital camera.

Whilst we waited for him to finish taking dozens of pictures I realised I'd not told Detective Voigt that the other bodies had been burned as well. I turned to him and found him looking into the trees.

'I see what you mean about being watched,' he said. 'It feels like . . . I don't know. Like knowing you're on camera.'

I glanced at Ethan, who was watching the uniformed cop with interest. He didn't seem to feel the same way. Or if he did he was keeping it to himself.

'I forgot to say, when I came back after the cabins burned down, the bodies in the woods were burned up too. Like someone lit a second fire there.'

I was expecting him to get annoyed but he only nodded, frowning. 'Makes sense.'

'What does?'

'From what you said, the two people didn't belong together. One in outdoor gear, one in business clothes. Unlikely a man in a suit came here without good reason.' He gestured to his own suit. 'But we are far from anywhere, somewhere many people don't go. A good place to get rid of a body.'

'You think someone dumped the bodies here? That they killed two people separately and hid them out here in a shallow grave?'

He nodded. 'Just a theory. But burning them would make sense if you didn't want them identified and also didn't want to find a new place to put them.'

'So someone knew I was here? They thought I'd found their dumping ground and wanted to keep me from telling anyone?' I felt cold all over. Now the fire made sense; it had happened right after I'd found those bodies. The sudden escalation had confused me but now I could see the logic. I'd seen something I shouldn't have and couldn't be allowed to live. There had been someone watching me. Not just anyone, a killer.

'It's a theory,' Voigt repeated. 'Equally it might have been something else. We need to identify the bodies.'

I led them into the woods. I'd had to find my way back to the bodies before and it didn't take long this time. Soon we were standing around the place where they'd been burned. The raw earth was covered in fresh snow, but the shape of the charred bodies was undeniable. Like a jumble of mannequin pieces under a white sheet.

'Jesus Christ,' Ethan breathed, then put his arms around me. 'Mils . . . You saw this?'

I nodded. 'It was worse before, when they looked . . . when they looked like people.'

Detective Voigt nodded, like he understood. I wondered how many bodies he'd seen in his career. The pouches under his eyes gave him a much older, sadder look than his age warranted. Like a new teddy left out in the rain.

He put on some gloves from the kit and began to sweep the snow aside. Looking at the ground critically.

'We'll need a proper team out here to inventory everything, collect it . . . but for now I think this confirms your story.' He looked up at me, then slowly lifted a blackened lump to show me. It was the watch, the glass shattered and the face warped, but still identifiable.

'We'll find out what happened to these people,' he said. The way he spoke made it sound less like a statement and more like a promise. A promise to me specifically, as the person who had seen these people, who had looked at their frozen features in complete horror.

'It will take time,' he admitted. 'It always does when the bodies are this . . . degraded. Even though you've given us the name of the woman, the man is . . . But we will find out. In the meantime, we will take a statement and you will be able to go home. You've obviously been through enough and there is no need for you to stay.'

We retraced our steps to the village, where Detective Voigt stopped and looked around at the charred wreckage. He put his hands on his hips, a frown creasing his face.

'Is there anything else you can remember about this place before it burned? Anything we should know?'

'Well, there's tunnels, under the cabins, they lead out into the woods, to this like . . . den. Other than that I don't think . . .' I stopped and remembered something. Though the thought of saying it out loud made me feel quite silly. 'There was this hole, in the wall of my cabin. Like a knothole but cut into the wood. I thought it might be a peephole but it didn't go anywhere.'

I glanced at Ethan, who had his head to one side like he was trying to work out what the hell I was talking about. The junior officer scribbled something on his notepad.

'This big?' The detective made a circle with his thumb and index finger.

'A bit smaller.' I showed him. 'One side was straight like a cut.'

The detective nodded and half turned towards the space where the cabin had been, where I'd pointed. He chewed his lip for a moment, eyes narrowed.

'How high off the ground?'

'Maybe . . . a few feet? I'm not sure. It's probably not important, I'm sorry if—'

'No no, it's . . . I think it might be, well, it sounds like a bullet hole. Only where someone dug the bullet out afterwards. So it couldn't be found and analysed.'

I blinked. 'Really?'

'I've seen it before with professional killing. They don't want the kills connected with forensics. I doubt we'll ever know now it's—' He indicated the ashes with a sweep of his hand. 'But someone may have been shot in the cabin. Maybe one of the people you found.'

I thought of all the time I'd spent in there. Of how I'd felt that hole with my fingertips. Had I been standing right where someone had died? I felt sick. There'd been so much dirt caked on the floor and it was so dark in there, I could easily have missed any stains on the ground. Had I slept on top of spilled blood? Jaqueline's blood? They'd both been so wrapped up in dark clothing that I might not have seen the blood on his suit or her coat. I shuddered.

The walk back to the car was subdued, an even greater tension in the air than before. I don't think Ethan really believed me until he saw the evidence for himself. I was surprised how much that hurt. That he, out of everyone, had been in Witwerberg, had felt the weirdness there and still didn't take me at my word. But then could I really say I'd have believed it if I hadn't lived it? Hell, even as I cowered in that cabin I'd had to constantly remind myself that I was afraid of phantoms that could not exist. And in the end I'd discovered that much of what I'd imagined was entirely wrong.

Detective Voigt had to turn the car around, crushing brush and knocking over frozen humps of snow. He managed to get us around the right way. Though the front of the car swung perilously close to the gulley. I held my breath, praying that we wouldn't slide down there. Even once the danger was over I found myself still gripping the leather seats so hard that my fingers squeaked.

I called out for him to stop the car when we reached the point ours had broken down at. We got out and looked down at the car way down in the gulley. It was nearly buried in snow by now.

The uniformed officer whistled. 'You got up and down here?'

'Up, further that way.' I pointed. 'But yeah, down here. Our luggage is still down there, our passports.'

Detective Voigt nodded, then looked expectantly at Ethan, who flushed and glanced down the slope.

'I can go,' I said, feeling a bit offended that they assumed I couldn't manage it now, when I had before on less sleep and less food.

'No, I'll do it. You should stay up here, just in case,' Ethan said.

He didn't say what 'in case' referred to. Maybe he thought I'd fall and break my leg or something. Or he was thinking about wolves being nestled comfortably in the back seat of our rental car. Anyway, he inched and stumbled his way down to the car.

Whilst he rummaged around, repacking the suitcase I'd left behind, I caught Detective Voigt watching me with an odd expression. The way you look at someone who's talking to themselves, trying to work out what they're about. Are they mad, or using a headset, or just a bit lonely? That was the way he looked: like he was trying to decide what he was dealing with. It occurred to me suddenly that he might be considering my guilt. I was the only one who could say what happened to the bodies. Maybe he thought I'd gone off the deep end and bludgeoned a pair of hikers for their energy bars.

Who knows, maybe after a few more days I might have. Still, I had an uneasy feeling about him after that. As he drove us to a police station to take my statement formally, I thought about what I was going to say. Was I really about to tell this man a tale of ghosts, shadowy figures and vanishing signs? Wouldn't that just make me look unreliable or untrustworthy?

Ethan interrupted my dire thoughts when he returned with the suitcase. His bag, which I'd had on me at the hotel, was already packed with our borrowed clothes.

'Did you get everything?' I asked.

'Most,' Ethan said, looking flustered and out of breath from the climb. 'Not enough room in the bag for everything.'

'I'll send back whatever's left,' the detective said. 'After we recover the car.'

'Thank you,' I said. That was one less thing to worry about. I didn't fancy trying to arrange a tow for the rental car. With our luggage back with us, we settled in for the long drive to civilisation.

I was quite excited when we reached a town. This was my first time seeing proper houses and shops instead of old cabins or the motorway. I must have slept through so much on our drive out from the airport. In the distance, high over the modern buildings and older townhouses, an honest-to-God castle branched out of the pines. It looked like an enormous, delicate mushroom, all pale and ghostly against all that dark green.

'If you ever come back to Bavaria, I hope you have a better visit,' Voigt said, catching my eye in the rearview mirror.

'I probably will,' I said, thinking it would be hard to have a worse one.

By the time we parked and Ethan hugged me for luck, I'd decided what I was going to say. Detective Voigt escorted me to a small room with a table and six chairs, all bolted to the floor. Two of the chairs were in opposite corners of the room. Probably for solicitors or extra guards. Just seeing them made me feel guilty, though I had nothing to hide.

I'd decided to tell the truth. All of it. From the moment we arrived in Witwerberg. I'd hold nothing back and gloss over none of my insane theories, delusions or paranoia. This detective was a professional. Lying would only make me look guilty and I decided I'd rather look ridiculous instead.

He left me alone for a moment and returned with plastic cups of coffee in a little holder and a couple of those airline waffles, wrapped in greasy plastic. I edged my cup towards me and removed the lid as he fiddled with a large combination recorder set into the wall.

'All right, Mrs Swift. Can you tell me what happened in Witwerberg on the day of your arrival there?'

I took a shaky breath and began to tell my story.

Chapter 30

We went through a lot of coffee and a pretty good ham sandwich before I was done with my statement. Detective Voigt was mostly silent and thoughtful, though he occasionally asked a question like 'Can you describe the height of this "figure"? or 'When you say a "chemical smell" was it like petrol or more like alcohol . . . ?' Eventually, though, we were done.

I met Ethan in the reception area. He looked tired and stressed out, which I'd expected. The table in front of him was littered with shredded bits of napkin and a food container he'd pierced a pattern on with a pen.

'All done?' he asked, glancing at the clock over the front desk.

I nodded.

'I think we have everything we need for the time being,' Detective Voigt said, eyeing the rubbish on the table with a frown. 'Thank you for giving us so much information. Hopefully a timeline of events will help us build a case. When we have a suspect. You might have to return as a witness if we take this to trial. But, for now, you have my contact information and I have yours. We'll be in touch.'

'Thank you, for everything. You've been really nice.' I blushed, because it sounded so small and stupid.

The edges of the detective's mouth curled in a small smile. 'Not something I am normally accused of but . . . thank you for talking me through what happened. That can't have been pleasant.'

'It wasn't, but . . . whoever was out there with me, whoever is responsible for those poor people, I hope you find them. Even if they're not the same person. I hope you get them.'

The detective nodded, then summoned another uniformed officer to drive us to the airport. We were quiet in the back of the car. I think Ethan and I were both preoccupied with our own thoughts. I was still thinking about Witwerberg, about Jaqueline and the man whom the police were now going to attempt to identify. Hoping they'd find their way to their families, that some peace would come out of all this.

I had no idea what Ethan was thinking about. Probably worrying that we'd miss our flight. We were meant to be back at work tomorrow. If we missed the plane we'd lose a whole day of business. We'd been closed long enough for the wedding as it was. The idea of going back to the shop tomorrow felt surreal. Such a weirdly normal thing to do after everything that had happened. I imagined our regulars coming in, like Cam the part-time DJ. How was that conversation going to go?

'How was Germany? Was the wedding good?'

'Oh, I actually got stranded in a ghost-town and found a bunch of dead bodies. I was alone for days with basically no food and the ever-present threat of my own death. That'll be £12.99 for the album, thanks.'

I would have to think of something I could actually tell people. Probably just that the trip was fine (a lie) and that the wedding was absolutely stunning and I was really happy for my sister (true).

It was quite depressing to think that I'd not have to tell the truth to anyone else. Ethan, Jess and Pete were my closest friends and family. The shop and all the admin around it – taxes, stocktaking, cleaning, sourcing inventory – took up almost all our spare time. I hadn't been out with the gang in ages. I couldn't even remember the last time they'd invited me out. I decided to send out a message when we got home and set something up. Though that thought was quickly followed by the realisation that I'd probably be on the phone to the car company all of tomorrow. We were so not getting our deposit back. I only hoped we wouldn't have to pay extra for the damage.

Finally we were in the airport and headed through security. We had no time to browse the gleaming, too bright shops. Our gate was open and half the passengers were already boarded. By the time I threw myself into the economy seat beside Ethan I was breathless and sweating from the sprint through the airport. Still, we had made it. Next stop, home.

I took Ethan's hand just after take-off and he looked up like he was surprised to see me. Then he smiled ruefully, clearly lost in his own head worrying about the journey and returning to the shop. I squeezed his hand gently.

'I'm so glad you're here, you know that? I couldn't have got through the last two days without you,' I whispered.

'I can't believe I lasted without you,' he admitted. 'Everyone was rushing around, trying to coordinate a search and I was just . . . helpless. I didn't know what to do. I couldn't even remember the name of the bloody village.' His free hand clenched into a fist and he punched the armrest.

'Hey, it's not your fault. I wouldn't have known what to do. Who would in that situation? You can't help what you do and don't remember, any more than you could control the snow covering the sign, or the car rolling away.'

'I never should have left you,' he insisted fiercely.

Privately, I agreed. But I didn't want to make him feel worse or start an argument on a plane that was packed to capacity. So instead I said, 'You didn't know what was going to happen. It was all just . . . cascading failures. Like, what if the car hadn't broken down, what if we'd had a mobile signal, what if the storm hadn't made us miss each other that morning? It was all out of our control.'

Ethan nodded, looking at the headrest of the seat in front of us. Through the gap in the seats I saw that its occupant, an older man, was already asleep with headphones on.

'I wonder how Jess is getting on?' Ethan said finally, changing the subject.

'The flight's like, what? Two hours to Barcelona? She and Pete are probably going to bed after their first afternoon of sun and sea.'

'I wish we were,' Ethan sighed.

'We'll be sleeping in our own beds when we get in. I'm looking forward to it. Well, that and having an absolutely filthy fry-up on the way to work tomorrow.'

'Ugh, work,' Ethan sighed. 'Back to the grindstone, fixing knackered Crosleys and trying to explain why we don't want to buy someone's entire collection of ancient Herb Alpert and his bloody Tijuana Brass albums.'

I giggled. It was an old, private joke and it felt good to indulge in it. Especially given everything that had happened. When we started the business we had a running competition of who could find the most Herb Alperts in auction lots and in charity shops. The tally of them was still in a frame in our back office. When we hit one hundred in total we instigated a flat rule: no more Herb. Our current competition was for Andrew Lloyd Webber soundtracks and Ethan was winning.

'I'll take a bit of normal right now,' I said. 'Anything that isn't snow, potential murder and creepy villages.'

Ethan gave me a sympathetic smile and put his arm around me. I snuggled in and tried to sleep the flight away. In only a few short hours I'd be back home, safe and sound. I could only hope that once I was tucked into bed in our tiny flat, Bavaria would seem like a bad dream.

Of course, in the travelling of it, those few hours stretched out to nightmarish lengths. First the flight, then the wait to disembark and find our way out of the airport. We'd pre-booked a taxi but it hadn't shown and Ethan's phone was dead, probably from watching tiktoks in the police station.

In the end we caught the shuttle bus to the town centre and picked up a local cab to get home. By the time we dragged ourselves and our luggage upstairs to the flat, we were both done in.

The flat felt strange after so long away. There's always that moment when you return home from a trip and find you can smell your own home. Normally you don't pick up on its unique odour but, in that moment of opening the door, it hits you. Our flat smelled like burned dust, stale coffee and sandalwood room fragrance. It had a weirdly dead feel to it as well. Everything was oddly still, flat and dark. Whilst Ethan snapped the lights on and rushed to the loo, I ran my hand over the kitchen counter, where a thin film of dust had settled. It felt abandoned, just like Witwerberg.

I tried to shake off that feeling. It would only take an hour or so before the flat felt homey again. Full of life and movement as we found our way back into its familiar routines.

I'd planned on ordering a pizza or something, maybe

just having a cuppa and some biscuits in bed. But my eyes felt sandy with sleep and I could almost feel my body shutting down. So I settled for leaving my clothes in a pile by the bed and crawling under the duvet. The bed felt vaguely damp. I wasn't sure if it was just the cold or if it had sucked up some condensation. Either way it felt odd. I tried to spread my warmth around, chasing the stale feeling from the bedsheets. I'd only changed them the day before we left.

Ethan came in and stripped down to his boxers. He brought with him the smell of hand soap and pine air freshener. Familiar, safe scents. Still, I had a weirdly out of sync feeling. Like the flat belonged to a stranger. As if we'd accidentally walked into a perfect copy of our home, only someone else lived there. I told myself it was probably stress related.

Ethan carried on a mostly one-sided conversation about the idiot taxi that hadn't turned up, the lack of coffee on the plane and the ever increasing security measures we'd had to navigate. I mostly contributed 'hmms' of affirmation, struggling to keep my eyes open. Finally he climbed into bed and turned off the lamp.

Annoyingly, as soon as the light was off, I felt wide awake. Not in a fresh and peppy way either. More in the grim travelling way, where you want to go to bed but have another two trains to catch and any loss of awareness will cause bag snatchers to swoop down on you. I was too wary to sleep. Even though this was the safest place I knew – miles and miles from Witwerberg, from the tunnels and fire and snow. Even though I knew nothing that I'd left behind in Germany could get me. I still didn't feel safe.

Just like when I was in the village, the most pressing fears were coming from inside me. My own paranoia and worry. I couldn't let go of the survival instincts that had kept me going.

Ethan's gentle snoring kept me company as I lay awake into the small hours.

Chapter 31

I didn't tell Ethan what happened at the wake.

He must have known something was up though because he kept touching on the topic. Dropping Jess into the conversation and letting her name hang there like a lure, trying to bring me out of hiding.

'How was everything – did Jess seem to be coping OK?'

'Has Jess told you where they're having the wedding yet?'

'Do you reckon we should wait for the gift registry or get something extra since Jess is your sister?'

I only shrugged or nodded. I didn't know how to tell my husband that according to Jess, I had no sister. That we were 'done' now that both our parents had been reduced to ash and deposited in a tiny plot by the crematorium. That I wasn't sure I'd ever see her again.

Ethan continued to probe, like he was afraid to just ask me what was wrong. It must have been clear that something was though. He could always read me, some-times better than I could read myself. Only this time he didn't know how to approach the subject. Something in my attitude must have been deeply changed for him not to know how to deal with me.

On the surface I tried to keep things as normal as possible. I helped with shopping and housework, went to work with Ethan as normal and did all the usual couple stuff. But inside I kept reliving that confrontation in the bathroom over and over again. Kept seeing Jess's agonised, furious face. Every day that passed with no word from her made the rift between us feel wider and deeper. Until I wasn't sure there was any way to cross it. I'd tried leaving a voice message to say I would be there to talk once she was ready. I'd sent a really long email apologising for everything I could think of. I'd even suggested we do counselling together. But it was like Jess had me blocked everywhere. I couldn't reach her.

A month passed and still no word from Jess, until one Sunday when Ethan was going through our weekly post. Anything important got sent to the business address or was online only. But once a week he opened our post-box at the flat and dumped the junk mail into the recycling, or updated our selection of pizza menus.

'Fancy' was his only comment as he passed me the envelope. It was thick and creamy with flower designs embossed into it. I knew what it was before I even prised up the wax seal – a wedding invitation. An invitation to attend the destination wedding of the sister who'd told me she never wanted to see me again.

I unfolded the sheet of paper inside, looking for a note or any kind of hint that Jess was ready to talk. Any kind of acknowledgement of what had happened at Mum's wake. But there was nothing.

'So . . . where is it?' Ethan prompted.

'Oh, umm, some ski resort they've been going to together for years. In Bavaria.' I flipped the invite over so he could read it the right way up.

Ethan whistled. 'Bet that costs a bomb. Can we afford it?'

'They're paying for the accommodation,' I said, hearing my voice but unable to feel my lips moving. 'The outfits, the food. Everything. We just have to cover the flights and getting there from the airport.'

'Not too bad then,' Ethan said, sounding relieved. 'I'll download some maps or something and we can rent a car. It's got to be cheaper than getting a taxi. I mean, the airport's not going to be up in the mountains is it?'

I nodded but I was barely listening. Jess was inviting me to her wedding. Did that mean she wasn't angry anymore? That her outburst at the wake was all it took to clear the air? Or was this just to save face, so she didn't have to explain to Pete that we weren't speaking?

Later that day, whilst Ethan was in the kitchen attempting to make shepherd's pie, I rang Jess. Shut away in our bedroom I expected it to go to voicemail, but she answered straight away.

'Hi, Mila, did you get the invitation? I haven't had an RSVP back from you guys?'

'I did. Sorry, we didn't check the post until today. It's usually just phonebooks and leaflets.' She sounded so normal and casual that it threw me.

'Ugh, I know, such a pain. We don't get that so much since we bought the house. Clearly junkmailers don't like coming this far outside the centre.'

Jess and Pete had finally taken the plunge and started looking for a house together a few weeks after the engagement party. I still hadn't been to see it. Jess hadn't invited me, but had mentioned they were gutting the place. Was that why? Or did she just not want me there?

'So you're coming?' Jess pressed. 'I just need to get the numbers to the resort as quickly as possible.'

'Yes, Ethan and I can come . . . if you're happy with that?' I asked, unsure how else to crack the layer of denial that encased our conversation.

There was a short but very sharp silence. Then Jess laughed.

'Well, obviously? Why wouldn't I be?'

And there it was, the silent ultimatum. Clearly Jess didn't want to address what happened at the wake. She was offering a choice, to forget it and carry on as we always had, or break this fragile truce. If I pointed out why I thought she might not want me there, I'd be the one responsible for continuing this fight. One she clearly wanted to forget ever happened.

'It's just . . . it's got to be expensive, having so many guests,' I said, coward that I was.

'Don't worry, Pete used to have a client who did a

lot of business with them, he knows the management and got us a great deal,' Jess said. 'Besides, I only plan on doing this once so we're going all out for the perfect wedding. The perfect trip for everyone else too.'

'Sounds great,' I said. 'You deserve it.'

A note of sincerity broke the happy-go-lucky tone Jess had taken since picking up the phone. 'I think after the year we've had . . . you deserve it too.'

Chapter 32

Eventually I managed to fall asleep. A surface sleep where I was still nearly conscious. So when our alarm went off and it was time to get ready for work, I felt almost as tired as I had the day before. Still, when I peeled myself out of bed the flat felt more like home again. Almost as if we'd never been away. The aches and exhaustion in my body were the only reminders of what I'd been through.

My phone was fully charged and I unplugged it from beside the bed to spend a few minutes scrolling my feeds. I hadn't done so in days and it felt so . . . ordinary. Comforting, to have that option again. The ability to step out of my own thoughts and just speculate on other people's lives.

'We've got nothing in for breakfast,' Ethan said from the doorway. He'd brought me a cup of tea made with the UHT milk we'd stashed for after our trip. Really it should have occurred to me to buy some cereal to go with it.

After a quick look around the kitchen I managed to find some bread snowflaked with mould. I'd used everything else up before we left.

'I'll pick us up a full English on the way in,' I said, already looking forward to a glut of grease and meat.

We walked into town and Ethan went ahead to open up the shop. I greeted Simon at the café, which was as usual full of end-of-shift workers and people with nowhere else to go. We were regulars and went there for hot drinks in the winter and slushies in summer. It was one of those high street greasy spoons that pop up alongside betting shops, off licences and blacked-out 'private' shops. Exactly the place to go for fried bread – the cheap white stuff, not artisanal sourdough.

'Mila! How was Deutschland?' he boomed, ladling beans in the cloud of steam by the counter.

'Pretty good,' I said, not willing to get into it. 'Two full English to go, please. One no beans, extra mushies.'

He was already filling the containers from the grill. It was the kind of food you'd bitch about at a hotel – sausages more bread than meat, bacon thin as a razor, rubbery eggs. But somehow I always craved it on a bad day. It reminded me of all-inclusive holidays and school dinners. A simpler time.

I thought of holidays and then of Jess with a pang, wondering what she and Pete were up to in Barcelona. Well, it was their honeymoon so, probably something I didn't want to imagine. But I hoped they were having an amazing time. I couldn't wait to hear about the places they'd seen.

'Must have been a bit of a shock for you,' Simon was saying as he cracked eggs onto the griddle.

I frowned. What was he talking about? 'Shock?'

'Yeah, when you heard about the—' He broke off, looking up from the searing griddle and bubbling eggs. 'Oh shit, did no one call you?'

'What do you mean? Call me about what?' I said, panicking now.

'Couple of nights ago it all kicked off down here. Some lads were drinking after the match and they started throwing shit and causing a scene. Police called and everything. Not that they turned up too quick, mind, had their hands full that night. I saw the lads from the flat upstairs. Wrecked the kiddie park, threw the bins and smashed a bunch of windows. I said to Janey, if I was five years younger . . .'

Despite the heat radiating from behind him, I felt suddenly cold. 'Did they . . .'

Simon nodded, his shiny pink face twisted in sympathy. 'They busted your window, messed around in there until they got hauled out by police. I don't know what they got up to but they did a few other places and it wasn't good. Mr Singh with the barbers said he had your number. I thought he called.'

'He only has our landline, in the shop,' I said mechanically. 'Oh Jesus, did anyone board it up?'

'Yeah, the emergency glazier came out and they did everyone. But you'll probably have a mess to clear up.'

I sighed, a familiar feeling of helpless dismay welling up inside me. This was just what we needed. Another catastrophe, another act of God. Or at least an act of drunken football louts. Why was this happening to us all at once? What had we done to bring this shitty luck down on ourselves?

'There you go, I've put some extra fried bread and hash browns in.' Simon pushed the two Styrofoam containers towards me with a wink.

'Cheers,' I said, and held out my cash.

He shook his head. 'On me, just this once.'

'Thanks, Simon.'

When I left the café and went further down the street, I started to see the signs of chaos. The kids' play park was just a few rocking animals and a slide on some coloured rubber flooring, but one animal was gone now. There were two bits of twisted metal there, wrapped with caution tape. The slide had been toppled and was missing two plastic steps. The bin outside the hair salon was dented and their window, normally full of wigs and bright bottles, was boarded over. A few shops, the ones with tougher windows, had cracked glass with tape over it to keep the weather out. There was dirt all over the pavement, I guessed from one of the big wooden planters. Someone had tried to sweep it up but at some point it had rained and the mud was stuck between the paving slabs.

Then I saw our shop and thoughts of overturned planters left my mind. Both our windows were broken and boarded. Without our bright chalk pen drawings of musical notes and glam rock stars I hardly recognised the place. It looked sad and down at heel. I balanced the containers carefully and pushed open the door.

Whatever I was expecting, it wasn't this. From what Simon had told me I'd assumed the windows would be the worst of it. A bit of mindless vandalism, quickly contained. But inside . . . the shop was ravaged. Clearly some of the football fans had discovered the frisby-like properties of records. There were empty sleeves everywhere and bare seventy-eights littered the floor. Some were smashed, others cracked. Two trays of country albums had been tipped over and a slew of Dolly Parton and Tammy Wynette raced like dominoes across the floor. One beaming portrait of Dolly had a filthy great footprint on it. Several rolled-up posters were lying, bent and abandoned, on top of a display table. Possibly evidence of a sword fight. One wall had a great big brown splatter mark on it. On the floor below was broken glass from a beer bottle and a heap of kebab salad. A limp, sickly yellow pepper hung from one of the fluorescents.

In the middle of the chaos, Ethan was having a meltdown.

Normally he was the cool, calm and collected one. In a crisis he'd be the first person to stand up, call for silence and say, 'Right, where do we start?' But today, whether because he was as tired as I was, or just emotionally exhausted from the past few days, he was clearly not coping as he normally would.

He kicked out at the naked records again and again, scattering bits of shattered vinyl and shellac. Finally he seemed to run out of steam. I watched as he rubbed his hands over his face, squashing his nose and pulling his mouth out of shape.

'Hey,' I said softly, not wanting to startle him.

Ethan turned around and tried to offer a smile, but it was so wan it slid off his face in an instant. I raised the containers of hot food and he waded through the wreckage to the counter. With plastic knives and forks in hand, we looked across the store from our naugahyde stools.

'Who the fuck did this?' Ethan said, spearing a fried tomato so hard it spurted bloody juice over his hand.

'Simon says it was lads from the football. They smashed up some other businesses and the play equipment.'

'I saw. But this . . . No one else was hit like this, surely?'

I chewed my lip as I sawed through the fried bread with a plastic knife. 'Maybe they were. They've had a few days to clear up. They might have been just as wrecked.'

Ethan grumbled in disbelief and I decided not to push the matter. I certainly didn't want to mention that most of the other units had better security than we did: shutters, wire glass and locked cases of merchandise. Whether or not our neighbours had been as affected wasn't my main concern. I was more worried about the cost of getting everything set right again. We'd need to replace the windows, not to mention the cost of the ruined inventory and replacement stock. I could see the numbers adding up higher and higher. We were already struggling – what if this was the thing that pushed us under? I wasn't getting my inheritance for a while yet, and we had rent to pay before then.

'I'll get onto the insurance after this,' I said. 'Or I suppose I should call the police first, get a reference number or something. That's what they'll ask for, right?'

Ethan nodded, but seemed stuck in his own thoughts.

'Hey,' I said, 'don't worry, we'll get it sorted out. It's not like we haven't had worse in the last week, is it?'

I was trying for a joke but it came out like confirmation of a curse. I'd acknowledged the black cloud over us and far from making light of things, it felt like I'd just closed the lid on a coffin.

'Why can things not just go right,' Ethan sighed, then looked up at me. 'Why does it always have to get fucked up?'

I shrugged, feeling helpless. I had no answers. We finished our breakfasts in silence, though instead of fortifying me, the greasy food made me feel a bit sick.

Obviously opening the shop was out of the question, so we were losing a whole day of business. Probably more. On top of the cost of the windows and the stock. We'd have to pay out for it all and try to get some insurance back but it was going to be a long process. I could feel it.

The clean-up operation looked like it would take all day, and then some. I would look up every so often, wiping sweat off my face, to find that we'd made shockingly little progress. There was stuff everywhere. For every mess I picked up, there was another one underneath. Even once the glass was all swept up and the broken bits of records bagged up with it, we still had to go over everything that had been taken out of its sleeve to check for scratches. Each record had to be brushed, its sleeve located, then replaced in the correct display. Some sleeves had footprints or sticky liquid on them and had to be wiped clean. The records had to be re-graded and sorted.

Ethan went at it like this was his own personal hell and a demon had a pitchfork to his neck. He didn't complain or even talk much at all, just went on cleaning and correcting. After a few hours though I was really starting to struggle. I'd only had two days of proper food and rest since escaping the village. And frankly neither day had been very 'restful', what with the wedding, the police and the torturous journey home.

Before long I started messing up – putting things in the wrong place, knocking piles of paperwork over, or getting fingerprints on records Ethan had already cleaned. The third time I did that he put down his brush and sighed.

'Mils, why don't you just go home?'

My face went hot and I felt in that instant both shamed and frustrated. This business belonged to both of us. This mess was our responsibility. But Ethan made it sound as though I were getting in his way. I wanted to help, but everything kept going wrong.

'We're nearly done,' I said.

Ethan looked at the complete chaos of the shop. It was almost messier now than when we'd started, what with the half-finished cleaning and half-sorted stock on every surface.

'I'll finish this, you can go home, rest a bit and do the phone stuff. Talk to the car rental place and the insurer – get a police reference number. All that stuff. You know I'm not good at talking to those people.'

He was throwing me a bone and we both knew it. Like giving a kid your broken controller so they think they're playing a game with you. But it was meant to spare my dignity and I let him think it worked.

I pecked him on the cheek, then got my bag and left the shop. On my way home I got an email from Detective Voigt. Just a note to say they'd had the rented car hauled out of the gulley. He ended by saying he hoped we'd had a safe trip home and that he'd phone with an update as soon as they identified the man's body or found a lead to whoever was in the village with me.

There was also a message from Jess. Just a picture of two pairs of feet as she and Pete lazed on a beach. I smiled at it, but once I'd put my phone away my low mood returned. Jess was having a great holiday whilst we swept broken glass out of our business. Worse, when she got back I'd have to tell her all about the bodies and the police.

So much for everything being over.

Chapter 33

The moment I closed the door behind me, I felt anxious. It took me a moment to realise that this was because I hadn't been alone since Witwerberg. Ever since my rescue I'd always had someone with me, my sister, Ethan, even the people passing me on the street as I walked home. But here in the flat, I was all alone again and it was far too quiet.

I quickly turned the TV on and let the chatter of a daytime antiques programme fill the living room. Still, I didn't feel entirely comfortable, so I did something I hadn't done since Jess and I were kids. I went from room to room and checked every hiding place: under the bed, in the boiler cupboard and the wardrobe, even behind the shower curtain. The electric ring of silence still somehow cut through the babble about Troika pottery.

As I went I kept glancing behind me, feeling like there was a presence there. A breath in the air or the slight heat from someone's skin as they stood too close. But there was nothing.

After I completed my check I closed all the doors and went back to the living room, feeling silly, but no less anxious. I sat down but then immediately got up and put the security chain on the door. My skin was crawling with unease.

I couldn't believe how quickly the feeling of normality had evaporated. Surrounded by people, it had been easy to push the fear and paranoia down, but here, alone, it rose up until it was a physical sensation. My skin pricked with goosebumps and my racing pulse was nearly painful. I dragged a blanket from the back of the sofa and pulled it tightly around myself. If I could breathe, just breathe, and stay still, it would be all right.

Eventually the awful knot in my chest began to loosen and my heartrate returned to normal. My actions when I first got home began to feel sillier and I managed to convince my hands to let go of the blanket. It was just a blip. A weird overreaction to being alone again, that was all. I'd got myself through it. Everything would be OK now.

I made tea and added three sugars. Sweet tea for the nerves, wasn't that a thing? I added a fourth sugar just in case. Maybe a biscuit too? I was hunting in the cupboard for some Hobnobs when I found the bottle of wine. Maybe that would help if I got a bit tense again? I put it on the coffee table, then sat with my hands wrapped around the mug of tea.

Feeling more myself, I took the paperwork for the insurance out of my handbag and found the rental car agreement in my emails. Phone calls to other human beings. The thought gnawed away at the remaining worry. I dialled the number for the call centre and listened, with a sigh of relief, to the recording that answered.

The calls kept me occupied for over an hour, in which time I finished my tea and drank another. The car rental place took the longest. It was hard to explain: 'we broke down and somehow the car ended up in a gulley, possibly because a murderer pushed it in.' But we got there in the end. It helped that the car had broken down and left me stranded in a dangerous, remote area. The implicit threat of a civil suit got me some excellent customer service.

I was feeling better by the time I put the phone down. It was just a little wobble, that was all. I was fine. Still, without anyone to talk to I could feel my anxiety climbing again. Maybe I should have pushed harder for a dog when we first moved in?

I eyed the bottle of wine and worried my lip with my teeth. One small glass to take the prickle out of my neck and the crawl from my skin. One tiny glass, like you'd have with lunch. I had that giant breakfast lining my stomach. It wouldn't even do much.

With a glass of white in my hand I cuddled up in the blanket again and let the banal intro to a gardening show wash over me. I'd sip my wine, watch some TV, then get started on a shopping list. By the time Ethan came home, exhausted from cleaning the shop, we'd have a proper dinner to sit down to and the flat would feel normal again. Lived in and secure.

The hammering on the door woke me up to canned laughter from the TV. The living room was dark except for the flickering of the screen. I twisted around, heart in my throat at the loud noise that had woken me up. When I saw that the front door was open, pushing against the security chain, I let out a strangled sound. The door wobbled back and forth as someone thumped on it. Fear went through me like an electric current and I stiffened, completely paralysed.

A hand shot through the gap to fumble with the chain, and I screamed.

'Mila!' It was Ethan, shouting at me through the crack. 'Open the fucking door!'

I struggled out of the blanket and set my wobbly legs on the floor. My tongue felt furry and the empty bottle I knocked off the table explained why. My head was swimming. I undid the chain and Ethan stormed in, shoving the door closed behind him.

'Jesus Christ, I've been out there for ten minutes,' he said, snapping on the overhead light. With a single glance I saw him take in the fallen bottle and crumpled blanket. He sighed and rubbed his face with one hand.

Shame made me blush, the awful seesawing feeling of being day-drunk making me want to be sick. The piece of paper that I'd intended to use for my shopping list was pasted to the coffee table by the tea I'd knocked over at some point. I grabbed a handful of tissues and started trying to mop it up.

'Leave it,' Ethan snapped. 'I'll do it, just . . . go to bed. Sleep it off.'

'I'm sorry, I was just . . .'

'Just what? Getting pissed in the middle of the day while I cleaned up the shit heap that used to be our livelihood? I said go home and rest, not drink a whole bottle of wine and lock me out. Did you even call the insurers?'

'Yes! And the rental car company, and the police. That detective emailed as well and said they'd recovered the car so hopefully we won't get fined or whatever on top of everything else.'

'And then? Did you get anything in for dinner? Because I've been on my hands and knees all afternoon scraping up broken glass and fucking kebab bits. Oh, and one of the bastards took a piss in the office kettle and turned it on, so it absolutely reeks back there. So maybe I could have done with some wine too.'

'I would have stayed to help, you told me not to,' I pointed out, getting quite snappy myself. 'And you never asked me to go shopping so why would you assume I'd do it?'

'Oh, I don't know, Mila – because you had time?' Ethan snapped incredulously.

'Yeah, I had time. I also had a fucking meltdown over being on my own in the flat, so maybe I needed to take a fucking moment, given everything that I've just gone through, because you left me!'

As soon as the words came out of my mouth, I regretted them. If I could have knocked them out of the air, I would have. Even if they felt like broken glass going down, I'd have swallowed them all. Every single

305

letter. But it was too late. I'd said it. The thing I'd been holding in since I saw Ethan outside the resort. The hurt I'd covered so well that I hadn't even felt it. I'd been trying so hard to be OK, for Jess, for the wedding. Now the cracks were starting to show.

Ethan seemed to deflate. He looked so defeated that I just wanted to hug him. But I was afraid to move in case it prompted another outburst, from either of us. We never fought like this, hardly even argued. I realised how incredibly naïve I'd been to assume that once we were back home, it would be like we never left. Something from Witwerberg had infected us and was seeping into everything. Ruining things. The stress, fear and pain of those few days overshadowed everything.

'I'm sorry,' I said, trying to keep things calm. 'I meant to go shopping but I was just so anxious and I thought a glass of wine would chill me out. But obviously I overdid it. I'll go to the shop and get something for dinner.'

Ethan shook his head. 'I'll go, it's dark out. You'll be all right here for a minute?'

I nodded and he left, shutting the front door almost silently on his way out.

Still a little shaky on my feet from the wine, I went to the bathroom and splashed water on my face. I had the urge to run after Ethan, anything not to be alone, but I held onto the sink and forced myself to stay still.

He came back a few minutes later, having gone to the corner shop rather than the supermarket. We only ever got emergency milk there because it was so expensive and most of their stuff was stale or cheap brands with crazy mark-ups. But Ethan had a whole bag of shopping: cereal and bread for the morning, microwave meals for dinner, a four-pack of beer and a Diet Coke – my go-to hangover drink.

Whilst he put the rest of the stuff away I microwaved us some pretty bland and stodgy carbonara. Ethan joined me in the living room, carrying a glass of Coke with ice. I accepted the peace offering and we ate in silence, the air still too raw for conversation. Afterwards I cleared up and took myself off to bed with a feeble 'Night then'.

I lay in bed and heard Ethan turn the TV up a little, then open a beer. I was asleep before he could crack a second. I slept so deeply, it was like falling down a hole that went on and on, without a bottom.

When I woke up I had a thundering headache, a mouth like the inside of a hoover bag and an empty spot beside me. Ethan was already up. I rolled over and tried to sit up, immediately feeling queasy. I couldn't really focus my eyes. Even the small amount of light knifing through the blinds made me want to stuff my head under a pillow. Jesus, I was never drinking like that again. I wasn't a teenager anymore.

It took a while before I could locate my phone, never mind being able to look at the bright screen without wincing. The numbers seemed to dance about as I tried to read the time. It was gone ten in the morning. The shop normally opened at nine.

Feeling like I'd been encased in salt all night, I

staggered to the bedroom door and into the living room. Ethan wasn't there. Neither were his boots by the front door. His wallet, usually left in the hideous glass punchbowl we found in a skip and kept keys and old batteries in, was missing. He'd gone to work, without me.

For a second I just stood there, then complete fury overtook me. How could he do this, again? I had shown him yesterday how his leaving me in Witwerberg had affected me. How upset I was, how much it had hurt. Now, less than twelve hours later he'd left me again. All right, so we weren't in a ghost village halfway up a mountain. But he knew how anxious I'd been when alone in the flat. Anxious enough to down a bottle of wine to myself.

In the kitchen I poured myself a glass of water and pressed it against my forehead. Then I noticed the note on the counter. It was scrawled on the mini-whiteboard from the fridge – *Gone to work, left you to sleep it off. Don't worry about coming in. Will handle it.*

I nearly threw the board across the room. So much for peace offerings and reconciliation. Apparently at some point during his four beers, the cans for which were on the coffee table still, Ethan had decided he was still annoyed over yesterday. Fantastic.

The only good thing about him going off and leaving me was that my annoyance kept me from feeling too vulnerable. In fact when someone knocked aggressively on the door, I hardly jumped at all. Though I did freeze, looking at the door but unable to move towards it.

How had I never noticed before that we had no peep hole? I'd been so lax about home security. Even the chain was left over from the past tenant, who probably still had a key to our locks. I'd have to sort that out or I'd never feel safe.

'Post,' came a voice through the door.

I reluctantly went and opened the door. It wasn't our normal postman, but a bored-looking courier. There was a small box on the floor by my feet, covered in stickers and thickly wrapped in tape.

'Name?'

'Amelia Swift.'

He tapped at his handheld gadget and walked off without saying anything. I took the box inside. It was addressed to both me and Ethan, but the sender was Karl Voigt. The detective. I frowned, wondering what on earth he would want to send us. Judging by the speed with which it had arrived, he'd made it a priority.

I cut through the tape with a kitchen knife, still too annoyed at Ethan to wait for him. Inside, the box was full of foam beads, with a letter poking out. It quickly became clear that this wasn't some kind of 'sorry you had such a shit time in our country' gift. It was just the stuff from our rental car that Ethan hadn't grabbed when he got our luggage. Still, it was really kind of them to get it back to us so quickly.

There wasn't much. The main thing was our satnav, which we'd taken with us instead of paying out for one when we reached Germany. I'd shoved it under the seat when I slept in the car, so Ethan had probably missed it. There were some charging cables, about thirty euros we'd withdrawn for tolls, snacks and tips, the packet of tissues that weren't ours and a box of allergy tablets. I frowned. Those also weren't ours, but unlike the tissues I hadn't seen them in the car before. They must have been left over from someone else that had used the car before us, probably tucked down the back of a seat or on the floor.

Anyway, that small bit of excitement was over with and I was back to being annoyed with my husband. I decided to take him at his word. If he didn't want me at the shop today, I wouldn't go. He'd just have to deal with it.

Chapter 34

Unfortunately, despite my intention to spite Ethan, I still needed to go shopping. Not only because we had almost nothing fresh to eat, but because it would get me out of the house and around people. Something I started to crave after about an hour on my own.

I scribbled a quick list, got dressed and headed out to get the bus. Our nearest supermarket wasn't actually nearby. It was part of a 'business park' about half an hour away by car. Which took over an hour and a half on the bus. That weekly trip was the only time I really missed having a car. Ours gave up the ghost ages ago and we'd decided we didn't use it enough to justify another. Ethan and I always had the same conversation about it: we didn't need one in a town, but it would be so convenient for the shopping. Then one of us would suggest delivery and the other would re-tell the 'beef broth' story and we'd be back to square one, taking the bus again next week. Just another one of our couple rituals.

Today, however, I was alone and the lack of this familiar discussion made me feel a bit off-kilter. Like half of me was missing. At least I was on a bus and surrounded by other people. It felt a lot nicer than being alone in the quiet flat all day. Hopefully the shopping trip would tire me out just enough to curb my anxiety by the time I got home.

I could only hope.

After trundling my way around the supermarket I struggled with the bags to and from the bus stop. Getting back up to the flat was its own trial, reminding me that only a few days ago I'd been practically starving to death. My body was still weakened, though improving. But I made it. Before I tackled the putting away I decided to have a cuppa and some biscuits.

I was searching for some biscuits, the same ones that had eluded me yesterday, when I knocked over a box of instant soup sachets. They were Ethan's. I hated the things, even the smell, so much so that he only made them when I was at the shop and he was ill at home. The box fell, hit the counter and spilled a bunch of white packets everywhere. But along with those came a tiny little blister pack of pills.

I picked them up, frowning, whilst the kettle rattled the mugs on their hooks behind me. Why were they in there? I read the name on the foil backing, then snatched up the box of tablets from the German package. They were the same make. Which was definitely weird, as neither of us was taking them.

The kettle ended its cycle and silence welled up in

its place. I looked at the two packs of pills and struggled to work out what on earth they were doing there. One set from our rental car, the other in our flat.

I'd assumed the first pills were from someone else renting the car, that they were so well hidden that neither the cleaners nor I had found them. But the question still remained, why were the pills in our home, when neither of us used them? And why were they hidden? Hidden, I thought, as I gathered up the soup sachets, somewhere only Ethan would have cause to look. I felt my skin prickle with unease. Why did I feel like I was somewhere I shouldn't be, as if intruding in my own home?

Biscuits forgotten, I typed the name of the medication into my phone. Maybe this was one of those tablets meant for one thing, that also helped with something else? Like taking the pill for bad cramps? Maybe Ethan was embarrassed about why he was taking them? I scanned the results. It was an allergy tablet used by people allergic to more common over-the-counter remedies. Good for all the usual suspects: pollen, dust and pets. No mention of alternative uses, just some side effects. Not something anyone would take for say, hair loss, or erectile dysfunction, the only two things I could think of that Ethan might not want to talk to me about.

Maybe Ethan had just discovered an allergy and not told me? We didn't obsessively share everything after all. If it was mild he probably hadn't thought it worth mentioning. But then, why hide the pills? I turned the packet over a few times, thinking. Maybe he'd just lost the box and put them there so he wouldn't lose them? He'd done something similar before when a bottle of squash started leaking in the office at work. I'd come in late and found a vintage decanter full of Ribena in the back room. His solutions didn't always make sense to me. Though normally practical he did have some odd solutions to problems.

Satisfied with this, I made myself a cup of tea and finally found the biscuits, stashed in the bread bin of all places. Possibly another one of Ethan's organisational brainwaves.

Once I'd had something to eat I felt a lot less shaky. Putting the shopping away didn't take long and I even had the presence of mind to drag the slow cooker out of hiding and get some beef noodles on the go for later. I wanted to think I was being kind and considerate, but the fact was it was all in the spirit of being petty. Ethan had made me feel about one inch tall, leaving me at home like I didn't contribute anything. Well, tonight he wouldn't have a thing to get on at me about. Dinner would be ready, the shopping done and I would have scored us some new stock.

The second bedroom of the flat, on the other side of the bathroom to the master bedroom, was more of a cupboard with a window. It just about fit a desk, laptop and printer. We'd put up shelves for folders of paperwork but they'd quickly filled up with anything we didn't have a place for in the rest of the flat. The desk was at the moment covered in tools from Ethan's attempts at fixing our own record player. I shifted the screwdriver set aside to make space for the mouse. The windowsill was covered in plants, two of which had dried out alarmingly whilst we'd been gone. I got up and went to put them in the bathroom sink for a soak.

Most of the stock for the record shop came from house clearance, online auctions and local selling sites. I sat myself down on the old roller chair and started to browse. Most of the stuff I came across was trash. Lots of orchestral music which didn't fit our target demographic. Eventually though I came across a good mixed lot of rock, country and some French pop that was just obscure enough for someone to want it. And it was priced amazingly low. The same person had a bale of old band t-shirts too. Nothing overly valuable and all a bit holey and moth-eaten, but with plenty of kitsch appeal. I put a bid in on both. We could get a bit of scaffold rail in the back and see if the shirts did well. I could maybe tie-dye a few or make crop tops for the festival crowd.

Pleased with myself I skipped out to the kitchen to get some instant noodles. Whilst the kettle boiled I picked up the rest of the stuff from the package and took it into the office to put away. I dropped the cables into the old shoebox of spare chargers. The satnav that had outlived our car went into the desk drawer. Then I paused, reopened the drawer and took it back out.

This thing had crapped out on us before the rental car did. That was how we'd ended up lost in the first place. It probably wasn't worth keeping. We didn't even have the car anymore. I weighed it in my hand. Maybe

I could sell it? Get twenty quid or so to put towards the work at the shop? If only I could work out what was wrong with it and either fix it or at least diagnose the issue for a buyer, then I could maybe get more.

I found a lead for it and plugged it into the computer. Maybe it just needed a software update? Or a new cable? Frowning, I tried to remember what Ethan said was wrong with it. I'd woken up in the car and asked if we were at the resort. Then he'd pointed out the broken satnav. The screen had been black, dead. Probably not a software update then. I sighed. Most likely it wasn't fixable, there was just something fried inside it that couldn't be replaced.

I jumped when the screen lit up and it played its obnoxious jingle at top volume. The screen was working! It showed where we'd been when it shut down – in Germany. I guessed it hadn't yet adjusted to its new location.

After pressing some buttons I decided it was working fine, but, if that was the case, what happened to it on that drive? Had it lost signal? But did that normally just turn off the unit instead of it telling you what was wrong? I had no idea. This wasn't my thing. Technology just sometimes screwed up and then was fine the next day. You turned it off, gave it a break and presto, it worked again.

It was still stuck on Germany though. I opened the options menu, trying to work out how to get it to check its location. I tapped 'recent locations', hoping to see our home address. Instead I saw the name of the resort

Jess's wedding took place at. But above that, more recently, the satnav had been set to 'Unnamed Road'. This was followed by a five digit code and the last part of a German address.

Now I wasn't just curious, I felt a prickling on my spine again. The same sensation that Witwerberg had taunted me with, a lesser version of which had tickled me as I held those packs of tablets. The feeling of being so close to a mystery that it could reach out and touch you. Or grab you by the throat.

Slowly, I opened a map window on the computer and typed in the address, code and all. The map shrank down before my eyes, zooming in on a bland screen of nothing but pale green with little cartoon tree outlines. The road cut through it, a hair thin white line. And right in the centre, where a little pointer appeared to show my destination, was a single symbol. A square house with a triangle for a roof, contained in a circle. With an X right through it. I hovered my cursor on it and a friendly little bubble appeared to tell me what it meant – 'Historic settlement – uninhabited'. I zoomed in and up close the word 'Witwerberg' sprang into existence over the same symbol.

I was very still. The word blurred in front of me as everything turned inwards and I finally started to see. The destination was altered after we got in the car at the airport and I set it for the resort. There was only one person who could have changed it, all whilst I slept innocently in my seat.

Different pieces came together. The whole thing

zooming in like the map until I reached my destination; the satnav that wasn't broken, the village we'd ended up at 'by chance'. Even the tablets I'd found. The tablets which the internet informed me, should not be taken whilst operating machinery, because one side effect of them was extreme drowsiness.

I'd slept so heavily on the plane out to Germany. I barely made it to the rental car before passing out again. Then, that first night in Witwerberg, I'd slept right through Ethan opening a trapdoor beside me and vanishing. I remembered him smiling at the airport, handing me my water bottle, now full of iced tea. So thoughtful of him to remember.

My stomach turned over when I thought about our fight last night. How Ethan went to the shop and brought me a Coke as a peace offering. One that sent me to sleep as soon as I put my head down. Sleeping so soundly I hadn't noticed him come to bed and then leave in the morning.

The more I thought about it, the more I let the possibility into my mind, the more I remembered other times. Other mornings I'd woken up with a dry mouth and bleary eyes. Days when I felt too sluggish to go in to work or on trips to buy stock, so Ethan went alone. Nights when I wanted to have a proper talk about when we wanted to start a family or where the business was going, and I left it because I was just so tired.

Had Ethan been . . . drugging me? I realised I was breathing too quickly, starting to get lightheaded. I gripped the arms of the computer chair and tried to get a hold on myself. Part of me was scoffing, telling me I was being crazy. But the part of me that had felt that presence in Witwerberg was saying something else. Screaming it.

Screaming at me to run.

I stood up, froze, then left the room. I froze again in the hallway. It was like being in stop-motion. My mind kept overruling my natural instincts and bringing me to a standstill. It kept coming up with questions, asking me why Ethan would do this? What possible reason was there? Why had he trapped both of us in Witwerberg? Why lie about it? What was he even trying to achieve? Did I really think he could do this to me?

Every question had me moving slower as I tried to work out an answer. I wanted to get somewhere quiet, somewhere small and dark and safe. I needed to think. To stop the questions and the rushing blood in my ears and the pounding in my chest.

Two things happened at once.

My mobile rang, making me jump. I was in the lounge by now and pulled it out of my pocket. Unknown, unfamiliar number. I swiped at the screen to decline the call, but I was already looking away.

The door was opening.

Ethan stepped in, an apologetic expression on his face and an iced latte in his hand. I'm not sure what my face did, but as soon as he saw me, he changed. Like an actor hearing the word 'cut'. Still in costume but somehow . . . dampened, the character allowed to drop.

He looked at me, and I looked at him – realising for the first time, that I was looking at a stranger.

Chapter 35

There was a moment, lasting about two seconds, where I almost convinced myself it was OK. That I was just freaking out again, like yesterday. That the way Ethan's face changed when he saw me was just him being worried, and not him reacting to the look of horror and realisation on my face.

It wasn't worry in his eyes though and it sent chills chasing over my skin. It was like his whole face emptied out. Like he was simply turning off the feelings I was used to reading there: the love, humour and frustration. Flicking a switch on them, the way you'd turn off a satnav, to make it look broken.

Then he nudged the door behind him closed and began to move towards me. He didn't say anything. Didn't look anywhere else but at me. Like he was holding me there by hypnosis. Which he almost was. I heard the plastic cup hit the carpet as he dropped it, reached out.

His hand closed around my wrist as I began to turn.

To run. He tried to jerk me back but only succeeded in knocking the phone out of my hand. I let out a scream and ran, bare feet sticking to the laminate floor.

'Mila!' he shouted my name, just once. Like I was the one who'd swatted the drink from his hand and he wanted an explanation.

I threw myself against the bathroom door, flung it closed behind me and scraped my shaking fingers on the tiny bolt. Like something you'd put on a doll house to fasten it. I pressed the button in the centre of the handle too, a second before it rattled. Just once, like Ethan was checking to see if the bathroom was occupied.

He didn't say a word and he didn't try to open the door again. I could feel him outside, just standing there.

'Ethan?' I called out, not recognising the panicked bray as my voice. 'Ethan . . . what is going on?'

'Can you come out?' he asked calmly.

'I don't know what's going on, please can we just talk?' I begged.

'Come out,' he said again, like he just wanted to show me a meme on his phone. Like it didn't mean anything at all. Yet it made my heart leap into my throat.

Tears welled up and slid down my face. I started to hyperventilate. There was no window in the bathroom. Only an extractor fan. No way out for me except through that door. Through Ethan.

I was almost amazed at how terrified I was of him. I'd known him for years, slept beside him, worked with him, brushed my teeth beside him in this very bath-room. Now I was paralysed by fear at the thought of opening the door that separated us.

I yelped like a scared dog when the light flashed on and off. For some reason, our landlord had installed the light switch outside and Ethan had flicked it on, then off. Like an impatient cinema worker trying to clear out the final stragglers from a screening.

'Stop it!' I almost screamed, slamming my palms on the door. 'Stop it, leave me alone!'

'You're worrying me,' he said. 'I want to see that you're OK.'

'I'm fine!' I yelled, then, with great effort put into keeping my voice level. 'I want you to leave.'

'Not until you talk to me. What is it that's got you in this state, eh?'

I started to feel wrong-footed. Was he being genuine? Had I once again let paranoia get the best of me? I tried to play back the last few minutes. My discovery of the satnav, the pills. Ethan's arrival. We'd looked at each other and he'd come towards me. Had I overre-acted by running away and shutting myself in the bathroom? It all happened so fast.

No. He knocked the phone out of my hand. Or was that an accident? Him just reaching for my hand and me dropping the phone in a panic? My brain was a soup of adrenaline and all my impulses were firing at once. Flight, fight, freeze. I couldn't make my thoughts stay still long enough to process them.

Ethan shook the door handle again and I sprang

back from the door as if he could reach through it and grab me. Was that just me being keyed up or was it proof that part of me knew to be afraid of him?

'Mila, if you don't come out, I'll have to come in there,' Ethan sighed. 'You've been behaving really erratically since those tourists picked you up . . . I'm worried about what you might be doing in there.'

It was like one of those horror films. The kind where an alien gets inside someone or copies their body. It looks and sounds like them but also . . . not. Like the thing pretending to be the person you love is playing with you. The way a cat mauls its food before devouring it. As if it amuses this predator to mock you with false tenderness. Yet the moment you stopped playing their game, or it ceased to be amusing for them, the mask would drop and you'd both know what was about to happen.

'Ethan,' I started, eyes still looking for any way out of the tiled cell I'd shut myself in. 'Could you . . . get me some water?'

I was hoping he'd do it, play along. Then maybe I could get out of the bathroom and shut myself in the bedroom. There was a window there. A third-storey window, but still. I'd take my chances. Maybe I could shout for help?

But Ethan was apparently tired of this game. He didn't respond but I heard him take a few steps, like he was pacing the hallway, then he came back.

'They sent the satnav back then.'

I didn't say anything. He'd been in the office. He

sighed and I heard the chipboard door creak as he leant against it.

'You know, Mils, you really do ruin everything. Not just for your sister, no. It's like . . . nothing can go right for anyone else when you're around.'

I felt sick, my knees almost giving out on me. I backed away until I felt the cold edge of the toilet against my legs, then sat down on the lid. The mask was off. This was the real Ethan talking, I could feel it.

'All you had to do was stay asleep,' he said, sounding progressively more frustrated as he went on. 'I had the perfect place picked out. I was going to drive up there, do it nice and quick – drop you down a gulley. No one would have found you. I was going to tell everyone you got lost while we were stretching our legs.'

He was talking about killing me. Saying it like it was no more of an inconvenience than driving to pick up some more records. Just another errand to be planned out and accomplished.

'Then you woke up, which was irritating enough. I had to think pretty quickly, turn off the satnav, pretend we were lost. Stop you asking questions. Obviously when the car broke down I was fucking pissed. How was I going to get to the resort, let alone explain everything? But I found a workaround . . . until you fucked that up too.'

I thought of the night we'd been stranded in Witwerberg. How I'd tried to start a fire in our cabin whilst Ethan searched for more wood. Was that when he'd found one of the trapdoors? Had he been gone so long because he was investigating the tunnel, realising that he could escape our cabin without leaving any evidence for me to follow, or for anyone looking for me to find?

'Why didn't you just kill me then?' I asked, almost without meaning to.

Ethan sucked air through his teeth, like this was a tricky one to answer. 'Well, I didn't really know what to do at that point. It was meant to look like an accident. What if I did something noticeable and someone found you before you had a chance to get all chewed up by the wildlife? They'd have been straight on to me. But finding that little den in the woods, that was . . . perfect.'

So he had seen it. He'd lied. Of course he had. He'd lied about everything.

'I thought, whoever left all this here isn't going to be happy to find people snooping around. So, if I left quick enough, they'd deal with you for me. That or you'd just freeze to death, starve. There were a lot of options.'

I closed my eyes. Here was my husband listing all the ways he'd imagined my death. How had I never realised how little he cared about me? Why hadn't I felt anything off about him, all this time?

'They must have cleared out most of their stuff by the time you found the place,' Ethan continued. 'Otherwise I think you'd have mentioned a couple hundred bricks of heroin. Or coke, whatever it was.'

Drugs. The tunnels were being used to store drugs.

Who for? Some kind of . . . gang? Cartel? Whatever they were called. Using the abandoned village as a store house. I thought of the two bodies I'd found. Was the guy in a suit a rival, or someone that betrayed them? And poor Jaqueline, had she just stumbled onto their territory, seen something they couldn't allow her to report?

The notes, spying on me, made more sense. Someone minding the place, wondering how to get rid of me and destroy the evidence, once they knew Ethan wasn't coming back. Maybe they were worried he'd bring the police with him. They'd probably have been relieved to know he had no such intentions.

'Why?' I asked. 'If you hate me this much, why did you have to kill me? You could just leave! You can still leave, I won't say anything – just please leave me alone.'

There was silence following my outburst. I wiped tears from my cheeks, embarrassed for cracking up in front of someone who so obviously didn't feel anything for me. Not even pity.

'Honestly I thought you were dead,' Ethan continued. 'It had been days and you had a hurt leg, almost no food. I even came around through the woods and rolled the car off the road, said I couldn't find the place, to give you enough time to shuffle off. It was a surprise when those people showed up with you. I thought for sure either the cold or some animal would get you, if the dealers didn't. But there you were,' he chuckled, but without humour. 'And you just had to insist the wedding went ahead.'

'The . . . wedding?' I wasn't following now. What did any of this have to do with my sister's wedding? There was an edge to the way he said it. That thin coating of casual chatter cracking apart, revealing anger and frustration. Why was the wedding so important to him?

'Yes, Mila, the wedding. The wedding that should never have happened,' he snapped. 'But now I'm going to fix it.'

Chapter 36

'Fix it?' I echoed, trying desperately to understand his logic. The cold, twisted type of logic that said killing me was easier than leaving me. That abandoning me to die a slow, painful death and be torn apart by wild animals was better for him than using his own two hands.

Ethan punched the door and I cried out, pulling my knees up to my chest as if that could protect me. I looked around me, desperately, for any type of weapon. Nothing but bottles of product and dried-out bars of soap and shampoo.

'Yes! Fix it! Which I wouldn't have had to do if you'd just let it go and let them rebook it. Or if you'd done your part right! I mean, who the fuck lets their sister marry a man with other women's nudes on his phone?'

I was lost in the flow of his angry words, and then suddenly, they swept me to the answer. I remembered that day, with Pete's phone. How I'd ended up with it instead of mine. Such a small thing that I'd never thought about it until now. Because it was Ethan that bought me that phone, out of the blue as a surprise present. A model we really couldn't afford. The same one Pete had. Then it was Ethan who handed me the wrong phone that day. Handed it to me so that I'd see the messages from a bunch of girls, sending nudes to Pete, and go running to my sister.

'You were trying to break them up,' I murmured, almost to myself. 'Why?'

'Because she's mine!' Ethan snapped. 'She was always meant to be mine! I thought if she saw that stuff on Pete's phone, she'd leave him, but she's too good for that. Too forgiving for her own good. So I thought I'd kill two birds with one stone – get the money I needed to impress her and stop the wedding. Because she was never going to go through with it when you were missing.'

Ethan was still talking, laying out his hope that they'd bond in their grief. But I could barely hear him. Jess. This was all about Jess. All this time Ethan had been using me to get close to her. She was the one he wanted.

I thought back to the start of our relationship. He'd been laid back, not possessive or clingy. He gave me space, is what I thought at the time. Looking back on it I could see it was disinterest. He called when he wanted sex or someone to listen to his terrible band play. That was all I was good for. Filler for a seat and for his bed.

I remembered the first time I took him home to meet my parents. He didn't want to go but I managed to lure him, cleverly I thought at the time, with the promise of fancy food and the chance of a hook-up in my parents' hot tub.

Jess was already there with Pete. They'd only been going out six months or so, but Jess was very driven. She wouldn't have gone on a single date with Pete if she didn't see him in her future. I'd been impressed with Ethan. With how charming and polite he was with my family, when normally he was a bit of a smartarse with an anti-establishment streak. Not something that would go down well with my Tory parents.

When we got back to uni after Christmas break, Ethan was much more keen. He cleaned up a lot, ditched the band as 'juvenile' and started calling me his girlfriend, wanted to know all about my family. About Jess. He spent a lot more time with me, bought me presents, and suggested we get a flat together for second year, start a business after graduation. Keeping me close, as close as possible. Waiting for his chance, which wasn't quick in coming because Jess and Pete only got more and more serious. I started thinking we weren't going anywhere and he proposed. He kept me right where he needed me. Waiting.

'This whole time, you wanted her,' I said, feeling numb.

Ethan was silent for a moment, probably surprised that I'd interrupted him mid-stream. Then he sighed in an almost pitying way.

'Well, obviously, Mils. Between the two of you . . . there's no contest.'

With one sentence everything in me turned to ash. It was everything I'd never wanted to hear and always secretly believed. That Jess was the successful one, the together one. Intelligent, beautiful, kind, neat and funny. She didn't have my mean streak, my wild, spoiled side. She made it all look easy; the clothes that hung just right, the manners, style and etiquette that were always perfectly aligned. The perfect daughter, whom my parents had scorned in favour of coddling their baby girl. The one who never thought anything through, was never more than average, only thought about herself and who never, ever, did anything right.

It had all been for her. Our entire relationship, our marriage. Every time Ethan touched me, he had to have imagined her in my place. Every smile he sent my way, every thoughtful gesture, just a tactic to win the game, to win her. Keeping me close like a bargaining chip, a consolation trophy.

I thought of him spotting that wedding tiara set, telling me it was perfect for Jess, and I felt sick. Would he have come back for it? Rescued it from the wrecked car and then, in a year or two, given it to her, once her grief had split her and Pete apart and left her alone and vulnerable? After Ethan convinced her to marry him. That their love could be the end to a story in which I was just a side character. A stop on the way to their happily ever after.

An odd cracking sound made me look up, sniffling and wiping tears with my sleeve. It took a moment to find the source of the noise. When I did my skin shrank in horror. It was the paint around the hinges. Layer after layer of landlord-special white gloss, crackling and shifting as the hinges moved.

I remembered then, the screwdrivers on the desk in the study. He must have gone to get one, that was how he'd spotted the satnav. That was why Ethan had kept up his monologue. Keeping me busy, drowning out the noise, whilst he unscrewed the hinges through layers of stiff paint. Quietly, so I wouldn't have a chance to fight back.

I looked around in a panic. Then I saw it, on the side of the sink; the metal cuticle pusher, its sharpened teardrop end just visible behind the soap dish. I snatched it up and held it close. Though what I was going to do with it was anyone's guess. I edged into the furthest corner of the room. Just as I pressed myself to the wall, Ethan jerked the door towards him. The painted hinges cracked apart without their screws and for a second it hung crookedly on the latch and bolt. Then the cheap metal fixings sheared off and the door fell down with a clatter.

Ethan stood there, holding the screwdriver in one hand, like a knife.

'Think how upset she's going to be, Mils,' he said, walking over the fallen door. 'She'll have to call off the honeymoon, when her little sister gets murdered by a burglar.'

I screamed and he flew at me.

My flailing hand knocked the screwdriver away but he slapped a palm over my mouth and tried to pin me against the wall. I lashed out in every way I could, arms and knees and feet all moving independently.

He knocked my head against the wall, once, twice, then swept my legs out from under me and sent me crumpling to the floor. I looked up at him as he examined a long scratch on his arm from the cuticle pusher, which I'd dropped at some point.

'Bitch,' he spat, and kicked out at me. I grabbed his foot and tried to unbalance him and he dropped to his knees with a snarl.

I struggled to get up, to half-crawl, half-stagger out of the bathroom, but he grabbed my hair. I could feel it ripping at the roots as he dragged me back by it. My strength was failing already. I was still too weak to put up a fight.

Ethan's hands closed around my throat and his thumbs dug hard against my windpipe. I retched, gasping for air that wasn't there. He pressed harder. I looked up, feeling my eyes bulge. Ethan's red, sweating face swam in front of me. His eyes locked on my throat, teeth bared. I clawed at his arms but he didn't react, even when my nail caught the slick wound and pulled. I knew then that he no longer cared about keeping his hands clean. He'd run out of patience. Afterwards, when he was left with my body, he'd panic. But right now, he wasn't going to stop until I was dead at his feet.

Black dots sprinkled across my vision and my arms dropped. My ears rushed as my blood pounded through my body, searching for air the way a trapped bird looks for an open window. My fingers trailed on the floor, felt something cold. I tried to grab it but it squirmed away from my fingertips, sliding on the linoleum. I tasted blood. My palm felt like it would tear across the middle, but I reached further.

As the world went dark at the edges, I snagged the cold splinter with my fingers. It rolled towards me and I grabbed it, swung my arm up, plunged it down.

The pressure on my throat was gone and I rolled over, hacking and spitting, gulping down air. Overhead Ethan was screaming, flailing, kicking out at me. I felt like a landed fish, unable to do more than flop on the ground, taking the glancing blows. He staggered away from me and I felt something warm and wet drip onto my face. I wiped at it and my hand came away bloody.

I crawled towards the door, used the frame to get upright. I turned back, a quick glance of fear. The sight nearly made me throw up.

There was Ethan, gripping the sink with one white knuckled hand. The other was reaching up and hovering an inch from the cuticle pusher, which I'd managed to drive through the inner corner of his eye. Blood was running from the wound and the eye was coated in it. It dripped into the sink, ran into his mouth.

I flinched away and ran through the flat. I didn't think of grabbing my phone or a weapon or anything other than reaching the door and getting out. I flew into the stairwell and slipped down several steps, feet skating on the carpet. I was shaking uncontrollably, my eyes blurring with tears. My throat burned with every breath and snot was running into my mouth.

I hit the downstairs door, fumbling blindly with the latch until it opened. Outside the fresh air and sounds of traffic were like another world. There was a roar behind me and I heard the front door to our flat slam against the wall.

Ethan was coming after me.

Then I heard sirens, close. Several police cars shot into the street and pulled up nearby. Within seconds two police officers were at my side. A third ran past, straight to the door I'd just come through. More followed. I heard Ethan, shouting my name on the stairs. Roaring in pain.

'Mrs Swift?' one of the police officers holding me up, a woman, asked. I nodded.

'Is there anyone in the flat besides your husband?'

I shook my head and my knees buckled.

'Where are you hurt?' she asked, the pair of them almost dragging me down the path to a car with its doors wide open.

'Throat,' I croaked.

'Yes, I see the bruising already, but where is the blood from? Are you cut anywhere?' she said, voice clipped and distant.

I shook my head. 'Not my blood. His,' I managed.

Behind me I heard a voice spitting out commands, giving the address and requesting an additional ambulance. The two officers put me in the back seat of the car with my legs dangling out uselessly. Like I was a toddler who needed to be physically folded into my seat. An ambulance howled into the street and I watched as green-uniformed paramedics rushed out and were escorted inside by the police.

'There's another ambulance coming for you, love. Don't worry,' the second police officer told me. 'Do you think you can give us a statement once you've been checked over? The 999 caller said they heard you scream and then your husband shouting at you?'

I nodded, not sure who'd called or why they hadn't come to check themselves. Whoever it was though, I owed them my life. If the police hadn't been there, I had no doubt that Ethan would have caught up to me and, in the state he was in, he'd have killed me even if there were people watching. Right there in the street. He'd lost it completely.

'Let's get you seen to first,' the female officer said, and I saw another ambulance enter the street from the opposite end. 'You look like you've been through enough.'

Chapter 37

The ambulance ride and the hospital were mostly a blur. They gave me water and painkillers for my throat but there wasn't any serious damage. Just a lot of bruising which would make it hard to eat or talk for a few days.

The two police officers stayed with me and I heard the man call his colleague 'Alice'. I eventually learned his name was Stuart when she brought him a tea from downstairs with his name on the cup. Their official titles had gone over my head in all the confusion.

Alice also brought me a tea, made strong and luke-warm with a lot of honey in it. So much that it made my teeth ache. But it went down like butter on a hot pan, soothing my throat.

Then for the second time in a week, I was in a police station, giving my statement. It hurt to talk a lot, but it was that or spend for ever writing it out in my terrible handwriting. I also couldn't leave out everything that happened in Germany, because it was all tied up in

Ethan and his plan. So I went for telling the whole story over again. The wedding, Witwerberg, the bodies and the tunnels. Ethan's detour, the pills, how he'd left me to be murdered by drug smugglers and, once his plan failed spectacularly, he'd had to bide his time until another opportunity presented itself. Only I'd found out what he was up to and he'd snapped.

They didn't believe me. Which was fair enough. Oh, they believed that he'd attacked me and that I'd fought back. That he had tried to strangle me and that the tablets and the satnav were where I said they were. But the rest of it was apparently a bridge too far. At least until I convinced them to phone Detective Voigt and have him tell them what happened.

If I'd been in a better mood I might have laughed when officer 'Stuart' came into the interview room with eyes like golf balls and said they'd confirmed my story. Detective Voigt also asked to speak to me, so they brought me out to use a desk phone.

'Are you all right?' he asked, as direct as I remembered him being.

'I'll live.'

'They said your husband attacked you? That he left you in that place on purpose?'

'He did, yeah.'

He said something sharply in German, which I assumed was a swearword. 'I'm sorry. For not realising that he was involved,' he said. 'If I had only looked at the things in the car properly, before I sent them, then perhaps . . .'

340

'It's not your fault.'

'I should have seen it. I should have protected you.'

There was a long silence, filled with the buzzing of the line.

'I wanted to say,' he began after clearing his throat, 'that we identified the man already. The man in the suit? The watch was easier to track down than I thought. He was a solicitor, Elias Bachman. Disappeared after he failed in his defence of a couple accused of smuggling heroin into the country. I think someone higher up in the operation wanted him gone. Maybe he knew too much, or pissed them off. But because of you his family aren't wondering what happened to him. You should be proud,' he said, so gently that I nearly burst into tears.

He seemed to understand that I was too emotional to continue. He said he'd check up on me again soon and to call if I needed any more information for my case, then he ended the call after wishing me a quick recovery.

After that it was back to giving my statement, now that the police actually believed what I was saying. I got it all out and by the end of it I just wanted to sleep. The only place I could go, though, was the flat and I didn't think I'd ever feel safe there again. I didn't even want to think about that place, let alone face the broken door and the blood in the sink.

'Your husband's still in hospital,' Alice told me when I was allowed to leave the interview room. 'The injury wasn't life-threatening but obviously needs a lot of care. He's also being guarded, so, he won't be able to leave and return home.'

'Am I . . .' I cleared my throat. 'Will I be . . . charged, with what I did to him?'

Alice glanced up at where a camera hung from the ceiling, noiselessly spying on us. Then she looked around in case anyone was within in hearing distance.

'I can't say, but, given the circumstances I would be surprised if the CPS pursued it. But maybe you should talk to a solicitor, just in case?'

I nodded, not really believing her that nothing would be done about it. I'd stabbed my husband in the eye. That wasn't something that just got glossed over.

'Do you have anyone I can call, anyone you can stay with?' she asked.

I shook my head. There wasn't anyone. Jess was on her honeymoon and I'd spend a week in prison before I spoiled that for her. I had some friends I could call, but the idea of explaining everything to them made me feel so very tired. They all knew Ethan, or thought they did. Making them believe me wouldn't be easy. I could maybe put a hotel on my credit card and pay it off when the inheritance money came through. That was looking like my best bet. At least then I'd be away from the flat I'd shared with Ethan. Away from all the pictures we'd taken together, the gifts we'd bought one another, the things we'd chosen together. All the lies he'd built, just to get at my sister.

'I'll book a hotel,' I told her.

'I can take you to the flat to get some things, then on to the hotel?' she said, like she was asking permission.

I nodded.

Alice led me out into the reception area and asked me to wait whilst she found keys to an available vehicle. I was left standing there, looking at a faded knife-crime poster. My whole body felt numb, right down to my soul. Everything that had happened since I woke up that morning felt like a horrible nightmare. I just wanted someone, anyone, to tell me it was going to be OK.

Alice returned with her keys and ushered me out of the station. It was night now and raining. Heavy, enormous drops that soaked me almost immediately. How long had it been since I entered the station? I had no idea. Time was stretching out on this endless, hellish day. I wasn't wearing a jacket, only a shirt over leggings. As we hurried towards the car I felt icy rain piercing through the thin fabric, right into my skin.

'Mila!'

I jerked at the sound of my name over the rain. Turning, I scanned the car park and the umbrella-wielding pedestrians beyond the iron railings. Rushing towards me, in a blur of bright orange and turquoise, was my sister. She was soaked to the skin and wearing a tropical print maxi-dress and trainers, sunburned and exhausted-looking.

'Jess?'

She came to a stop and threw her arms around me. She smelled like cheap air freshener, coffee and sun

343

cream. How on earth was she here, looking like she'd just swum from Barcelona?

'I got on the first plane with seats available,' she blurted, as if reading my mind. 'Pete's coming back too but he had to take a different flight and it has a stupid number of stops.'

'But . . . how did you . . .' I couldn't quite process what was happening.

'I rang you, from our room. You picked up but then I just heard a scream and Ethan yelling your name, and I thought you must've dropped the phone because there was all this static and banging. I was calling out, trying to work out what was going on, then I heard you shouting at Ethan and him telling you to come out of the bathroom. So I called the police and said you were in trouble.'

Ever since I'd been picked up off the street by the police I'd thought one of our neighbours had called them. But it had been Jess. Jess who called me from that weird number and then rang the police for me.

'But how did you know it was that serious? How did . . .'

'I just had this feeling.' She stepped back from me, not seeming to care that she was still getting soaked, her hair running like ink across her face. 'I got this weird feeling when Ethan showed up to the resort without you. I basically accused him of abandoning you, but I thought it was him being selfish and cowardly. Then when I heard you on that call . . . I just knew he was up to something. I never trusted him.' She cupped my face in her cold, wet hand. 'He was never good enough for you.'

That broke me. My whole body shuddered with a sob and I let Jess hold me upright in a fierce hug as I finally let out the misery and shame that had been boiling inside me all day. She had no idea that I had brought Ethan into her life. That he had nearly ruined her relationship twice over, because of me.

Alice, who'd been hovering unobtrusively, cleared her throat. I heard her ask Jess if she wanted to come to a hotel with me, or if she'd made other arrangements.

'I'm taking my sister home, but thank you.'

'I can't go back there,' I managed to whimper, my breath coming in fits and starts as I heaved with sobs. 'I can't face it.'

Jess shushed me and squeezed me tighter. 'Not back to the flat, home with me. Where you'll be safe.'

Somehow Jess managed to hail a cab and get me into it whilst I clung to her like a lost child. We were both completely drenched and soon began to shiver. For me at least the discomfort couldn't compare to how I felt inside. Like something rotten lived under my skin. A barrage of awful thoughts kept me company on that journey. How I'd ruined Jess's honeymoon. That she was such a good sister that she'd probably spent hundreds on a last-minute ticket to come and be with me. That she was so obviously the better of the two of us that I should have known Ethan would want her over me. That this was all my fault.

Part of me knew I shouldn't be thinking these things.

That Ethan was the one responsible for his actions, for his scheming. That he'd hidden everything from me and that I couldn't have known. And yet there was Detective Voigt practically admitting he'd felt something was off and Jess saying she'd had a bad feeling about Ethan all this time.

How had I not known? How had I shared a home and a business, a life, with him and never once suspected that it was all a means to an end for him? How had I thought he loved me, when he'd seen me as nothing more than a tool? A tool that had become disposable.

When the taxi finally came to a stop outside Jess and Pete's house, I was bone-tired and yet somehow had never been further from sleep. We got out and when I heard how much the cab was I nearly started sobbing all over again. Jess paid it without a word and shepherded me up the path to her suburban home.

'Wait here one minute,' she told me, then ran upstairs and returned with pyjamas and towels. We changed right there in the hallway and she took our wet things to the kitchen and stuffed them in the washing machine. Then she put the kettle on and took me gently by the elbow, leading me to the lounge like I was likely to get lost on my way.

Once she had me tucked up in a throw on the sofa she brought tea in and snuggled in beside me. Somewhere I faintly heard the boiler roaring and realised she must have turned the heating on.

'We don't have to talk about it right now, if you don't want to,' Jess said, finally, once the energy from her flurry of activity drained out of the atmosphere. 'But you can stay here as long as you need. You never have to go back to that flat again, OK? I will get you anything you need.'

I couldn't stop the tears that choked me when she said that. She hugged me whilst I sobbed into her shoulder, feeling guiltier and guiltier with each tender thing she did for me. In the end though, when my tea was cold and my body ached from crying, I managed to gather myself. I sat up slowly and wiped my face with the back of my hand.

'This is all my fault. I've ruined everything for you again.'

Jess looked surprised, then her expression softened into something that could only be pity. She exhaled a long, slow breath and took my hand.

'Mila . . . none of this is your fault. Ethan is the one who attacked you. I knew from the moment he showed up without you that something was . . . but none of that is on you. It's on Ethan. Even if we never know what on earth possessed him to do it, none of it is your fault.'

I shook my head, crumpling back into tears.

'What is it? What's wrong?' Jess asked, panic lacing her voice.

But I couldn't tell her, couldn't find the words to say, that she was the one he'd wanted all along. And that I'd brought him right to her.

Chapter 38

Jess stayed up with me until I cried myself to sleep. I woke up to find her sprawled on the sofa beside me, a strand of rat-tail hair hanging over her face. The coffee table I had my feet up on was a wasteland of crumpled tissues, empty cups and blister packs. Jess had made me cup after cup of tea, then given me water and more painkillers for my throat. Finally, when I'd devolved to the hiccupping stage of my crying fit, she gave me brandy to sip. That was what had finally knocked me out.

In the light of day her living room was almost like a doctor's waiting room. Not an NHS waiting room, but one of those fancy ones you only see in films where celebrities buy new faces or get secretly committed. Everything was white or pale grey, plush and soft. Not a speck of dust on any of the gleaming glass and polished chrome surfaces. Although there were cream candles all over the place, in glass orbs, lanterns and bowls, none of them had ever been lit. There wasn't a single drop of wax out of place.

I took all this in through eyes slitted against the daylight coming through the blinds. It all felt so safe and controlled. So perfectly Jess. Maybe she'd never invited me here in case I messed it up. My sore eyes started to well up again, but I bit my lip until the tears filtered away, back into my body. I couldn't go on like this for ever. The shock of yesterday was over, and now there was only a horrible ache radiating through me. It wasn't better, but it was at least more manageable. I no longer felt like I might die from the pain of it. Only that I'd have to live with it inside me for a very long time.

I was only stirred by the need to pee and to wash the tearful crust off my face, I didn't want to move. Jess was asleep and I didn't want to wake her up. But I peeled off the grey waffle blanket she'd draped over me and crept upstairs.

In the bathroom I found a folded flannel and a toothbrush still in its plastic packaging. She must have laid them out when she dashed upstairs for towels and pyjamas. I felt a wobbly smile tug at my lips. Even in the middle of a crisis, Jess was a perfect hostess. Beside the sink she'd left some miniature bottles of face cream, mouthwash and soap.

After using the loo I looked out of the window and saw that the garden was full of building materials. Sacks of sand and piles of paving slabs ready to be laid. Maybe that was why I hadn't been invited over – Jess wanted everything to be perfect. How long would it be until I gave her the benefit of the doubt instead of assuming the worst? I sighed and picked up the toothbrush.

Looking in the mirror was a special kind of shock. My neck was purple and black. I could make out the shape of Ethan's fingers, imprinted on my skin. I laid mine over the top and suppressed a shudder. If I hadn't managed to get away from him, I'd have been dead only seconds later. The police might not even have reached me in time.

Where was Ethan now? In a police cell or still in hospital having his eye seen to? I realised that there was probably going to be a court case. I'd have to give evidence. Immediately my stomach started to churn. The idea of being in the same room as him, hearing his voice, never mind seeing him, filled me with terror and nausea. I clung to the sink and stared into my own panicked eyes, imagining how he'd feel to look at me like this and know he was the cause. How I could ever look at him again, knowing what he'd done.

'Mila?' Jess tapped lightly on the door. 'Are you all right? Do you need anything?'

'I'm . . .' I gulped, watching my lips flap like I was a fish gasping for water. 'Fine. I'm fine. Be down in a minute.'

I heard her hesitate, then her footsteps padded away. Moments later the clack of the kettle lid springing open echoed up the stairs and the pipes whined as she filled it.

I was going to have to tell her. Today. It had to be before Pete turned up, before I lost my nerve. The longer

I kept the secret the easier it would be to say nothing, for it to become one of the many things we never talked about. I couldn't deal with that. More importantly, I didn't think Jess would be satisfied until I told her everything. If I didn't she'd always think I didn't trust her.

With that decision made, I washed my face, brushed my teeth and tried to make myself feel a bit more human. Downstairs I found my sister scooping tissues into a white wicker waste basket. She paused when she saw me.

'I hope you got some sleep?' she said. 'How's . . .' She gestured at her own neck.

'Not great,' I croaked. 'Bit less swollen but the bruising's taken over.'

She winced in sympathy. 'I was about to make some breakfast if you felt like something? I could pop to the shop for some Greek yoghurt and honey, which should go down easy? Or I can make you some scrambled eggs—'

'I need to tell you something,' I said, interrupting.

'What is it?' Jess nibbled her lip, clearly anxious.

I didn't want to drop the bomb on her. What if she'd be happier not knowing?

'It's . . . about Ethan. About what he said yesterday. I don't know if I should say because it's sort of . . . about you, about you and me and the wedding.'

Jess's eyes widened. 'Whatever it is, you can tell me. You don't have to pretend that . . .' She slowly stopped talking. A thousand tiny expressions filtered across my

352

sister's face. Like flickers of a light in a cinema. In that moment I watched every interpretation of my words go through her mind. Then every moment she'd spent near my husband. Everything he'd ever said to her, the things she'd half-noticed and dismissed in the way he looked at her. It was exactly the same series of revelations I'd gone through the day before, when he told me. Seeing all that time again at high speed, this time noticing where his attention was, how he said things, what he said and how he was with her.

Jess sat down on the sofa with a soft thump.

'Mila . . . Are you saying he . . .' She looked at me cautiously, expecting me to deny it or correct her.

'He wanted me gone, so he could try and get with you,' I said, the words coming out robotically.

'Ethan . . . was after me?' she said, seemingly unable to take it in.

'I think, given what he said to me. And everything I've thought back on since then. That he wasn't interested in me, ever.' It hurt so much to say it that for a moment I was breathless. The pain inside me so intense that I felt as though my ribs were breaking. 'He was probably just using me for a bit of fun. But then I brought him home for Christmas and he met you . . . After that he got serious. He kept me around, but I think he was just waiting for a chance with you.'

'Mils . . .' She let out a shocked exhalation and shook her head. 'I don't know what to say . . . I'm so sorry.'

'Don't!' I saw her flinch at my sudden outburst. 'It's

not your fault! I would never, ever think that. He was . . . is . . . a monster. If anything *I'm* sorry, for not seeing it, for not stopping it. Even when you guys got engaged he was suddenly so interested in the wedding. I just thought he was worried about the cost of the trip. I had no idea what he was planning.'

'Planning . . .' Jess said, slowly. 'So, when you got stuck in that village, he planned that? He left you there . . . because of me?'

'Not because of you,' I insisted. 'He was the one who did it. He was the one who sent Pete those pictures,' I said, sitting down at a safe distance, giving her space to process. 'He handed me Pete's phone that day so I'd find them and tell you. Then, when that didn't break you guys up, he . . .' My voice trembled. 'He drugged me so I would stay asleep and he was going to take me out into the woods and –' I fought to get the words out '– push me into a ravine so it would look like I fell and he couldn't find me. So that you'd call off the wedding and he could . . .'

I had to stop because Jess's face clenched up, like she was trying not to be sick. She leant forward and put her head in her hands, shaking it slowly back and forth.

'Yesterday,' I made myself say, 'I found some things that made me realise some of what he'd done. He must have seen on my face that I knew and he just . . . I'm not sure what his plan was otherwise. He'd been drugging me before the trip and even when we got back here. Maybe just because he didn't have the patience for the act anymore. But he was probably planning something else. I just got in the way and he lost it.'

Jess stayed frozen with her head in her hands.

'I wasn't sure if I should tell you,' I said, feeling my chest constrict with guilt. 'I shouldn't have. This isn't something you should have to know about.'

Her head shot up and she looked at me like I was mad. 'Of course it is! Mila . . . I would have heard it anyway in court – at least now I get to take it in here and not with him watching me.' She sounded disgusted at the thought.

'Court?' I echoed.

'Well, obviously he's going to court. He tried to kill you, twice. God only knows what else they can get him for.'

'But I didn't think you'd—' I stopped midsentence at the sight of her aghast expression.

'You didn't think I'd be there, with you?'

'I . . .' I cleared my throat which was suddenly thick with unshed tears. 'I thought maybe you'd prefer not to get caught up in another one of my messes.'

Jess reached out and took a firm hold of my arms. Looking me directly in the eye she seemed to be working herself up to saying something.

'Mila, I know what all this has been about. Pushing for us to still have the wedding, working so hard on it when you had to have been exhausted. The tiara set, which must have cost . . .' She shook her head. 'I know, all right? And with what happened at the wake . . . I

355

shouldn't have tried to ignore it. I should have sat down with you before now and explained.'

There it was, the unacknowledged rift between us, finally out in the open. I felt my whole body prickle with shame. Jess sighed and clasped her hands together in her lap, twisting them together.

'Mila . . . I don't really know how to explain it. I didn't know – when we were kids, they never told us but . . . she wasn't my mother.'

I couldn't breathe. I felt like the earth had been snatched away from under me. And yet. Somehow, it all seemed to fit into place, into all the holes and dark places in our past. I could feel the truth in what Jess was saying. As if I'd known all along somehow that there was a secret burning away under our perfect little family.

'They thought they couldn't have children,' Jess said quietly. 'That she couldn't anyway. Dad cheated on her and the woman got pregnant. I'm not sure how it happened or where he met her but, based on the papers I found when I was clearing out their house, I think Dad convinced . . . Mum, to pay that woman off. So they could raise me as their own.'

'But . . . she never treated you like her own,' I finished.

Jess only looked at me sadly, then shook her head. 'I never knew why. You came along when I was five and for the longest time I just thought it was normal, that you were the favourite because you were the baby. But it was because you were *her* baby, and I was just proof that her husband cheated on her.'

I remembered Mum throwing that cup at Jess in a dementia-fuelled rage. Calling her a homewrecker. Had she been thinking of Jess's bio-mum when she said that? Remembering her from years ago? All the times she'd told me I shouldn't wear this or want that, because it was 'common' or 'tarty' – was that all down to the spectre of Dad's mistress, Jess's mother, hanging over us?

'You found out before they died,' I said. 'Why didn't you tell me? I could have been there for you.'

Jess swallowed, her eyes shining with tears. 'I found the paperwork and . . . I didn't know how to feel. Never mind how to tell anyone. Pete doesn't even know. Then the wake and having to pretend that I was saying goodbye to my mum when she was never anything like a mother to me . . . I snapped and you just happened to be there. I'm sorry.'

'You don't need to apologise,' I said quickly.

'I do,' Jess said, then pulled me into a hug. I was too surprised to do anything but when she released me I must have looked shocked, because she sighed.

'Mila, I appreciate everything you've tried to do. I know it hasn't been easy between us for a long time. But, I haven't blamed you for that in a long time either.'

I could hardly breathe. It felt simultaneously as if a weight was being lifted off my chest, and a fire lit in me all at once. An unbearable tenderness that made me want to cry and laugh at the same time.

'Mum – your mum – and Dad put you first a lot. I'm not saying I never blamed you, because I did, when you were a teenager and constantly getting in these situations that pulled them away. But that's what teenagers do. They fuck up and they get in trouble. Especially if they have overprotective parents trying to dictate their every move. And when that happened . . . they chose to prioritise you. You didn't force them to. And when I found out where I really came from, I finally understood why. Wow.' She huffed a humourless laugh. 'If you only knew how much I've spent on therapy to be able to say that. But it's true, they could have done things differently. Dad especially. Because I was his daughter, but he let her treat me that way. I don't blame you for being caught up in all that. None of it was our fault.'

'I'm sorry,' I said, my voice wobbling. 'I think about all those times – your graduation, for fuck's sake – and I feel awful.'

'Me too,' she admitted. 'But that's the past and now they're gone.'

'What about her, your birth mum?' I asked, gently.

'I have no idea. To be honest I don't really care where she is. She was never family to me and she never left any information that I could find. They gave her some money and she signed me over to them, like a pet. So I don't need her. Now it's just us and I don't care about who got what and making it even. I don't care if we're half-sisters or not. I don't want you to sacrifice anything for me, to make me happy. I just want you to be my sister, so I can be yours.'

I blinked and two fat tears slid down my cheeks.

Jess's eyes were gleaming too and she sniffed delicately, trying to control herself. It lasted until I nodded, then she half-sobbed, half-smiled, and we hugged each other tightly. For the first time in years I was with my sister and there was nothing hanging between or over us, and that was all I cared about.

Chapter 39

Eleven Months Later

I was late to the first day of Ethan's trial.

It was at least very on-brand for me. Also, in my defence, I had established a great punctuality record with the people who mattered to me. I was, for example, early for Jess's baby shower and accompanied her to the hospital when she went into labour. I even remembered to bring all the aromatherapy stuff and the white noise machine. She didn't use any of it because she immediately changed her mind about an epidural. But the thought was there and so was I. Pete was too, but he spent a lot of time crying tears of joy and not being very useful. It was very sweet though.

In fact I'd learned that Pete was a bit of a softie all round. Ever since he'd flown back from Barcelona he'd been very careful of me. Very considerate. I think it was because he'd been a bit pissed off about the phone incident and now felt really guilty about being angry with me for it. To be honest I was in the same boat.

But it was kind of nice to have him as a friend now, after everything that had happened.

This was Ethan's first day in Crown Court. The first day of the trial that would, we were ninety-nine per cent sure, end with him in prison. The CPS had assured me that with what they had, it was very unlikely the jury wouldn't convict. Jess was going to testify what she'd heard on the phone. We had the satnav record showing he'd taken me to Witwerberg intentionally, the police and paramedics who heard Ethan ranting about me on the day of the attack – and of course I would be giving my account as well.

That didn't mean I was ready to see him again.

It was what had kept me up all night, every night for the past week now. Despite the effort I'd put in to dress smartly I knew I looked a complete wreck. My eye bags were too dark to conceal and my lips were bitten raw.

Sitting in a back room I awaited my turn to give evidence. It was very quiet back there and smelled of furniture polish and stale instant coffee. I couldn't keep still. Kept getting up and pacing the room. I was going to see Ethan soon, for the first time since the day I stabbed him. I hadn't gone to the magistrate's court. Hadn't seen him charged. It was too soon and no one forced me to go. They'd offered me a screen for today, so I couldn't see him and he couldn't watch me. Or maybe I'd prefer to do this via videolink? I'd considered it, but in the end I decided I had to face him. Not because I had something to prove, but because I wanted him to see me.

The thing was, Ethan had never really respected me. I knew that, had talked about it with the therapist Jess recommended. He saw me as a useful idiot. Someone to use for sex, to get close to Jess, to keep him amused whilst he waited for her. Like I was the human equivalent of a dentist's office magazine. Mildly entertaining but ultimately disposable.

But today, even if he didn't look at me, he'd know that I'd survived him. That he wasn't the centre of my universe and that my life hadn't crumpled without him. In fact, it had improved, massively.

Jess helped the most. She came to look at flats with me, brought Pete along to pack up the shop when I ended the agreement with our landlord. The only thing she hadn't done was accept the inheritance money I'd offered to split with her. Though she didn't know I'd set up a savings account for baby Edgar. Mostly to make up for the fact she'd called him that.

As for the rest of the money, I'd opened a small shop in a trendier part of town. Not a record shop, a vintage clothing boutique – Amelia's Attic. I had a little flat nearby and a side-line in recycling curtains and bedding into new clothing. It was bringing in more than the record shop ever did. Enough that I had a little holiday booked for myself and Jess over the summer.

'Amelia Swift?'

I winced, hearing my married name. It was a constant reminder that even once the trial was done with, there were other hurdles in getting Ethan out of my life for good. Although I'd applied for divorce he'd opted to fight it. Maybe because he thought it would keep me from doing what I was about to do – give evidence against him. Or else he was clinging to that one last connection to Jess. Hopefully once he was convicted, I'd be able to push it through, with or without his agreement.

My legs felt like water as I was escorted into the courtroom. Suddenly all eyes were on me. I barely made it to the witness chair before my knees gave out. Then there was the swearing bit and I fumbled my words. This was not the impression of strength that I wanted to project. Then I was asked to begin my account and as I did so, I looked up at Ethan for the first time.

He was at the other end of the room in a Plexiglas box that looked big enough for two football teams to share. On either side of him a uniformed guard hovered unobtrusively. He looked like a political hopeful about to give a speech. They'd got him a suit, not one I'd ever seen before. All his other things were in a storage space somewhere. Pete took them for me and I'd never asked where they were or what was going to happen to them. I didn't want to know.

Ethan looked grey, which I supposed was fair, given he'd been locked up for nearly a year. Bail was denied, given his attack on me and the evidence they found on his laptop. All the pictures of Jess he'd saved. Many of which he'd taken himself, not at events he was invited to, but by stalking her. Probably on the days he'd drugged me stupid and gone off on his own. Pictures taken through the window of the home she shared with

Pete, outside her gym, whilst she was on site as a surveyor. That was creepy enough. When the police uncovered the box of 'mementoes' he'd stashed in our wardrobe, I thought I was going to be sick.

The box was marked 'family pictures' and I'd never looked inside. But I'd moved it several times when looking for other things. I'd handled a box of my sister's things —lipsticks, underwear, private letters, her old diaries. All things Ethan stole thanks to me giving access to Jess's space. Dating right back to when I was in uni.

Today, Ethan looked even worse than I felt. Aside from his grey skin he'd lost weight. Weight he couldn't afford to lose. His cheeks were shadowy and his eyes looked huge. I guessed they'd tried to clean him up for the trial, but he had a look about him that was slightly unkempt. Hair too long, stubble that ought to have been shaved again. A clammy, unpleasant sheen on his skin. Like he'd spent the night on a sofa in someone's back room, sleeping off a heavy session.

The thing that really caught my attention however, wasn't the way he looked. Wasn't even the fact that he was wearing his wedding ring. Like a cheap trick on the jury. No, it was the way he wasn't looking at me. Not because he couldn't face it or he wasn't able to meet my eye. He wasn't looking at me, because he only had eyes for Jess.

She was sitting right at the back in the furthest corner from me. This was because I'd told her she didn't have to go and she probably interpreted this as me not wanting her there. But she'd come anyway, just in case I needed her. Possibly also because she wanted to face Ethan just as I did. He'd hurt us both after all.

She had her long, dark hair scraped back in a ponytail and was wearing a sombre work suit. Clearly trying to be as unobtrusive as possible. Yet Ethan's eyes had found her and they weren't letting go. Even though he kept trying to look away, like he knew this looked bad to the jury. It was as if he couldn't help it. Like he was trying to drink her up and savour the image. It made my insides flare hot with anger. My voice stopped stuttering and I straightened up, telling the court everything. Yet even as I gave the evidence that he had to know would convict him, he didn't look at me once.

Jess hadn't noticed, or at least, she wasn't acting as if she had. Even as Ethan's gaze never left her, hers never left me. She watched me with a soft, encouraging look I could read all the way across the courtroom. My sister, beaming me support and strength with her eyes. The heady combination kept me going as I told the jury everything, ripping right down into my soul for the worst moments of my life.

Finally, after Ethan's solicitor had tried and failed to win back some points, I was allowed to get down. As I was ushered back out through a rear door I turned. For the briefest instant I saw Ethan's eyes on me. Then I realised it was just an illusion. He was still looking at my sister. Only his blind eye was on me, wandering without his intent.

Outside, I found a bench in the fresh air and took

long, steadying breaths. It hadn't gone as I'd imagined, but I wasn't upset by it. I only felt tired. Like I'd finally crossed the finish line in a race I had no chance of winning, but at least it was over and I could now fall to the ground and rest.

Jess was at my side a moment later, her arm around my shoulders.

'You were amazing,' she said fiercely. 'They're going to send him down for sure.'

'Thank you for being here,' I said, holding her hand on my shoulder.

'That's what big sisters are for.'

She squeezed me as she said it. Weirdly we were closer now than we'd ever been, despite knowing the truth about our family. The knowledge that we were half-sisters hadn't driven a wedge between us, but removed one that was already there. One created in part by a bitter and hurt woman who'd raised us so very differently. I couldn't find it in me to hate our mother, my mother, but I definitely thought of her and Dad differently now. Perhaps just more realistically. They hadn't failed Jess by accident, but they had made mistakes. Ones that I hoped one day I'd be able to forgive, as Jess had done.

'I'm going to go get a bottle of water. Do you need anything?' Jess asked.

'I'd love a tea, please.'

Jess gave my hand a final squeeze and dashed off towards the coffee kiosk. I sat and watched her go, knowing how lucky I was to have her.

'Hello again. Do you mind if I sit?'

I looked up at Detective Voigt in complete shock. He looked just as he had when I saw him in Bavaria, only now minus his heavy coat. He was wearing a suit with a wrinkled grey shirt and had the slightly dazed look of someone who's just travelled a long way on public transport.

'Sure, how are you . . .' I wasn't sure if I wanted to end that sentence with 'doing' or 'here', so I let it drop.

'I'm well,' he said, dropping into Jess's vacated seat and answering the first of my incomplete questions. 'I flew in this morning,' he offered, to answer the second.

'They made you come all the way here to testify?' I asked, thinking that if they'd offered me videolink he should have had the same.

'No,' he said, but didn't add anything else by way of explanation.

'Oh . . . I just gave my evidence,' I said.

He nodded. 'Was it how you expected?'

'No,' I said, wondering how he'd managed to jump onto my train of thought so easily. 'But it wasn't bad either. Just, different. Like it's finally over, but it doesn't feel . . .'

'As good as you hoped?' He nodded again at my look. 'That's how it felt when we finally got Jaqueline Forbes' killer. I got to tell her parents and they had closure . . . but that meant telling them what happened to her. That she just stumbled on someone killing a solicitor and for that she had to die.'

So they'd found him. The man from the woods. The

person who'd tried to burn me, who'd killed two other people that we knew of. But, as he'd said, it didn't help. I still felt awful about her death, the way her body had been burned out there in the woods.

'Did you get a confession?'

Detective Voigt nodded. 'After a lot of questioning and some very tedious evidence gathering, yes. We did.'

'So he's going away. But it doesn't help?'

'It helps because he can't hurt anyone else and because he's going to give evidence against some other people who are far worse. But no, it doesn't help me feel better about it. He chased that poor girl through the woods and shot her through a door when she thought she was safe. I still think about how afraid she must have been.'

We sat in silence for a moment and I caught a waft of coffee and cologne from his rumpled suit. People moved around us, in and out of the courthouse and thronging the coffee kiosk. I saw Jess glance back at us and frown, obviously having no idea who the man next to me was. I smiled and waved a little so she'd know not to be worried. My protective big sister.

I knew, a fraction of a second before he spoke, that he was about to ask if he could see me again. And before he'd uttered half the invitation, I knew I was going to say yes.

Acknowledgements

Everyone needs a Jess in their life, sister or no. I'm very fortunate to have my own. Vander, you may not be my literal sibling, but without you, I don't make sense.

Given how hard times are at the moment for everyone, I owe a massive debt to my parents. Without their support I wouldn't be able to write nearly so much or as often. This year has been incredibly trying what with health concerns and the stress of organising a major move, but even in the thick of it, I'm glad to be here with you. I can't imagine a life where I don't get to see you every day.

Thank you to my brother, Jack, especially. Not only for regular coffees but also for at least pretending to listen to my plot brainstorms, if only so you can get me to pretend to listen when you talk about anime. Thank you too for leaving such a lovely review of my last book, even after saying you weren't going to. I bet you thought I hadn't noticed, didn't you?

I owe a huge thanks as usual to my wonderful agent

Laura Williams at Greene and Heaton for her advice and support during the writing and editing process. It was especially nice to finally meet in person again, what with my first two novels having come out during the height of Covid precautions. Laura's insightful suggestions always improve the final draft and I am amazed at how often she picks up on things that I didn't even know had crept into the story, and brings them to the fore. *The Resort* is no exception. Without Laura's input, Jess would be half the character she is.

Thanks also go to Cara Chimirri my editor, for not only working so hard to promote my previous novels, but also making sure this one came together smoothly. Her input into the setting greatly informed the direction of the story and for that I'm incredibly grateful. I can't imagine Mila's story taking place anywhere but the Alps now that it's written. Especially as without the Bavarian setting, there would be no Detective Voigt – unthinkable! Likewise, thanks to everyone at Avon for their outstanding work on bringing the book together, particularly the excellent cover art.

Many thanks to the Ware branch of Hertfordshire Libraries again for use of their internet and study space when writing the first draft of this novel. Even if I did get disturbed by a live robin flying around in the gallery, which will probably make its way into a book at some point.

Lastly, I cannot stress enough how much I owe to the NHS, particularly the staff at the Lister Hospital in Stevenage and those operating the mobile mammogram centre. Early detection of cancer is so important and were it not for routine screenings and the care of our local doctors and nurses, it's incredibly likely that neither of my parents would be alive today. It's because of the NHS that they received the care they needed and for that I owe them a great debt.

You'll want to stay. Until you can't leave . . .

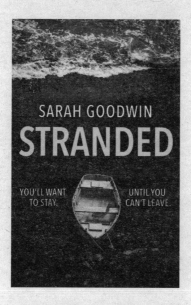

A group of strangers arrive on a beautiful but
remote island, ready for the challenge of a lifetime:
to live there for one year, without contact with
the outside world.

But twelve months later, on the day when the boat
is due to return for them, no one arrives.

**Eight people stepped foot on the island.
How many will make it off alive?**

A gripping, twisty page-turner about secrets,
lies and survival at all costs. Perfect for fans of
The Castaways, *The Sanatorium* and *One by One*.

'Because he chose you. Out of thirteen girls.
You were the one. The last one.'

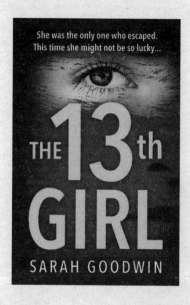

She was the only one who escaped.
This time she might not be so lucky...

THE 13th
GIRL

SARAH GOODWIN

Lucy Townsend lives a normal life. She has a
husband she loves, in-laws she can't stand and
she's just found out she's going to be a mother.

But Lucy has a dark and dangerous secret.

She is not who she says she is.

Lucy is not even her real name.

A totally gripping, edge-of-your-seat thriller with
twists and turns you just won't see coming.
Perfect for fans of *Girl A* and *The Family Upstairs*.